THE
RETURN HOME

WITHDRAWN

THE
RETURN HOME

JUSTIN HUGGLER

Published in 2017 by Short Books
Unit 316, Screenworks
22 Highbury Grove
London N5 2ER

10 9 8 7 6 5 4 3 2 1

A CIP catalogue record for this book is available from the British
Library.

ISBN 978-1-78072-202-3

Printed and bound in Great Britain by CPI Group (UK) Ltd,
Croydon, CR0 4YY

Cover photograph © Michael Trevillion / Trevillion Images
Cover design by www.asmithcompany.co.uk

To Anuradha

"It was meet that we should make merry, and be glad: for this thy brother was dead, and is alive again; and was lost, and is found."

Luke 15:32

Chapter One

The Ghost in the Chimney

THE FIRST TIME I ever heard my parents argue was when Uncle Jack got injured in the war. In autumn, the wind used to blow so hard around our house it would rattle the windows like someone trying to get in, and moan in the chimney like the ghost of some poor soul who had been bricked up alive and was trying to get out. It drove the sea mad against the cliffs below, and brought something to life that would thrash about in the trees outside my bedroom window; and I would lie awake listening, too frightened to sleep. Sometimes it got up so strong it would steal in through the gaps in the old wooden window frames and stir the curtains about, and I would watch as they sent shadows scuttling across the ceiling, convinced they were being moved by the spirits of the restless dead. When it got too much for me, I used to slip out to the top of the stairs and listen for the sound of my parents below; I knew every creak and whisper of the landing, and how to move across it without making a noise. It was cold the night I heard them talking about Uncle Jack, and I can still feel the floorboards under my bare feet. I'd have gone back to bed as soon as I heard them talking below, but there was something in their voices that held me at the top of the stairs, shivering as I was.

"He can't stay here," my mother was saying. "I know what he's going through, and I feel for him, I really do. But I'm sorry, we've got to put the children first."

"He's got nowhere else to go," my father said. I'd never heard their voices hard like that before, and I clung to the banisters, the ghost in the chimney forgotten.

"He's got plenty of money," my mother said. "He can take care of himself."

"It's not about money, for Christ's sake! Who else has he got?"

"And whose fault is that? Let's face it, he's driven away anyone who's ever given a damn for him."

"What am I supposed to do? Throw him out in the cold?"

"Don't be so dramatic, Tom; he's got a home of his own. And keep your voice down; you'll wake the children."

"Oh, I'm sorry for living!" my father said, and I heard a sound like his table being knocked over. "This is my *brother* we're talking about," he said more softly. "I can't abandon him."

"No one's asking you to abandon him. We'll do

what we can for Jack, of course we will. It's just that he can't come here, not with the children. You must see that. We wouldn't be able to take proper care of him anyway."

I wondered what had happened to Uncle Jack: I knew he'd been away in the war; it was what he did for a living, so I thought he might have been injured. The banisters pressed against my head; and my feet had gone numb from the cold.

"I know he can be an ignorant bastard sometimes," my father said; "no one knows that better than me. But I grew up with him, Sarah, he's my flesh and blood, and he's got no one. Christ knows my mother can't take care of him; she can barely take care of herself."

"What about Sandy?"

"Not after the last time."

"Not even after this?"

There was a pause, and my father sighed.

"I called her," he said. "She'd heard from Rachel. Of course *he* hasn't spoken to her, hasn't called or anything. She's really cut up about it, but she says she's not letting him back into her life."

"Well, I can't say I blame her."

"Can't you give it a rest, just this once?"

Sandy was Uncle Jack's girlfriend, but from what my parents were saying, it sounded as if they'd fallen out. I was sorry about that: I'd liked her when they came to visit in the summer.

"Does Valerie know?" my mother said.

"There's no chance there. Not any more."

"No, of course—but has anyone told her?"

"I called her."

"And?"

"She didn't want to know."

"And Alex?"

"She said Jack made up his mind a long time ago."

There was a silence.

I didn't know who these other women were, but I guessed they must be some of Uncle Jack's friends. He had a lot of women friends.

"So you see," my father said, "we're all he's got."

"We can't, Tom. It's not fair to the children. You know what he's like."

"I'll speak to him."

"It's not just that. I...I don't want them to see him. Not like this."

"He's my brother. How do you think I feel about it?"

"They're only children."

I wondered what could have happened to Jack that was so terrible my mother didn't even want us to see him. I heard the sound of my father's chair being pushed back and his voice growing louder as he came towards the hall, and I was about to slip back to my room when the sitting room door opened. I crouched down as low as I could, hoping he wouldn't see me.

"They'll have to find out sooner or later," he was saying. "We can't shield them all their—" He was looking right at me. "Ben, what are you doing up? You'll catch your death out there on a night like this."

"Couldn't sleep."

"Poor love," my mother said from the doorway, "was it the wind again?" Her voice was back to normal, all the hardness gone from it: you'd never have known they'd been fighting.

"I'll go," my father told her, starting up the stairs. "Come on," he said to me, "let's get you back to bed. You're freezing. You can't sit out in this weather."

I looked over his shoulder at my mother below, her hair golden in the light that spilled out of the sitting room.

"There's nothing to be scared of," my father said, as he tucked the blankets around me, "just the wind making noises in that old chimney again."

"Wasn't that," I said.

"What then?"

"Nothing."

I didn't want to say it; I was afraid of the answer.

"Come on, you can tell me."

I turned away from him, towards the wall.

"Why were you fighting?" I asked.

"Fighting? We weren't fighting; your mum and I were just talking."

"You were shouting."

"Is that why you were sitting out there in the cold?" He put an arm around me and hugged me close. "We weren't shouting; we were just working something out. We weren't fighting."

"Promise?"

"Promise. Now go back to sleep, it's the middle of the night."

It wasn't till he'd turned off the light and was halfway out the door that I remembered to ask what had happened to Uncle Jack.

"Nothing," he said, but his voice was different. "We'll talk about it in the morning."

When I reached up to push my hair out of my eyes I could feel grooves in my forehead where I'd been leaning against the banister. The rain had started up against the window, and I fell asleep to dream that it was machine-gunfire and I was in the war with Jack. The wind in the trees was the sound of the tanks moving, and the boom of the sea against the cliffs was the bombs getting nearer. In the dream we were trying to get home, but we couldn't find our way out of the war, and I remember I woke up once sweating with fear.

The next morning I wanted to tell Martin and Roz what I'd heard, but before I had a chance my mother made us all sit down at the breakfast table and told us she had some bad news.

"It's your Uncle Jack," she said. "He's been hurt badly, in the war. He's—well, he's lost his leg."

I'd never heard anyone use that expression before, and for a moment I had a crazy image of Uncle Jack forgetting where he'd put his leg and hopping around looking for it, until I saw her face and realised what she meant. I looked over to where my father was standing, looking down at the floor, and I started crying—I don't know why, I just felt it was what I was supposed to do.

"Now that's not going to help your dad," my mother said. "His brother's been badly hurt and he needs you to be strong."

I went over to my father and put my arms around him, and he ran his hand through my hair and gave me a sad smile. But the next thing my mother said surprised me: she must have changed her mind or backed down after I'd gone back to bed the previous night, because she told us Jack was going to come and stay with us for a while.

"Just until he's feeling a bit better," she said. "so we're going to need you all to be really good and help out."

"What happened?" Roz asked. "How did he...I mean—"

"It was a terrible accident," my mother said, as if that was all she was going to say. But my father looked up then, and cut across her.

"He stepped on a landmine," he said.

It sounded to me as if Jack had fallen down a mine, but I didn't see how that would make him lose a leg. The others all looked solemn, though, as if it made sense, so I didn't say anything. I don't think I really took in what had happened; I was just happy my parents weren't fighting.

Chapter Two

Egypt Wood

I WAS EIGHT years old in 1983 when Uncle Jack came to stay because he had nowhere else to go and, young as I was, I still think of it as the year I began to grow up. I went back to visit our old house a few weeks ago, and when I walked down through Egypt Wood to the sea and saw the old memorial Jack struggled so long and hard to reach, those days came rushing back to me: the way he blew into our sheltered island life on the autumn wind, and seemed to bring all the troubles of the world with him. I'm forty now and have children of my own, but for a moment back there in the wood I was eight years old again, watching my crippled uncle shambling down the path; and, though it was a hot summer day, I could feel the cold wind of that vanished winter, gone for ever now.

I came back to Jersey just as my own life started to fall apart. The call came in the middle of the night. My sister's voice, frightened. It was my mother, she said, she was going to be alright but I might want to come over. My wife moved in her sleep and murmured something, so I took the phone out to the landing to avoid waking her. It was a heart attack: not a big one, the doctors said, but a warning. She was in the hospital. I told my sister to go and take care of my parents, said I'd be there as soon as I could. I didn't wake Naomi; there was nothing she could do for me. I went downstairs and switched on the computer to book a flight. One seat, no point Naomi and the kids coming. I sent an email to work to say I had a family emergency and wouldn't be in for a couple of days, put some coffee on and sat down to wait in the grey London dawn until it was time to wake Naomi and tell the children.

It was a call I'd known would come one day, but I hadn't let myself think about it. You deal with it when it happens, I'd always told myself, but now that it had I had no idea what to do. My mother had always been the one who'd held us all together; now I supposed one of us would have to take her place. I'd heard it in Roz's voice, already trying to hide her fears the way my mother would.

It wasn't until my plane was coming in to land that I realised it was the first time I'd been back to visit Jersey without Naomi and the kids. Another thing I'd have to get used to, I thought. She'd been great when I woke her, said she'd take care of the kids and told me just to go. But I couldn't forget what I'd seen.

There was no one waiting for me at the airport; I'd

told my sister I'd come straight to the hospital. There was a queue at the car hire desk, and it was so long since I'd driven anywhere on the island I couldn't find the way. There was some problem with the signal on my phone and I couldn't get the GPS to work. Jersey's a small place, only nine miles by five, though it grows a mile when the tide goes out, but it's an easy place to get lost, with its narrow roads and hidden valleys.

When I tell people I'm from Jersey, they sometimes get the idea I'm an American, and I have to explain that I'm not from New Jersey but from the old, the first and original. I travel a lot for my work, and in some parts of the world people seem surprised to hear it even exists, which makes me wonder how they think New Jersey got its name. I don't want to give the impression we're an old Jersey family, because we're not — although my brother, sister and I were all born on the island. The old Jersey people can be a little unfriendly towards newcomers: I remember once when we were children we got home to find a strange car blocking the way, and my father had to ask the driver to move.

"Why should I?" she said. "My family's been here longer than yours."

At school, the other children would tell me we had no business being on the island. My brother Martin told me to explain we'd only come because the hospital had needed a new cancer specialist and my father had got the job. That tended to satisfy them.

It was Martin who named me Ben, and I suppose I should be grateful for that, because my parents had called me Aubin John Merryweather. I'm not saying Martin couldn't manage my name; I think he just couldn't be bothered. It's pronounced *oh-bin*, by the way. My parents had thrown themselves into their new life on Jersey with such enthusiasm they decided to name us all after places on the island. My sister was called Rozel, after a harbour on the north coast, and Martin got away lightly with the name of the first parish they lived in, but I got stuck with Aubin, after the village of St Aubin, largely, I think, because it was the site of one of my father's favourite pubs. I should probably count myself lucky: he could have chosen Brelade or Ouen, two other saints who are big in Jersey. At any rate, my brother's version caught on, and I've been Ben ever since, except for a few months after we first saw *Star Wars*, when I became Obi-Wan for a while.

Eventually I got the GPS working and found my way to the hospital. I was directed to the fourth floor, to a private room, naturally, for the wife of a retired head of department. My father was waiting in the corridor. He looked old and vulnerable, diminished.

"There you are," he said with a sad half-smile. "I was beginning to get worried. Was your flight delayed? It landed an hour ago on the internet."

"I got lost. How's Mum?"

"She's okay. In pretty good shape actually,

considering. Come and see her."

She was lying propped up against the pillows, pale and confused, a blanket drawn up around her despite the warm weather. Her hair was dishevelled in a way I had never seen before, and that brought what had happened home to me: the gold may have long faded to white, but she always took care of her appearance. Roz was sitting by the window, almost as pale as my mother. She must have brought the flowers by the bedside, my mother's favourites. I wished I'd thought to bring some.

"It's good of you to come," my mother said, trying to sound cheerful, her voice weak.

"How're you feeling?"

"I'm fine, love. A bit tired, but that's to be expected. Be alright in a day or so."

She smiled at me the way she had when I was a child. She was still trying to protect us from the truth after all these years, but I didn't need an overheard conversation to work out what she was hiding. Her hand was lying on top of the hospital blanket, the skin almost transparent. She was connected to a heart monitor, and I tried to keep my eyes off the spiky green graph of her heartbeat.

"Matt and Anna send their love," I said. "Anna wanted me to give you this." A home-made get-well card she'd drawn while I was packing, a drawing of my mother on the front.

"Ah, they're good kids. Tell her thank you. I'm sorry

to drag you all this way. You should be with them."

"They're fine, Naomi's taking care of them."

"Come on, you know you're not supposed to worry," my father said, smoothing her hair back from her forehead. He motioned me to the door with his eyes. "Jenkins says she mustn't get stressed about anything," he told me in the corridor. "The new cardiologist here."

"What happened?"

"Her blood pressure. He's got her on medication. But it's best if we keep the numbers in with her to a minimum, so she doesn't get worked up about anything. Come and meet him."

He leaned in the doorway of the nurse's station as if he still worked there.

"Jenkins around?" he asked.

"I'll page him for you, Dr Merryweather."

A reply to a doctor, not a worried relative: it was like he'd never left. He hadn't wanted to retire; they'd practically had to force him out, and now he was back in his kingdom. But I was being unfair, I saw: he was trying to hold things together the only way he knew how. There was a time when I'd thought he could hold the whole world together.

"She'd just had a bath," he told me, "and was drying her hair. You know how long she can be with that thing. If I hadn't gone up to check. She was on the floor."

When Jenkins arrived you could see he was a little

in awe of my father. I'm not sure he would have been dealing personally with my mother's case to this extent if she hadn't been married to one of the hospital's longest-serving former doctors.

"First and foremost, your mother's going to be fine," he told me. "This was a small heart attack. I don't want to downplay it, because no heart attack is minor, but this was what I'd call a wake-up call. A warning to change a few things around. In your mother's case, there aren't really any lifestyle issues: she doesn't smoke, she's in good shape for her age. This could be nature's way of saying it's time to slow down. We'll have to keep her here for a couple of days to monitor her, but I don't foresee any problems. She just needs lots of rest. The heart is resilient, but it needs time to recover."

Roz said she'd take me down to the canteen for lunch. I wasn't hungry, but I could see she wanted to get me on my own.

"Christ, I'm glad you're here," she said as we waited for the lift. "It's been a total nightmare. She's looking a bit better now, but you should have seen her last night. I thought, this is it."

"God."

"I'm telling you, at one point I thought I'd be calling to tell you she was…gone."

"How long have you been here?"

"Since they brought her in, whenever that was. Some time around ten. It's alright now she's talking. And the doctors reckon she's going to be okay. The only problem now is how much more I can take of Dad's quiet competence act. He's been second-guessing everyone here. I can't believe they put up with him."

"He is a doctor."

"He retired eleven years ago. And he was an oncologist: when's the last time he treated a heart patient? Medical school?"

"It's just his way of coping"

"I know. If he hadn't been there she could have died. He won't tell you, of course."

She was more like my father than she realised. I bought two coffees and a bacon sandwich, though I didn't feel like eating anything.

"I wish Martin was here," she said.

"I know."

"He'd have been good at this. Better than me."

"You're doing fine."

My sister was the star of the family. She'd founded her own company a few years after she left university, made a lot of money in the first dotcom bubble and got out just in time. She'd started another company in the second internet boom, but never quite repeated her first success.

"How's Naomi?" she said.

"She's fine," I lied. Under the table, I felt the wedding ring I was still wearing in spite of everything. "How's Neil?"

"He's been fantastic. I don't know what I'd have done without him."

Roz was married to a local GP—I suppose one of us had to end up with a doctor, given no one in the family had followed my father into medicine.

"He's with the kids now; he's been great explaining all this to them," she said. "How are Matt and Anna taking it?"

"I haven't told them. Not the whole story. I just said Mum was sick. I thought it was best that way, with me being away. Anna was upset."

"She's like you were at her age, a worrier. She'll be alright. Naomi's great with her."

It was true: Naomi was good with the children, but that didn't make the decision I was facing any easier.

Roz sighed. "I suppose we'd better head back up. Life gets complicated, doesn't it?"

More than she knew.

Up in the room, my mother was asleep. She was frowning slightly, like a child having a bad dream, and she reminded me of Anna when she'd been sick.

"Why don't you go on to the house and get yourself settled?" my father said, holding out a set of keys to me. "Freshen up after your journey. Mum knows you're here. Best not to let the room get too crowded."

Roz was ready to argue, but I agreed before she could say anything. I wanted to get out of there anyway, away from the heart monitors and hushed nurses, and the sensation of death watching over us. Everything had happened too fast.

I didn't want to risk getting lost again so I went the long way to my parents' house, hugging the coast and keeping the sea in view. When I saw the house I wondered why my father had ever agreed to move there. It was everything he hated: a white house in a row of white houses right on the main road, noisy and not much in the way of privacy. There was nowhere to park, and I had to leave the car down the road and walk back. The house looked out over Green Island Beach, where we used to go swimming as children. In those days it was packed with holidaymakers on a warm afternoon; I remembered days when there wasn't space to put your towel down. Now it was deserted, except for a few dog-walkers and a solitary family playing in the waves. The tourists had long abandoned Jersey for cheap flights to Spain, and left the island to the millionaires and bankers.

Inside, the house was frozen in the moment when my parents had left for the hospital. My father's dinner was sitting cold and half-eaten by his armchair in the living room, the television playing silently, a table in the hall lying on its side where he must have knocked it over. The lights were still on, and I went from room to room switching them off. Upstairs, I hesitated outside the door to their bedroom. The chair in front of my mother's dressing table had been pulled out of place, and the hairdryer was lying on the floor. The book she was reading was lying on her bedside table, her glasses on top. I picked them up: she might need them. Beside the book was a misshapen pot I'd made for her when I was ten years old; on the wall above it a rather more accomplished painting of Roz's.

I left my bag in the guest room and went downstairs to make myself some tea. The house was quiet, the only sound the grandfather clock in the hall. It felt wrong to be there without my parents, a rehearsal for a future without them I didn't want to face. I tried to watch television but couldn't concentrate. I couldn't go back to the hospital yet, but I couldn't stay in that house either, so I went out for a drive.

I'm not sure what it was that drew me back to our old house, the one I grew up in. Perhaps it was some sense of a place of safety, or maybe I just found myself out in that part of the island. Jersey may be small, but it was a world to us as children, the more so because the place where we lived is called Egypt. I've no idea why it's called that; it's the most unEgyptian-looking place you'll ever see, cliffs plunging down to the sea and trees bent over from the wind. The road was even narrower than I remembered: the verge brushed against the car on both sides. We lived right out at the end, where the road runs out. I don't know what I expected to find, but I was relieved to see the house was still standing. Only the name had changed: the old wooden sign was gone and in its place was a new one that said Maison Bellevue or something like that. All the old Jersey houses have French names, but in our time it had been called La Tempête, which was exotic even by island standards. My father fell in love with the place the moment he saw it, and refused to listen when everybody told him it was falling down. He called it Tempest House.

On closer inspection, I saw the house had changed after all—or rather I had. In my memories it was a castle on the cliffs, but I saw now it was just a dilapidated old farmhouse that had been added to so much over the years it had lost any shape or design. To get to some of the rooms you had to go through others, and even on the same floor some parts of the house were on different levels, so you had to go up a step here, and down a couple there. There was a tower in one corner I'd been convinced was left behind from an old fort, but now I saw it for what it was: the faintly ridiculous addition of a former owner who'd wanted to make the house look grand. Martin's room was at the top of the tower, and I remembered how we used to sit at the window looking out to sea, lying to each other that we could see ships in the distance. He used to tell me what size gun we'd need to sink them: even then he'd wanted to be a soldier.

This was the last place I'd been truly happy, I thought, before the paper walls of childhood were torn down. The garden was better cared for than it had been in our time. The old greenhouse, with its windows starred with holes from the time Martin got an airgun for Christmas, was gone. He'd denied all responsibility for the holes, of course, and claimed a neighbour must have done it, but my parents didn't believe him and took the gun away.

There was a movement from one of the windows, a woman looking out suspiciously at me. I didn't feel much like explaining myself, so I went on to where Egypt Wood began. There was nothing much to give it away, just a dirt path that began at the end of the road and didn't look like it led further than the next field. Egypt Wood is probably too grand a name: it's just a small stretch of trees running down a steep hill to the sea between the headlands, but it was a forest to us as children, and it was one memory I found untouched by time. Even now, as the trees closed overhead and I found myself wrapped in the cool mossy scent, the only sounds the hidden stream and the waves breaking below, I could have been miles from anywhere.

About halfway down the hill, the stream emerged from the undergrowth and flowed across the path, dropping away in a small waterfall where Martin and I used to hide from Amazonian bandits. At the bottom of the wood there was a hidden cove; Martin said the old Jersey smugglers used to hide their ships there, and he was forever coming home with his clothes soaked from scrambling across the stream to get down to the beach.

I never went down to the cove, because it meant

going past an abandoned cottage with boarded-up windows at the bottom of the path. The place was fenced off; there was a sign on the gate that gave its name as the Wolf's Lair, which terrified me as a child. I thought a werewolf lived there—who else would build a house down there, cut off from everyone? Opposite the cottage was a memorial that looked like a gravestone, and I was sure the only reason anyone would be buried there was because they weren't allowed on holy ground. But Martin said the cottage was named after one of the Jersey smugglers, who'd called himself the Wolf to frighten people away.

I stood looking out to sea, the lost years piled up behind me, wondering what was left of the child I'd been in Egypt Wood. The wind stirred in the trees as if trying to whisper something, but whatever it was, I couldn't make it out: the days were gone when my mind could find voices in the air and fill the shadows with ghosts. Of all the memories that lay sleeping among those trees, I don't know why it was that of Uncle Jack, limping down the path with the stick my grandmother gave him, that came back to me: Jack, and the year when everything changed.

The wind stirred the branches, the waves broke upon the shore. My mother lay helpless in a hospital bed, my father and sister were driving themselves crazy with worry, and I was harbouring the secret I couldn't tell them, not now. That my marriage was falling apart and the reason I'd been awake when my sister called to tell me about my mother was that I was deciding whether to walk out on my own children.

Chapter Three

Uncle Jack

UNCLE JACK MANAGED to get me in trouble at school before he even arrived—though to be fair, it wasn't really his fault. Martin and I both went to St Edward's; I always wondered why they'd dragged Edward into it when Jersey already had plenty of saints of its own, what with Aubin, Brelade and the rest. The main building had once been a country house, and there were steps up to the front door covered in ivy, and an attic room that stuck out from the roof, where the older kids said the family used to keep a mad uncle locked up. I sometimes wondered if they'd forgotten to let him out and he was still up there, but Roz, who'd been at St Edward's before she moved to secondary school, told me he'd have died years before. Everyone was always on about what a big deal it was to go to St Edward's, but we only went there because my mother was one of the teachers. Martin was in her class, which I thought would be great until he said she was tougher on him than on any of the others. But I noticed whenever she'd been particularly hard on him at school, we'd get his favourite food at home, or he'd be allowed to stay up late to watch TV. At any rate, he was better off than me, because I was in Mrs Maudsley's class, and everyone agreed that she was the meanest, toughest teacher in the whole school, and probably in all of history. When Martin heard I'd been put in her class, he told me the year would be living hell, and that my best choice was to end it all, and take my own life, or at least give myself some horrible injury so the school would have to take pity on me.

The day before Uncle Jack was due to arrive from London, Mrs Maudsley got us all to tell the class what we were doing for the weekend. I usually hated speaking in class, but for once I had real news, and knew everyone would be interested.

"My uncle's coming to stay," I told them. "He's been injured in the war. He trod on a thing called a landmine"—Martin had explained to me about landmines—"and it blew his leg up, and now he has to come and stay with us until he gets better and learns to walk with a wooden leg—"

"Aubin Merryweather," Mrs Maudsley cut me off, "in this class we do not tell lies."

"But—"

"We all know you have a good imagination, Aubin, but in my class you do not make things up."

"But—"

"And it is not nice to pretend your uncle has had a terrible injury just to impress the others."

"I'm not lying," I said. I hadn't made up any of what I'd told them that morning, except the bit about the wooden leg, which I admit I'd added in a moment of inspiration.

"And where is your poor uncle supposed to have had this dreadful misfortune?"

"In the war, in—"

"Are you British, Aubin?"

Jersey was part of Britain, but it wasn't part of the UK; it had its own government, but it wasn't a country. It was all very confusing, so I just said "Yes", because it was what she seemed to want me to say.

"And is Britain involved in any wars?"

I wasn't sure about that, but I could see which way the conversation was going.

"So how could your uncle have been injured in the war?"

"He was in Afghanistan. He—"

"*Afghanistan*! Is the British army in Afghanistan?"

"No, but—"

"Well, then," Mrs Maudsley said, "hoist by your own petard."

I didn't know what a petard was, but I was pretty sure I hadn't been hoist by one, because Uncle Jack wasn't a soldier, and I'd never said he was. But Mrs Maudsley wouldn't let me explain.

"You can't let her get away with that," my friend Matthew Micklethwaite told me after class. "Tell your mum, get her to report the old bag to the headmaster. I think she forgot your mum works at the school. She's bit off more than she can chew."

Matthew really spoke like that, repeating things he'd heard from his father; I think it was because he was an only child. Matthew was my first real friend. I didn't like to run about or play football in the playground with the other kids: I preferred to play on my own, imagining I was a space explorer or a man like the one on TV who could transform himself into any animal. One afternoon I was pretending I was a spy when I noticed a small boy watching me from under a tree. His uniform fit him perfectly, unlike mine, which was a hand-down from Martin. After a bit he came over and asked me what I was doing. We started spending break times imagining together; I suppose the others thought we were boring, but while they chased each other, we walked on the surface of Mars, and captained nuclear submarines.

Matthew was wrong about my mother, though: she never interfered with our lives at school. She used to say we had to learn to stand up for ourselves. I wasn't bothered anyway; for the first time since I'd joined her class, I had bigger things to worry about than Mrs Maudsley. The sound of my parents arguing in the night came back to me, and I watched them as the day of Jack's arrival drew nearer. I hung around the kitchen when they talked in the evenings, and crept out onto the landing at night, listening for any sign of trouble. I didn't say anything to Martin or Roz; I'd never told them what I'd overheard that night. I was afraid to talk about it; I felt saying it out loud would make it more real.

Though I did my best to hide it, I was nervous about Uncle Jack coming to stay: I'd known him as far back as I could remember, but I'd never felt easy around him. He could be fun when he was in the right mood, but you had to be careful with him. He wasn't a soldier, whatever Mrs Maudsley might have thought; he was a journalist: he worked for a newspaper which sent him around the world to report on wars and disasters. Matthew said that meant he was a war correspondent, but when I asked Jack he laughed and said he was a fireman. I thought he was joking, but he told me that was what his job was called, because he had to drop everything and rush straight to the scene, just like a real fireman. You could see he and my father were brothers, though Jack was taller and thinner, and still had plenty of hair— women often seemed bothered by Uncle Jack's hair, and would reach up to fix it, but he didn't seem to mind. He brought a different woman friend with him each time he came to stay, and he always seemed more interested in them than he was in us; Roz said he used to bring his wife when I was too small to remember, but they'd been divorced for years. He'd muddle up which books and films we liked, and give us the same Christmas presents he'd given us before, and he could be frightening if you caught him at the wrong moment.

But there was one thing I loved about Uncle Jack's visits. When you grow up on a quiet island where nothing much ever happens, you live for stories, and no one had stories like Jack. When he started talking about the places he'd been I couldn't help but listen. He told us about Berlin, where there was a wall that divided the city in two, and you could get shot if you tried to cross it; about Iran, where they had paintings of missiles on the sides of the buildings and all the woman had to cover their faces; about Beirut, where there were tanks in the streets and different parts of the city were controlled by different sides in the war; and about a place in Africa whose name I've forgotten, where he once drove six hours to get to a bridge where a soldier took his passport away and refused to return it until Jack gave him a hundred pounds, and then told Jack he couldn't cross the bridge anyway.

And Russia. We were all afraid of the Russians, but Jack was the only person I knew who'd actually been to Moscow and met them. They were as scared as we were, he said. A couple of government spies had followed him around the city, and he'd had to give them the slip by ducking into a shop and leaving out of the back door. His favourite country, though, was always Afghanistan: you could see it from the look in his eyes when he spoke about it. He told us how he'd travelled there with the

Mujahideen after the Russians invaded, walking for days through the mountains. There was no electricity in the villages where he stayed, and sometimes it was so cold he woke up with ice in his hair. The Mujahideen had no money, they had no cars or planes and they travelled everywhere on foot. Some of the people were so poor they couldn't afford shoes, but they shot Russian helicopters out of the sky. If an Afghan agreed to be your friend, Jack said, he'd risk his life to keep you safe. It sounded a very hard country to me, but Jack loved it, and it seemed sad to me he'd lost his leg there.

I'd been given my middle name after Uncle Jack, and though he often frightened me, I'd always felt I had a sort of connection to him. It felt strange to hear about his accident, because I had a bad leg of my own: I had been born with a club foot. It was operated on and straightened when I was a baby, and you can't see anything much wrong with it, apart from a long scar that runs from my heel almost to my knee, but I get tired easily, and I can't run all that fast. Sometimes, the other kids would laugh, and adults would look sorry for me, but I've never felt bad about my leg: it's part of what makes me myself, and not one of them. I wondered if Jack's bad leg would be on the same side as mine.

He was supposed to arrive at the weekend. My father flew to London to pick him up from the hospital, but a few hours after he left one of Jersey's fogs descended, covering Tempest House in a shroud of white and smearing its wet fingers along the window panes. Usually I liked the fogs, which came on fast and made it feel as if the house had been picked up and deposited on another planet, or in some wasteland at the edge of time, but I was worried their plane wouldn't make it back. Martin and Roz were both staying over with friends for the night—I think my parents had wanted us all to be away when Jack arrived, because I was supposed to stay with Matthew, but he was sick. My mother was getting Jack's room ready, and I offered to help, but she said I'd be most useful if I kept out of the way. My father thought the stairs would be too much for Jack at first, so they'd turned his study into a sort of downstairs bedroom; they'd moved the desk out, but it was a small room, and with a fold-up bed, armchair and television all crammed inside, I wondered if there'd be room for Jack.

My father called to say he'd picked Jack up and they were on their way to the airport, but outside the fog was thicker than ever. I watched it through the window: every now and then it cleared a little and the trees showed through at the end of the garden, only to vanish again as it drifted back. I imagined I was an explorer on a planet shrouded in permanent fog—I suppose Mrs Maudsley would have said I was daydreaming: she had a thing about daydreaming, she was always on about it, but it was the weekend, so I reckoned I could do as I pleased. When my father called again to say the flight was delayed, it was already dark. I wanted to stay up and wait, but my mother said it looked as if they might have to stay in London for the night, and sent me to bed.

I don't know what time the fog cleared, or when they got in, but it was night when I woke to the sound of them below. I slipped out of my room to listen: there was no wind, the ghost in the chimney was silent and my father's voice carried clearly up the stairs, telling Jack where things were, and how to get to the bathroom. At first I heard no reply, and I wondered if Jack's injuries were worse than my parents had said, before I realised he was speaking, but his voice was very soft, which wasn't like Jack at all. I couldn't make out what he was saying, but he sounded tired. My parents wished him good night, and I crouched down to keep out of sight as they crossed the hall to the living room and closed the door behind them. I was about to go back to bed when I heard a strange, tapping noise from below. I looked down through the banisters. Jack had come out into the hall, and as he moved into the light I saw he was on crutches. His leg was missing from the knee down—the left, I noticed, the same side as my bad leg—but that wasn't what shocked me. He was a lot thinner than I remembered him, and he seemed to be struggling to get around on the crutches; his arms were shaking with the strain, and his hair was stuck down on either side of his face with sweat. He'd grown an untidy beard, and he seemed terribly pale, almost white. When he looked up I saw his face was gaunt, so that his bones stood out and he looked older. But none of that was what shocked me.

It was when he stopped to rest during his slow, painful progress down the hall, steadying himself against the bookcase. It was as if he sensed my presence, because he raised his head and looked straight at me. I smiled down at him and waved. I'm sure he saw me, because he was looking right into my eyes, but he didn't smile back. He gave me this hard, unfriendly stare, as if he didn't recognise me at all.

Chapter Four

The Face in the Mirror

THERE WAS ONLY one photograph of Jack in my parents' new house. It was in the dining room, on top of the old upright piano none of us had ever successfully learned to play, between a shot of Roz getting her degree and a picture of Martin posing with the new bicycle he'd had with him the day he went missing, all those years ago.

My parents only ate in the dining room on special occasions like Christmas; the rest of the time it was a museum of memories, almost every inch of available space taken up with pictures of Roz, Martin and me. I saw the acts of my life, from wide-eyed childhood to my wedding, and the births of my own children. After that, I faded somewhat from the scene, my part played, relegated to a supporting role as smiling parent while Matt and Anna took up the drama. In London, they would be back from school in a few hours, home to a home without me. A vision of stolen weekends stretched before me, every moment with them negotiated in advance. Everything passes in this life but our love for our children, the one wound we carry to the grave.

There on the piano was the picture of Jack. I must have seen it a hundred times over the years without stopping to think that it was the *only* photograph they had of him. There had been a time, I was sure, when there were more, but Jack and my father had fallen out over thirty years ago and hadn't spoken since. I never knew what had come between them; whenever I tried to ask, my parents changed the subject. My father didn't just stop talking to Jack; he didn't mention him at all, and neither did my mother. It was as if Jack stopped existing. He was disappeared from family history the same way Stalin was collectively forgotten by the Soviet Union—an analogy he'd have liked. Except for me: I never forgot Jack; I just learned to keep my memories to myself and observe the family code of silence. I'd often wondered what could have made my father cut Jack out of our lives so completely. It wasn't like him to do that to anyone, let alone the brother he'd nursed through the loss of his leg. He'd spent so much time taking care of Jack, the first time I heard someone call him an oncologist I'd thought the word was uncle-ogist.

The photograph was a group shot of my father's family. Perhaps that was why he kept it. They were all there, except my grandfather, who'd died when my father was still a child, just as I remembered them: Aunt Ruth mischievous, with a sadness I never understood; Granny

Merryweather imperious, scowling at the photographer for daring to suggest she smile; Jack louche, almost absurdly good-looking. The picture was from before he lost his leg and he'd managed to pull off the perfect pose, lounging back against a railing as if the camera had found him there by chance. He and my father had their arms around each other's shoulders, and my father's head was tipped back in laughter. In my memories, there was always a distance between my father and Jack, even before they fell out: a sense my father didn't quite approve of his younger brother, loved him but was critical of his failings. But here there was no distance at all; they were as natural with each other as Martin and I had been. Perhaps it was some trick of the camera, a split second given a significance it never had because it was the moment that happened to be preserved.

I went upstairs to shower before heading back to the hospital. The guest room was crowded with furniture from Tempest House. The antique dressing table and heavy carved wardrobe looked out of place in the airy, modern house. When I opened the wardrobe, I found it was crammed with childhood relics: my first school uniform hung beside Martin's beloved camouflage fatigues. He was always dressing up as a soldier. I reached out and touched the cloth. Everything seemed so much smaller than I remembered.

In the bathroom, I caught sight of myself in the mirror, an ornate monstrosity that used to hang in the hall at Tempest House, all curves and gilt. I used to look at myself in it as a child and dream of the grown-up I was going to be—for some reason, I always pictured myself with swept-back hair. One thing was certain: I'd never imagined the face that stared back at me now. Naomi always said I'd kept my looks: I hadn't lost my hair like my father and I was only beginning to turn grey at the temples. But the man who gazed out at me was a stranger; his eyes were knives, no forgiveness in them. Was this the face Matt and Anna saw? I hoped that they at least could still draw some gentleness from me. Where was the child I'd been? There was nothing of him left, and I had the disquieting feeling my memories could have been anyone's and it wouldn't have made any difference: my past had nothing to do with who I was. Time is a thief, not a healer. I thought of my mother's hand on the bedclothes; my father waiting in the hospital corridor. They had grown old and I hadn't even noticed. Time steals everything.

When I arrived at the hospital, my mother was sitting up in bed. She'd brushed her hair and put some lipstick on, and looked more like herself.

"Oh, you are good," she said when I gave her the glasses I'd found on her bedside table. "Of course, you can trust your father to forget them and leave me half-blind."

"Sorry for worrying about saving your life," he said. "Next time I'll ask the ambulance to wait."

"Listen to him. He's saved my life and he's never going to let me forget it."

She sounded weak, but their affectionate bickering was a relief after the hushed whispers of the morning.

"Are you alright to be here?" she asked me. "The kids won't be worried?"

"They're fine."

"You won't get in trouble at work or anything?"

"I think the world of human rights will manage to get along without me for a day or two."

She looked doubtful. It was like her to worry about me when she had bigger things to deal with.

"How are things at work?" my father asked.

"Good," I said, another lie. "I've got a conference coming up in DC. So long as you're feeling better, of course," I added to my mother.

"Oh you must go. I feel bad enough as it is."

I didn't tell her Washington was the last place I wanted to go. The truth is that I fell out of love with my job long before my wife fell out of love with me. I work for Asylum, the human rights organisation, in international advocacy and government relations—which means I fly around the world telling governments what to do and generally making a nuisance of myself. But I'm a fraud. We're supposed to be making the world a better place, but these days I'm just in it for the money. The job's all about conviction, and I don't believe in it any more.

We agreed that Roz would stay the night with my mother and I would take my father home so he could get some sleep, but when the time came he didn't want to leave.

"I can stay the night here," he said. "They'll give me a blanket and a sofa in the staff room."

"At your age?" my mother said. "Don't be daft."

"I've spent plenty of nights in this hospital."

"Thirty years ago. These days you have trouble enough sleeping in your own bed. Imagine the state of your back."

"I'm not leaving you alone."

"I'm not alone, Roz's here. Now come on, Tom, the doctor said no stress."

"I might as well jump out the window."

"If I had a penny for every time you've said that."

He was quiet on the drive home. He was never an easy passenger; he sat as he had throughout the twenty-three years since I passed my driving test, holding on to the grab handle as if I was about to crash at any moment, despite the fact we were doing a steady 20mph in traffic.

"She's always been a good healer, your mother," he said. "She'll soon be back to her old self. For a moment the other night I really thought..." He broke off, staring out the window. He had never confided in me; I didn't know what to say.

"She's going to be okay, Dad."

Night was falling; it was already dark out to sea.

When we got into the house he went upstairs to take a shower. I slipped out to the terrace at the back of the house to call the children. The beach was lost in darkness now, but I could hear the waves breaking below. Naomi answered on the third ring. I wanted to hang up when I heard her voice.

"How's your mother?" she asked.

"She's okay, I think. I don't know. The doctors say she's going to be alright."

"Well, that's good then."

"Yes, I suppose so."

"They know what they're doing."

"I know."

"Tell her I sent my love and said to get well soon. How's your dad?"

"He's...coping. In his way."

"I miss you, Benny."

Do you? And when you feel his arms around you, do you miss me then?

"I wish I could be there with you."

And lose these days with him?

"Me too. How're the kids?"

"They're fine. They miss you, that's all. When do you think you'll be back?"

I'm never coming back. Not to you.

"In a couple of days, I think. When she gets out of hospital."

"I mean, there's no rush, of course. Take as much time as you need."

Of course.

But I didn't say any of it. We'd been through the arguments too many times, and I knew it led nowhere.

"I love you," she said.

"I love you too."

And it's true. I wish I didn't, but I do.

To my relief, she put Matt on, and I was able to deal with uncomplicated love. He was full of the part he'd been given in the school play, and made me promise I'd come and watch him. He was so excited he only remembered to ask about his granny as an afterthought—which was how it should be. When Anna came on, though, that was the first thing she asked about.

"I was worried," she said.

"There's nothing to worry about, sweetheart, Granny's fine," I said.

"Did she like my card?"

"She loved it, it's on her bedside table. She asked me to thank you."

"Can I speak to her?"

"She's still in hospital. They're keeping her in for a few days, just until she feels better."

"When are you coming back?"

"Soon. In a couple of days."

"Mummy misses you."

Sometimes I had the feeling Anna guessed the truth

about me and Naomi. She had a way of knowing things she shouldn't. My mother said she reminded her of me.

My father was still in the shower. I found a couple of frozen pizzas and put them in the oven. There was a bottle of wine open on the counter, and I poured myself a large glass. I was drinking a lot. Too much, probably.

When my father came down he dropped a Perry's guide map of Jersey in front of me, so faded and dog-eared it could have dated from my childhood. "So you don't get lost again," he said.

I don't know why, of all the things I'd been through that day, that brought tears to my eyes. We ate as much pizza as we could stomach, but neither of us was hungry. My father wanted to be up to relieve Roz in a few hours, and went straight to bed. I switched the lights off and walked through the house by moonlight, locking up the way he had when we were children. Everything was still, apart from the sound of the sea.

I remembered the first time I brought Naomi to meet my parents. They were still at Tempest House, and we'd been afraid to make love in case they heard us, and had lain laughing in each other's arms instead. What happened to our laughter? I thought of my parents bickering at the hospital. Matt and Anna would never get to see us grow old together.

Looking back, it had started to go wrong a long time ago, before either of us realised. As long as the kids were babies, we'd both been too wrapped up in them to notice anything else. When Anna started at school, I couldn't blame Naomi for resurrecting her career, but a part of me resented her eagerness to go back to work while I was stuck in a job I hated. Perhaps if I'd been braver I'd have tried changing job. Instead I took on more work and agreed to more foreign trips, until I was away one week in three. And I let the trips stretch, leaving a day early to get a good sleep, staying an extra night to fly at a "civilised hour". We began to lead lives that were a little too separate: with the long hours we were both working, there were weeks we hardly saw each other. But that wasn't what undid us.

It was a spring evening when Naomi invited Richard over to dinner. I'd bought her roses on my way back from the airport just the day before, and I remember their scent spilling over the dining table. He was a colleague of hers from work: I got on with him well enough, though he'd never struck me as particularly interesting. But that evening their laughter was a little too private for my liking, the looks they gave each other a little too knowing. I didn't say anything, but in the days that followed I noticed his name kept coming up: when she brought home a bottle of expensive wine, Richard had recommended it; when she started reading a book, Richard had lent it to her. There was something about the way she said his name, as if she enjoyed the sound of it. Still I said nothing, but I began to watch. She closed her emails when I came into the room, took phone calls on her own in the bedroom—to get away from the sound of the television, she said, but I heard her laughing through the door.

She went to a conference in Basingstoke, leaving me to take care of the children. When I called her at the hotel, she said it was noisy in the bar and she couldn't hear. She called me back a little later, but I was sure I'd heard Richard's voice in the background. I thought of all the lonely hotel rooms where I'd sat up waiting for her call.

When she got home, as she was unpacking, a couple of toothbrushes fell from her bag. Both used. She laughed, said she must have taken one by mistake. For once I was not silent. Had they shared a room, I asked, or had he slipped over to hers in the night? She denied it, of course, grew angry, said she'd never accused me of anything all the times I'd been away.

After that the fights started. Naomi said it was my imagination, my male insecurity. I told her I didn't have time for amateur psychology. She refused to cut contact with Richard. It would be unprofessional, she said; she wasn't going to let my paranoia interfere with her career. The poison spread to everything. It had never bothered me before that we didn't agree about things like politics or religion; now I felt she was deliberately taking the opposite view on everything. We did our best to hide it from the children, but they must have noticed how often we fell silent when they entered the room, or went in the bedroom to talk while they watched television. There were times when I believed her and was plagued with guilt. Until, one day, she forgot to sign out of her email. I read the messages, hating myself for it: there were several from Richard, and they left no doubt. I confronted her; she admitted it. She'd only done it because I was away so often, she said, to prove to herself she could still be loved. She begged for forgiveness, said it would never happen again, promised to cut contact with Richard. I told her I was leaving her.

The next day she phoned me at work and said she needed help. She'd gone out to fill up the car and got into a fight with another driver. The petrol station attendant had taken her keys and was threatening to call the police. She put Matt on the phone: he sounded scared. I dropped everything, of course, and went to get them. She was standing by the roadside with Matt cradled against her body, her make-up tear-streaked. She didn't say much on the way home. Matt was badly shaken but I managed to convince him it was the other driver's fault. I said I'd never let anything happen. That night Naomi broke down in tears, told me she couldn't live without me. And I forgave her. I told myself I was doing it for the children.

She really did stop seeing Richard, and I let myself believe it had been a temporary crisis. Things were better between us than they'd been in years. I cut short my trips and looked forward to getting home. It was almost a year later when I managed to get out of a meeting in Paris ahead of schedule, and caught an early train back to London. I was a few streets from the house when I saw her from the taxi window, coming out of a restaurant. I was about to call out to her when I saw Richard behind her. She leaned into his arms and rested her head against his shoulder.

I got the taxi to drop me in another part of town, walked the streets in the rain for an hour. How long had it been going on? When I got home I said nothing. I wanted to drag her by her hair and slam her head against the wall, but I wasn't going to do it. I wasn't going to be that sort of man. That night, I lay awake beside her wondering what to do. It wasn't her infidelity that hurt, not then. It was the way she'd played me along, promising to give him up, and all the while going on behind my back.

That had been a week ago, but still I'd done nothing. I knew I should leave her, but I couldn't do it to Matt and Anna. It would tear their world apart. They would never have the happy childhood I'd had, they'd become children of divorce, products of a broken home. I never saw how sad that phrase was before: home, the safest place in the universe, broken.

I looked at my phone: it was past eleven. Anna had trouble sleeping, the way I did at her age, and often lay awake with the light on until one of us came to reassure her. I hoped Naomi hadn't forgotten to check on her. She was nine, already a year older than I was when Uncle Jack lost his leg and came to stay.

Chapter Five

The Resident Ghost

THERE WAS NO sign of Jack at the breakfast table. I could still remember the look he'd given me the night before, and I was relieved he wasn't there. My mother said he was tired and not to disturb him; she was in a bad mood, already washing up instead of sitting over breakfast with my father the way she usually did. He was hidden behind his newspaper, and I could tell neither of them wanted to talk. Roz and Martin were still at their friends', so I ate my cornflakes in silence, looking at the wall opposite. Jack was lying on the other side of it. He must have lost his memory from the shock of the landmine, I'd decided: that would explain why he'd forgotten who I was. The window had fogged up, and when I rubbed a small patch clear with my sleeve my mother told me to stop smudging it, which didn't make much sense to me, since as far as I could see I was cleaning it. Outside, the real fog was gone. I hoped Martin or Roz would get home soon; I was worried my parents would start fighting again. My mother knocked a plate over and swore, which she normally never did, when it fell to the floor and broke. My father got up to help her with the pieces, but she waved him away.

"I might as well jump out the window," he said, and went upstairs. He often said things like that, and I knew he didn't mean them, but all the same I was relieved when he came back down and said he'd take me for a walk in Egypt Wood. I think he just wanted to get out of the house for a while.

It was one of those cold mornings when the air's so bright you can see everything in more detail: the sun flashed on the stream and the sea where it showed through the branches. The wind was moving in the trees and leaves were falling all around. It had rained in the night and there was a carpet of wet leaves on the path. I knew I only had to get my father on his own for a bit and he'd tell me all about Uncle Jack; my mother believed there were things children shouldn't be told, but my father would tell you just about anything if you asked him—maybe it had something to do with being a doctor. On the way down the hill, though, he wanted to talk about school: he asked me things I'd told him before, and didn't listen to the answers. I could tell he was thinking about Jack, but when I tried to ask he changed the subject. I was beginning to worry there was something seriously wrong with Uncle Jack—something they hadn't known about. We stopped at the bottom of the hill, and he crouched down and started moving the leaves from the grave-stone outside the Wolf's Lair. I drew back, nervous.

"Don't be afraid," he said, turning to look at me. "Do you know what this is?"

"A grave."

"No," he said, smiling, "it's a memorial. I suppose it's a bit like a grave, but there's no body. They put it up in memory of a British soldier who died in the war. He was killed by a land-mine."

"Like the one that hurt Uncle Jack."

I looked at the writing on the stone where he'd cleared the leaves away: there were a lot of long words I didn't understand.

"What happened to Uncle Jack?" I said.

"It was a terrible accident," he said, getting up.

"Yes, but how did it happen?"

"I'm not sure you're old enough."

"I won't get scared, I promise."

But he turned away and we walked on in silence, past the empty Wolf's Lair, to where the trees cleared and you could look out to sea: the wind was stronger out there, whipping at the tops of the waves.

"I suppose you should know," he said, "if Jack's going to be staying with us."

He fell silent again, and I'd given up hoping he was going to tell me anything when he began. He was looking out to sea, where the gulls were fighting the wind to stay up.

"It was in Afghanistan," he said. "Jack was in the mountains, in a tiny village miles from anywhere, travelling with the Mujahideen, when they got a warning that the Russians were out looking for them. There was only one road in and out of the village, and the Russians were coming that way. The only other way out was through a minefield. If they'd stayed, or gone back the way they came, the Russians would have captured them."

"So they went through the minefield?"

He nodded.

"Did Jack know about the mines?"

"The Afghans told him they knew a way through."

"Is Uncle Jack angry with the Afghans?"

"No, I don't think so. They were the ones who got him out. They carried him through the mountains for days."

All the same, I thought, Uncle Jack wouldn't have been there in the first place if it hadn't been for them.

"Is he very sad about his leg?"

"It's hurting him."

"Can't you give him medicine?"

"The hospital gave him some painkillers. They help."

"Will they give him a wooden leg?"

"A wood—well, not exactly. They'll give him a prosthetic leg."

"What's a prophetic leg?"

"No, a *prosthetic* leg." He explained, "He'll be able to walk, but he won't be able to run, or go for long walks."

He wouldn't be able to go to Afghanistan either, I thought. Out at sea, the gulls were still struggling to keep up. I thought they would probably be better off giving up and waiting until the wind died down, which it always did, sooner or later, but they kept fighting just to stay in one place, and giving out their strange, sad laughter.

On the way back up the hill, we passed the memorial for the British soldier again, and I asked why it was down in the wood where nobody would see it.

"Because this is where he was killed," my father said.

That came as a surprise. We all knew Jersey had been taken over by the Germans during the war—it was one of the first things you learned growing up, even before you went to school—but this was the first time I'd heard of any British soldiers being killed on the island. I didn't think there'd been any fighting: the British had decided Jersey was too small and too close to France to defend, so they'd left it to the Nazis. It turned out they hadn't abandoned it completely. One Christmas in the middle of the war, my father told me, a small team of commandos was sent to the island to find out what the Germans were doing. They came by boat in the night, landed in our hidden bay at the bottom of Egypt Wood and climbed up the same path my father and I were walking on. This was incredible news, and I forgot all about Uncle Jack: there had been a secret wartime mission in our wood, right below my bedroom window, and I couldn't wait to tell Martin. The commandos had looked around in the night and spoken to a few local people, before trying to slip away unseen, but on the way back down through the wood their commander, Captain Ayton, stepped on a landmine. The others managed to get him back to the boat before the Germans came, but he died of his injuries. I didn't like the sound of that so much: the leaves were thick on the path, and I began nudging them gently aside with my foot before I put my weight down, in case there was a landmine that had been forgotten.

"Don't worry," my father said when he saw what I was doing, "there are no mines now; it was all cleared years ago."

All the same, I trod carefully. I imagined I was one of the commandos who came that night, feeling for landmines with every step I took. It was a cold crossing we'd had, on the look-out for patrol boats all the way, the spray needles on our faces, the water bone cold as we waded ashore. The path was dark under the trees and I heard whispering in the leaves. German soldiers came out of nowhere, only to turn to branches moving in the wind. The smell of smoke came from a chimney ahead, and I thought of my family huddled around a Christmas fire far away, while I was out here in the cold, hunted by men I didn't know. I stumbled and imagined how it must feel: the sudden touch of something half buried, knowing there was nothing you could do, that it was going to happen. I suppose Mrs Maudsley would have said I was daydreaming again, but I thought of Uncle Jack, and how he must have made the same lonely walk in the mountains of Afghanistan: did he see Russians in the shadows? Did he feel the mine beneath his foot and know what was coming?

Martin was back when we got home. He was disappointed Jack was still shut up in his room, and I told him what I'd seen the night before, but I didn't mention the way Jack had looked at me—I don't know why; somehow I felt it was something I shouldn't speak about. The morning stretched on but Jack's door remained closed, and there wasn't a sound from inside. At one point the fire alarm went off—my father, who loved gadgets, had installed it himself, but he'd put it too close to the kitchen and it went off sometimes when my mother was cooking. Even that didn't wake Jack, and I began to wonder if the journey had been too much for him and he'd died in the night.

When Roz got home my mother told us to lay the table for lunch. My father had gone to check on Jack, and I tried to be quiet so I could hear what was going on, but Roz got upset with me for putting the knives and forks the wrong way round—I could never see why it mattered; people could switch them easily enough. Martin wanted to pour the wine, and my father got back just in time to stop him breaking a glass. He said Jack would join us in a bit, but when everything was ready and the food was on the table getting cold, there was still no sign of him. My father went to check on him again and came back shaking his head.

"I'm not sure he's up to it," he said.

"I suppose we'd better start," my mother said, as if Jack's failure to turn up was the most natural thing in the world. "I'm sure he'll join us when he's ready."

"What's wrong with Uncle Jack?" Martin asked, helping himself to potatoes.

"He's just tired," my father said. "I'm not surprised, after the trouble we had getting him through the airport. The airline insisted he come in a wheelchair—for insurance, or something like that. But you imagine trying to get Jack to sit in a wheelchair. I thought he wasn't going to come at one point."

"Yes, well, we don't need to go into all—" my mother started to say, but she broke off at the noise of a door opening down the hall. It was followed by a tapping I recognised as the sound of Jack's crutches.

"Jack?" my father called out, getting up, "need a hand?"

But before he could reach the door, it swung open and crashed into the sideboard.

"Sorry," Jack said, swaying into the room out of

breath, "not quite...used to...these yet."

He looked as wild as he had the night before, his face pale and sweaty. His trousers, I saw, had been cut away just below where his leg ended, the edges frayed and jagged as if he'd done it himself. He moved awkwardly around the table, waving away my father's offer of help, though his arms were shaking with the effort. My father took the crutches while he lowered himself into the chair next to mine. As he sat down, his stump came into view, wrapped in a thick white bandage. He had an animal smell, as if he hadn't washed in a long time, and I could feel the heat coming off his body.

"Sorry'm late," he said. "Roast beef! All through...'fghanistan...told myself 'Keep going...keep going...and you'll...get one'f Sarah's roasts'."

"You've grown a beard!" Martin said.

Jack rubbed his chin.

"Not up to shaving," he said. "Sorry. Not at my best, Ben."

Martin's face fell, and Jack realised his mistake. "Martin," he said, "sorry. Not myself. The leg, y'see."

"Who'd like some gravy?" my mother said, to break the silence. Jack reached across the table for the wine.

"I'm not sure that's a good idea, Jack," my father said.

"I am," Jack said, pouring himself a glass.

"Those painkillers you're on, it's not a good idea to mix them with alcohol."

"What difference does it make?"

He drank off the whole glass, and filled it back up from the bottle.

"Seriously—" my father began, but my mother spoke over him.

"How's the beef?" she said.

"D'licious."

"We thought you could do with a good roast to fill you up after the hospital food. I was going to do chicken, but Martin said it had to be beef."

I think my mother said that to make Martin feel better about Jack forgetting his name. If she did, it worked, because Jack said, "Quite right!" and soon Martin was telling him how he'd been picked for the school football team.

"Will you come and watch my match?" he said.

"Sure," Jack replied without looking up.

Despite what he'd said about the food, I noticed he wasn't eating much, just pushing it around his plate. He seemed more interested in drinking.

"I'm going to be starting sailing lessons this summer," Roz said. "Will you come out on the boat with me, Uncle J—?"

Her voice trailed off as she realised what she'd done. Jack loved sailing—he'd often said he wanted to get a boat and keep it in Jersey—but he didn't look like he'd be going back out on the water any time soon.

"Who wants dessert?" my mother asked.

Jack was staring into the empty fireplace as if he could see something there invisible to the rest of us.

"Sure," he said, in a hoarse voice. "I'll come sailing with you."

He reached for the bottle and filled his glass. When my mother brought in the apple crumble, he didn't even make a pretence of eating. He had started sweating again.

"May I be excused?" Martin said.

"Wait till everyone's done," my mother replied.

"Yes, Martin, wait," Jack said. "Learn to be a polite young man." His voice sounded thick and strange, and his hand shook as he lifted his glass, spilling wine on the table.

My father looked at my mother. "I think we should probably let the kids go," he said.

Martin and Roz got up to leave, but I hadn't finished my crumble. Jack was swaying slightly from side to side.

"Are you alright, Uncle Jack?" I asked.

"Your uncle's fine, he's just tired," my father said. I looked at Jack again, and abandoned my crumble and fled.

At school, whenever Matthew asked about Uncle Jack and what it was like having a wounded hero in the house, I told him Jack was doing well, that he was bearing up against cruel fate and had laughed off the loss of his leg, that he was his old self and sat up joking with us every evening—in other words, I lied. Jack was doing anything but well, and even I could see it. Roz put it best: she said that it felt as if his ghost had come to stay, and in that first week he became a far more convincing resident spirit than the one in my chimney. He spent days on end shut up alone in his room, and all we'd see of him were fleeting glimpses when he'd glide through the hall on his crutches, staring straight ahead as if we didn't exist. Once I tried saying "Good morning", and he muttered "What's so good about it?" without even looking at me. He left signs of his presence in the hall: there were empty bottles outside his door each morning, and the smell of cigar smoke drifted out in the evenings, although my parents didn't allow smoking in the house. And in the night he cried out. The first time I heard it, I understood why old books talk about your blood curdling, because that's exactly how it felt, as if my blood had turned to lumps the way sour milk does. When the wind was still at Tempest House, you could hear the pipes whispering secrets to one another and the floorboards grumbling, and Jack's cry was all too clear. I lay awake with the light on for hours after. When I told Martin the next morning he laughed and said I'd imagined it, but my mother said she'd heard it too, and that it was just Jack having bad dreams. I wondered, though, what dreams could make a man cry out like that.

He couldn't stay shut up for ever, and after a week

or so he began to sit with us in the evenings, but the way he behaved was so weird I found myself wishing he'd stayed in his room. He didn't join in with whatever we were doing, but would sit in the corner muttering to himself, pulling at the threads of an old Afghan shawl he kept wrapped around his shoulders. I could never quite make out what he was saying; there was one word he repeated all the time that sounded like something between "shuffle" and "traffic". At other times I heard him murmur "I'm no good" or "All my fault". He had an amazing ability to ignore the television; he would sit staring at the wall instead, almost as if he was watching an invisible television of his own. Sometimes he seemed to be reacting to it: his head shaking, his eyes wide with fear; once, I even thought he forced himself to look away. At other times he would laugh out loud for no reason at all. With his shawl draped over his shoulders, and his hollow eyes, I thought he looked like a wounded old eagle brooding on its perch. The shawl was covered in dark stains and had a musty, unpleasant smell, but when my mother tried to wash it he wouldn't let her.

"These are noble stains," he said.

My father told me not to stare at him, but one evening he did something so strange I couldn't help watching: I saw him reach down below his stump and claw with his nails at the empty air. It looked as if he was scratching his foot—only the foot wasn't there. I glanced up at his face to see if he realised what he was doing and his eyes met mine across the room.

"Got an itch," he said, "in my foot."

I thought he must be going mad from the shock of having his leg cut off. My parents pretended there was nothing strange about the way he was acting, but I could see they were on edge—though sometimes I thought they worried about the wrong things. My father seemed more bothered by the amount of whisky Jack was drinking than anything else, which didn't seem all that fair to me, since he'd been drinking more himself since Jack arrived—though nowhere near as much as Jack, who kept the bottle beside him, and used it to wash down the pills he took every few hours. My father kept telling him he shouldn't mix them, but I wasn't sure the pills were doing Jack much good anyway: as far as I could see they just made him sweat. My father could be hard on Jack at times: he couldn't manage the stairs on his crutches at first, but my father insisted he try a few steps each day. His arms used to shake with the effort, and once he'd have fallen if my father hadn't been there to catch him. We didn't have a bath or shower downstairs, just a toilet, so my father took a bucket of hot water and towels to Jack's room each evening to help him wash. Jack often said his stump was sore and wanted to leave it, but my father insisted on cleaning it and changing the bandages every day, and I heard Jack gasping with the pain behind the closed door. My mother told me not to hang around outside his room, but something drew me there in the evenings, and I'd hear him and my father talking inside. Some of the things he said just made me more convinced he was going mad.

"My foot's still there," I heard him tell my father one evening; "it's still there but it's dead. I can feel it right now. It hurts sometimes, in the night. When it itches I can't scratch it. An itch you can never scratch, that can drive you mad: it must be how it feels to be dead."

He talked about death a lot, which scared me. "It's like a piece of your own death, losing a leg," he told my father another time. "Part of me died early, and the rest's just waiting to join it."

There were things I wished I'd never heard. "I watched a man die once," Jack said. "It was in Afghanistan. I remember the look of surprise in his eyes. The blood made a neat trail in the dust as they carried him away."

I wasn't afraid of the ghost in my chimney any more: I had worse things to keep me up at night.

Roz came back from school one afternoon excited that she'd come top of her class for something she'd written about the war between Iran and Iraq—I hadn't even realised they were different countries; it seemed ridiculous to me they were at war when they had almost the same name. Roz could be a little full of herself at times, but there was no need to put her down the way Jack did. She was telling us what she'd written when he interrupted.

"Nonsense," he said, "you can't reduce a war to good guys and bad guys."

I think we'd got so used to him ignoring us by then that we didn't think he was listening.

"When it comes to war, it doesn't matter which side you're on," he went on. "All that matters is being trapped in the middle."

"But Mrs Stanhope said—" Roz began.

"When was she last in Ahvaz?"

"That's not fair," my mother protested, but Roz interrupted her.

"It doesn't matter," she said, blushing, "it's only an essay."

She ran out of the room. Jack stared after her in surprise.

"Try to remember they're only children," my mother said.

Jack didn't join us for meals after that first lunch; instead, my mother would send one of us to his room with his food on a tray. He never let any of us into the room, but would tell us to leave the tray outside, and I began to think there was something he didn't want us to see—perhaps that his leg had gone bad and was turning green under the bandages. Roz told me not to be stupid—our father would hardly let his leg turn green. I would knock on the door and watch the cigar smoke drifting out from underneath as I waited for him to answer—my mother said we couldn't really ask him to go outside to smoke, not with his leg. But one evening he answered almost as soon as I knocked, and said to come in.

He was sitting up in bed, the bandage unwound and lying in a mess. And in the middle of it, uncovered and open, was what was left of his leg.

"Oh, Ben," he said, looking confused, "sorry, I thought it was your dad." He pulled the duvet over his stump, as if it was something to be ashamed of.

"I—I brought your dinner."

"God, is it time already? Thanks, you can, uh, leave it there."

I put the tray on his bedside table and got out of the room as quickly as I could. His leg hadn't gone bad, and it wasn't gruesome the way I'd thought it would be: you couldn't see the bone poking out or anything like that. But somehow that made it worse. There was a row of black stitches where they'd sewn the skin back up, very neat and tidy. They'd left a useless little bit of leg below his knee, and as he'd turned to look at me it had moved pointlessly. Like a cruel joke of a leg.

Chapter Six

The Tower

"OF COURSE WE have to make allowances for Uncle Jack," Martin said, "after what he's been through."

We were sitting upstairs in the old German watchtower at Les Landes and Martin was telling his friend Harry Grainville about Jack, while I looked down at the sea tearing itself apart on the rocks below. The wind moaned in the tower, and at times I could have sworn I heard a human voice calling out. My parents would never have allowed us in that old watchtower on our own, but Harry's father was more relaxed about that sort of thing. It really was a tower: seven floors high, like a mini-skyscraper with concrete walls thick enough to stop bullets. The Nazis built it when they were in Jersey during the war. It was right on the edge of the cliff, and to get there you had to scramble down a loose dirt path where the wind blew so hard I worried it would hurl us into the sea. There was a sign by the entrance that said "Danger", and the place was supposed to be kept locked up, but someone had broken the lock off the door. It was empty inside, the only sign of human presence the names scratched on the walls. The door was halfway up the tower and there were stairs down to a lower level, but Martin led us to the top where the view was better. I thought of the German soldiers who had once stood where we now sat, and what their ghosts might do to us.

Harry was alright. He was Martin's best friend, and like everyone else he wanted to know all about Jack. Martin was playing it up, talking about how Jack had nearly died in the minefield, and repeating something my mother had said about making allowances, when I knew he was really put out Jack hadn't made it to his football match the day before. I don't know why it bothered him so much—the rest of us had all been there.

The wind died down, and in the quiet I heard a scraping sound from below. I glanced at Martin, but he didn't seem bothered and I didn't want to look frightened, so I turned back to the narrow slit of window to take my mind off it. This was where the German guns had been thrown down the cliffs at the end of the war.

The wind picked up again. Harry and Martin talked on, untroubled by the past closing in all around us. I thought of the room as it must have been in the war, crowded with radar screens, maps and charts; the German soldiers staring out to sea, straining their eyes for ships on the horizon. They were talking to each other in low voices; one sat hunched over a radio in a uniform that was too big for him, his fingers on the controls, thinking of his home in Germany. I could feel the fear and anger in the room as they stared out to sea, ready to open fire on any ship that came near. I thought of Captain Ayton and his men slipping past outside on their way to Egypt Wood.

The wind dropped again. Martin was telling Harry how the Afghans had carried Jack out of the minefield, and I wondered if they had watchtowers in Afghanistan. There was a thud from below and I looked up in alarm.

"What's wrong with you?" Martin said.

"Nothing."

"It's just the wind, " Harry said.

But the sound only came when the wind died down. I was sure someone was below, listening to us. A convict escaped from prison, looking for a place to hide, or the ghost of a German soldier returned to find his tower open and unguarded.

"Scared?" Martin said, with a nasty smile.

"No, I just wondered what it was, that's all."

"Dare you to go and find out."

I hated it when Martin got like that. He was just showing off to Harry, but I didn't want to admit I was scared. They were both watching to see what I'd do.

"It was probably nothing," I said, "just the wind."

"So why don't you go and make sure?"

"We have to go out that way anyway."

"Then you may as well go and see."

"Let him be," Harry said. "He doesn't have to go if he doesn't want to."

But Martin knew he had me. "Alright," he said. "But he has to admit he's scared."

Their eyes were on me, waiting. I thought of everything that might be waiting below, but I knew I couldn't back down. Martin would never let me forget it. I crossed to the top of the stairs and looked down. The wind was louder here, and seemed to be humming in the walls of the tower.

"And don't forget to check the bottom floor, below the entrance."

I thought of the stairs disappearing down into darkness, and hid a shiver. I started down, hardly believing what I was doing. What if I was right to be scared? I told myself there would be nothing, just another empty room. When I reached the floor where we had come in, I saw the old iron door was moving in the wind, swinging against an old block of concrete that had been left there to hold it open, and making the thudding sound I'd heard from above. Relieved, I started down to the floor below, knowing I'd proved myself to the others and would find nothing. But as I came round the corner of the stairs, my stomach dropped with fear. There was something lying on the floor in the middle of the room. I stared at it, too frightened to move. It was a sleeping bag, with what looked like the remains of a fire beside it.

There was the sound of a door slamming shut from above and I was running back up the stairs before I knew what I was doing. Martin and Harry stood laughing beside the closed door.

"You *idiots*!" I said. "I could have had a heart attack and died!"

"You should have seen your face," Martin said.

"Yeah? Well, someone's been down there! There's a sleeping bag and everything."

"Nice try."

"Honestly. See for yourself if you don't believe me."

Martin shrugged and went down to look, while Harry dragged the concrete block back in place to hold the door open.

"Blimey, he's right," Martin called up the stairs. I wanted to leave but Harry went down to look as well, and I didn't want to be alone so I followed, wishing I hadn't said anything. I was afraid the owner of the sleeping bag could come back at any moment, and I didn't want to meet him. Martin was prodding the sleeping bag with his shoe, while Harry examined a couple of empty beer cans he'd found beside the fire as if he expected to find the answer written on them. The wind was different down here, more muffled. The thought of an escaped prisoner hiding in the tower came back to me, and I imagined him returning with a freshly killed rabbit for his lunch, a knife in his hand.

"Probably just older kids, messing about," Harry said.

"Yeah, probably," Martin agreed.

I was relieved when I heard Harry's father calling us from outside, and we had to leave with the mystery still unsolved. Martin wanted to go back the next weekend to see if the sleeping bag was still there, and swore me to secrecy, but I was pretty sure this only applied to the world of adults, and told Matthew what we'd found. He was convinced the sleeping bag must belong to a mad old German soldier who didn't know the war had ended and was still guarding the tower with an old machine-gun. I told him that was stupid, but he said there were Japanese soldiers lost in the jungle who were convinced World War Two was still going on, and he brought an old magazine to school to prove it, with a picture of a man who'd been found in the middle of nowhere, still fighting on his own.

A couple of nights later, Uncle Jack tried to kill himself. It was Roz who found him. I feel bad about it now, but that evening I was glad he stayed in his room and didn't come and sit with us: one of my favourite programmes was on television and it was easier to watch without him muttering in the background, or the feeling he could do something weird at any moment. It was a rotten night: the trees were restless outside and the ghost was moaning so loud in his chimney you could hear him over the television. It was Martin's turn to take Jack's tray that night. Somehow my mother had managed to get his dinner ready just as our programme was about to start, and Martin raced down the hall with her calling after him not to spill any of it. It wasn't till later he admitted there'd been no answer when he knocked on the door; the programme was about to start and he'd just left the tray outside. An hour or so after, Roz got up to go to the bathroom and noticed it still lying untouched outside Jack's door. She told me later she wouldn't have said anything if it hadn't been an ad break when she came back in. My mother told her to go and check if Jack was alright. She was asking Martin why he'd left a perfectly good dinner to go cold in the hall when Roz cried out. We looked at each other. My father got up and I ran down the hall after him. The wind was rattling the front door like someone trying to get in. Roz was staring into Jack's room.

"Christ!" my father said.

"Is—is he?" Roz stammered, but my father pushed past her without answering.

That was when I saw Jack. I thought he was sleeping at first: he was lying across the bed, the clean bandage my father had put on earlier still neatly wound around his stump. But then I noticed his lips had turned blue. My father was taking his pulse.

"Call an ambulance," he said to my mother, who was standing behind me. "Tell them it's an overdose."

He was very calm. He was always like that when

it was something medical. He could get stressed over the tiniest things, like not being able to find a book, but when he had someone's life in his hands he was the calmest person in the world. He pointed to the empty pill packets on the bedside table.

"I need to know how many he's taken." Martin started counting them. Roz looked terrible: she was swaying from side to side as if she might faint.

"He's okay," my father said, "he's breathing."

Martin said Jack had taken twenty of the pills. My father didn't comment, he just nodded. My mother came back to say an ambulance was on the way.

"He's going to be alright," she told Roz. "You did really well finding him. Now I want you to take the boys and go and wait in the other room."

I could see Martin was hurt Roz had been put in charge, but he came without arguing.

"Well?" I heard my mother ask my father behind us.

"I hope that ambulance gets here fast," he replied.

The television was still on. Martin turned the sound down so we could make out what was going on, but my mother had closed the door to Jack's room. Roz was hugging herself as if she felt cold.

"What's wrong with Uncle Jack?" I asked.

"He took too many of those pills," Martin said.

"But I thought they were supposed to make him feel better."

"Not if you take too many."

"What's going to happen to him?"

"He might die."

"Shut up," Roz said.

"Will he be alright?" I asked her.

"How should I know? Just shut up, the pair of you."

The sound of sirens came. No one stopped me when I went to the door and watched the ambulance men carry Jack out on a stretcher. He already looked like a corpse.

Chapter Seven

A Difficult Man

I SEARCHED THE internet for Uncle Jack but I couldn't find anything. I was a little more successful when I tried his formal name, John Merryweather: some of his old archived newspaper articles came up, from before he lost his leg, but nothing more recent. It seemed he hadn't just disappeared from our family history, but from the wider world as well. The last entry I could find for him anywhere was a dispatch from Afghanistan, on the advance of Soviet forces into Mujahideen territory in the mountains, and their brutal repression of the local population. He must have sent it a few days before he set out across the minefield. After that, there was silence, as if he'd died there in the mountains or succeeded in his suicide attempt a few weeks later at Tempest House, instead of recovering and returning to make our lives still more complicated.

I'd slept well for the first time in a week—so well I forgot where I was and woke to the sweet delusion I was in bed with Naomi back in the early days of our marriage and all was still right between us. It was a double awakening when I reached for her and found only cold sheets: to the memory of Naomi in Richard's arms, and to the reason I was back in Jersey. My head was pounding from the wine I'd drunk: I'd been waking up with hangovers for months, but they didn't seem to get any easier. Roz called from the hospital to ask me not to come in that morning, but to take the afternoon shift instead so she could see her kids. My mother came on the phone. She still sounded weak but there was more life in her voice.

"I'm fine," she said, "I just want to get out of this place."

I had a couple of hours to fill, and I looked through a few more of Jack's old newspaper pieces. It was strange to read his description of events I knew as history: the Khmer Rouge, the end of the Vietnam War, the Iranian Revolution. I could hear the words in his voice. He was a good writer, better than I'd realised, with a vivid direct style. On a whim, I sent an email to the newspaper asking if they had a contact address for him, or knew where he had ended up and how I could get in touch. I felt a little guilty, betraying the family code of silence, but I told myself the chances were nothing would come of it: the newspaper editors probably had no idea where Jack was—if they even bothered to reply to my message.

There was a message from Matt in my inbox, a

joke that had been doing the rounds at school, which he hoped would "cheer me up". He was more sensitive than he liked to let on: as I'd left the previous morning, he'd run after me to the door and said, "Don't worry, Dad, be happy!" There was an email from work, about our new Syria report, but I couldn't face opening it. I had enough to worry about without getting involved in a project that was close to dragging us into taking sides in a civil war.

In many ways, it was because of Jack that I'd become a human rights campaigner. When I emerged from university with a second-class English degree and no qualifications that could reasonably be expected to earn me a living, and began to look around for something to do with my life, all I could think of were those stories Jack used to tell of the places he'd been and the things he'd done. I wanted a life like that. I was already infected, and though I'd never have dared mention it to my family, I wanted to be Uncle Jack. The moral ambiguity of journalism, though, was not for me. I wanted to know which side I was on, and one alcohol-emboldened night, despite my complete lack of experience and apparent unsuitability for the job, I sent Asylum an application for the position of field researcher. No one was more surprised than I was when I was invited to London for an interview. I must have seemed very young and gauche to the man who interviewed me, overdressed in my one good suit beside his jeans and open-necked shirt. I remember him trying not to smile as I gave him some drivel about Asylum being the "conscience of the world". But I must have said something right, because a couple of weeks later they offered me a place as a trainee. Sometimes, I wonder who I might have become if they'd said no.

I volunteered for all the most dangerous assignments. I even made it out to Afghanistan, though to be honest I couldn't see what it was Jack had loved so much about the place. There was, I think, something else driving me on to those places: as a child I'd always been hopeless on the sports field because of my leg. In Kosovo and Gaza, I was proving to myself that I could be a man—or what I thought a man was.

I was happy enough in those early days at Asylum. I was travelling the world, visiting places most people only got to see on television and doing what I believed was valuable work. One of my reports was mentioned in parliament, another came up at a White House press conference.

It all changed, though, when Matt was born. With the responsibilities of a father, Naomi and I agreed, I couldn't go flying off to war zones any more. I'd had an episode of post-traumatic stress disorder after a near miss with a rocket in Afghanistan. It embarrassed me: I didn't feel my experiences justified it, compared to other researchers I knew who'd discovered mass graves. But it gave me the excuse I needed and Asylum agreed to let me move to advocacy and government relations. I could try to blame it on Naomi, but it wouldn't be true. She'd been trying to stop me going to dangerous places for years, but the moment I held my son in my arms I knew I was never going back. From that day on, I had my own world to protect.

To any outsider, it must have appeared that I'd gone up in the world: I'd swapped air raid shelters and emergency generators for five-star hotels and international conferences. The trouble was I just wasn't suited to advocacy. For one thing, it bored me. I suppose the irony should have occurred to me sooner: I was drawn to precisely the sort of places we wanted to fix, but it was the things that were wrong with them that I liked. I wasn't at home in the sort of well-ordered, just world we were trying to build; I missed the high stakes of war and upheaval. Still, if that had been the limit of the problem, I could have lived with it, but there was a more serious fault line. As a researcher, all I'd had to do was uncover human rights abuses, but pointing out what was wrong wasn't enough in my new role. Now I had to get something done about it and that, I had found, involved compromises I wasn't ready to make.

The new Syria report was one of them. The idea had been fine when my former colleagues in the research team first brought it up. Everyone was talking about the Syrian civil war but no one had any idea of who the different factions were, or of the things they'd done. What we were proposing was a report detailing the human rights abuses, faction by faction, chiefly to discourage the West from making the mistake of siding with any of them.

But as soon as the British government got wind of what we were doing, I was summoned to a meeting with a junior minister at the Foreign Office. I was paid to lobby the government, but it quickly became apparent that it was the minister who was lobbying me. He asked which group was going to come out best in our report. I tried to explain the aim wasn't to choose a side, that we weren't in the business of endorsing human rights abusers, but he brushed that aside. He wanted us, he said, to consider holding back on our criticism of one particular faction.

"Of course, we're not expecting you to give them your *approval*," he said. "Dreadful people. But we need someone to sort the place out, and frankly they're better than anything else on offer." A couple of years before, the minister had been one of the leading voices calling for Britain to join air strikes. "We're just asking you to bear it in mind," he said, with a television smile. "After all, we're all on the same side here."

And that was the problem. It had been ever since the Iraq War. We'd spent so long crying in the wilderness about the things Saddam Hussein did to his people that when someone came along promising to do something about it, a lot of us were too willing to sign up to their war. We'd disowned it since, of course, but it's not so easy to escape. When you've opened negotiations with Mephistopheles, it's a long way back to the high ground.

At the hospital, my mother was looking more herself. Some of the colour had returned to her, and some of the fight.

"I'm just fed up with being stuck in here with all these wires running out of me," she said. "And if one more person tells me not to worry, I'll scream."

"Take it easy," my father said. "We'll have you home soon." He was exhausted, and I told him to go home and get some sleep, but I knew I was wasting my breath. There was no prising him out of that room.

"I'm sorry to drag you away from Naomi and the kids," my mother said. "You must be bored out of your mind, stuck over here with nothing to do."

"I'm fine, it's good to get a break." I didn't tell them it was Naomi I was glad to get away from for a few days. What was it Dr Jenkins had said? The heart is resilient, but it needs time to recover.

"I dropped in on Tempest House yesterday."

"Tempest House? You didn't tell me." My father's face lit up at the name of the place; I wondered why he'd ever left. "What were you doing over there?"

"Just had a look for old times' sake. It's years since I've been."

"I can take you over there if you want to see it. Of

course the new owners have wrecked the place."

"They have not," my mother said, "all they've done is change things to suit them. It's their house now. Not everyone has to keep things the way you want them."

"No, they've *ruined* it. Do you know what they've done? They've taken out the fireplace in the sitting room, and all the plastering—"

"For heaven's sake, Tom," my mother interrupted, "he doesn't want to hear about all that."

"He's the one who said he wanted to go over there."

There was a time when Naomi and I were like that with each other, I remembered. Now we were painfully polite, we trod softly around each other.

I listened to them bicker, and tried to ignore the muffled sound of the heart monitor. Outside the door, nurses padded along the corridor in soft shoes, other visitors murmured in hushed tones. We were all trying not to attract Death's attention, pretending we couldn't see him watching us, hunched and silent in the corner of the room. Through the window I could see traffic queuing at the lights, life going on, oblivious to the drama that played out here, not even daring to raise its voice.

Dr Jenkins came to check up on my mother. She was making excellent progress, he said; she'd be home in a couple of days. After, he went out to talk with my father in the corridor. I watched them through the glass panel in the door, trying to decipher what they were saying.

"Are they analysing every last beep and flicker out there?" my mother said.

"You know Dad."

"Ah, whatever keeps him happy."

"Does it bother you, the monitor?" I asked.

"No, I ignore the stupid thing. What does it know? When your time comes, it comes."

When my father came back in, he was happy. "You're making a fantastic recovery," he said. "I told Jenkins you were a good healer."

Roz came to take over from me in the early evening. She tried to get my father to go home with me, but he still refused to leave my mother's bedside. I left the hospital and filled my lungs with clean sea air, grateful to be back among the living.

I stopped at a pub for a beer on my way home. The place was full. Outside the gulls were chasing each other over the beach.

"Over on holiday?" the barmaid asked. I looked up in surprise. "You've got hire plates on your car," she said.

"Oh. No, I'm just back visiting family."

"You local then?"

"Originally. But I left years ago."

Her eyes were pale blue, and she was wearing some scent that reminded me of summer fields. I watched her work the beer pumps, thinking of all the lives I could have led if I'd never met Naomi.

"What brings you back to the Rock then?" She leaned forward and smiled at me under her eyelashes. She had a mole on her left cheek, just below her ear.

"Family illness."

"Sorry to hear that."

I ran my thumb along the back of the wedding ring I was still wearing as she finished pouring the beer.

"You going to be over long then?" she asked, placing it in front of me.

"Thanks. Just a couple of days."

I took the beer and moved off to a table, feeling her eyes on my back. I waited until I was sure she was busy with another customer before I glanced back over at the bar. It was so long since I'd flirted with a woman I wouldn't have known what to say. I'd spent years trying to be Uncle Jack with women, but the truth was I'd never been that good at it. When Naomi came into my life I'd thought I'd left all that behind.

Roz invited me over for dinner that evening. My father had insisted on staying with my mother, so we thought we might as well take the chance to catch up. The children were in bed and we sat on the terrace of their house overlooking the millionaire's view of St Brelade's Bay. It was the antithesis of Tempest House: clean lines, open spaces and plate-glass. Roz was trying to prove to herself she wasn't my father.

Watching her and Neil together, I felt my own failure. Like my parents, they had successfully negotiated marriage, while I was left staring at the wreckage, and couldn't even bring myself to admit it. When they asked about Naomi I smiled and lied. I was used to keeping things hidden. Even with my own sister, I felt so alone she might as well not have been there.

After a time Neil slipped out to check on the children, and left us to talk.

"She's going to be okay," Roz said. "I know she is."

"I know. She's tough; it'll take more than this to stop her. I still can't believe it, though. She always seemed indestructible when we were kids."

"She was too busy taking care of us. She didn't have time to get sick You don't realise it till you have your own, do you? Whenever any of mine give us trouble, I reckon it's karma for all the grief I gave Mum and Dad."

"You weren't any trouble. Martin and I were the ones who were hard work."

"I wish he could be here."

"Me too."

"Remember the time he crashed Mum's car?"

"I thought she was going to kill him."

"It was a good thing he hit the gate before he got out on the road. What was he doing driving anyway? He was only ten!"

"He wanted to prove he could do it."

She offered me another glass of wine, but for once I said no. My father had agreed to let me take over from him at my mother's bedside at ten; the hospital was on the other side of the island, and I didn't want a drink-driving charge.

"What about the time we made our own raft?" she said. "I nearly drowned!"

"That was your fault—you took her out too fast. Martin and I worked so hard on that thing, we were sure it would float."

"It did. So long as no one sat on it."

I looked at her and wondered. Surely I could break the code of silence with her. "Do you remember Uncle Jack?"

She stared at me, and hugged herself as if it had grown cold.

"What about him?"

"That time he came to stay, after he lost his leg."

"How could I forget? I can still remember finding him that night, after he took the overdose."

"What happened between him and Dad? Why did they stop talking?"

"I don't know. Some sort of row."

"Doesn't it strike you as a bit odd? They used to be so close."

"Who knows? It was a long time ago. Look, I know what he did for us, but sometimes Jack frightened me.

There was something about him. To be honest, I was relieved when he left."

"I liked him."

"You always seemed to have some sort of connection with him. I never got it—it's not as if you had anything in common. Although you're beginning to get quite a look of him these days. Must be the hair."

"It just think it's a shame we've lost touch."

"I don't. He was a difficult man."

Night had fallen over the bay and we looked out over the lights shining at the water's edge below.

"You were very young in those days," Roz said. "You don't remember. I know what happened afterwards, but that time he came to stay was pretty rough for all of us."

But that wasn't right: that wasn't how I remembered it at all.

Chapter Eight

Annie

UNCLE JACK DIDN'T die. They brought him home in the morning, his face still pale as bone.

He didn't say a word, but went straight to his room and closed the door. My father had been at the hospital with him all night; he said they'd had to pump Jack's stomach up with air or something. Whatever it was, it sounded painful. My father had to go back to work after breakfast and I didn't get a chance to speak to him alone until the evening.

"Dad," I said, "you know those pills, the ones Uncle Jack took?"

"Mmm," he said, searching for something in his black doctor's bag.

"What were they?"

"Painkillers. Medicine to stop his leg hurting."

"Why did they make him sick?"

"He took too many of them. You have to be careful with medicine."

"Do you think he meant to take them?"

He looked up at me. "What?"

"Did he do it on purpose?"

"Who told you that?"

"No one, I—"

"Your uncle would never do a thing like that. Never. He got confused and made a mistake, that's all."

He seemed upset so I didn't mention it again. There were other things to worry about: my parents were fighting again. They didn't shout or anything, but you could see it in the way they were with each other. They'd stop talking when I came into the room. "This isn't the right place for him, he needs help," I heard my mother say, and another time: "It's not fair to the children. You can see it's affecting them."

I wished there was some way of showing them I wasn't bothered by what had happened. Martin and Roz didn't want to speak about it. Roz told me I was too young and didn't understand. I knew what it was, though, the thing no one wanted to mention. It was something only crazy people did, and that just made me all the more worried Jack was losing his mind. He never spoke to us about that night, but I hung around outside his door in the evenings when my father went to wash his stump, listening for their voices.

"I don't know," I heard Jack say, "perhaps it was what I deserved."

"Don't talk like that," my father said. "You didn't deserve to die."

"Ask not who deserves to die, but who deserves to live."

"You didn't deserve what happened to you."

"Losing my leg, you mean? What makes you think the rest of me has any right to be here?"

It was around this time that Annie turned up on our doorstep in the rain.

When the bell rang, I remember I ran down the hall ahead of my mother just to see who was mad enough to be out in weather like that.

Through the water streaming down the window I saw a young woman dressed in white, holding a plastic bag over her head in a hopeless attempt to keep the rain off. When she saw me looking out she smiled at me, and not in the way adults sometimes smile at children because they feel they have to. She had a sort of hold-all with her, and I wondered why my parents hadn't said she was coming to stay.

"I'm Annie," she said when my mother shooed me out of the way and told her to come in, "Annie Le Sueuer. For John Merryweather."

I thought she must be one of Jack's woman friends. When my mother asked her to wait in the sitting room, she started unpacking her hold-all. I wondered why she'd brought such odd things with her: a rubber mat, some tiny weights and a sort of sleeve-like thing with lots of straps hanging from it. She noticed me watching her and smiled up at me.

"Are you Uncle Jack's friend?" I said.

"No, I'm the new physio," she said.

"What's a fizzy-oh?"

"A sort of...special trainer. For people who have problems like your uncle. I'm here to help him get his strength back."

Someone like this had come before, I remembered, but Jack had refused to see him.

"What are those for?" I asked, pointing at the weights.

"They're for exercises. To get your uncle ready for his prosthetic leg."

"Do you always come out to people's houses?"

"Sometimes. When they're badly hurt."

"I've got a bad leg too."

"Really? They both look fine to me."

"It's okay now. I had an operation."

I showed her my scar. It made her look sad, so I told her it didn't bother me.

"Jack's very upset about his leg," I said.

"Well, we'll have to see if we can cheer him up then."

I thought she might be taking on more than she realised. I heard the sound of his crutches coming down the hall, and he appeared in the doorway wrapped in his Afghan shawl.

"Hello," Annie said, getting up and holding out her hand. "You must be Jack."

"Mr Merryweather. I'd shake your hand but I'd probably fall over."

"Jack!" my mother protested.

"No problem," Annie said. "We'll just have to see what we can do about that." She was trying to keep the brightness in her voice, but I could see she was upset.

"If we must."

"Why don't you sit down here, and tell me about your leg?"

"Got blown up."

"Well, we'll leave you to it," my mother said, drawing me away. "Just call if you need anything."

She closed the door behind us, but it wasn't long before it swung open again and Jack swept past us, muttering, "No bloody point anyway."

"We'll try again tomorrow," Annie called after him, but the only reply was the door to his room slamming.

"You alright?" my mother asked.

Annie nodded, but she didn't look it. "It's hard at first for amputees. He's been through a lot."

"Yes," my mother replied, "and he's determined to put everyone else through it."

It was the same every afternoon that week: Annie would come and unpack her hold-all in the sitting room, and Jack would refuse to do the exercises and tell her they were a waste of time. He said she didn't know what she was talking about, and once he even called her a silly girl. I felt bad for her; she was only trying to help.

But I felt sorry for Jack too: everyone was pushing him as if he just needed to try a little harder, and I wondered why none of them could see that he wasn't being difficult, he really couldn't do the exercises. He was just too proud to admit it.

"I think you might need to get another physio," my mother told my father after a few days. "Someone more experienced."

"She comes highly recommended," he said. "Bill says she's the best he's had in years." I thought Annie would make the decision for them: towards the end of the week I saw her packing up her little weights, and she looked so sad I was sure she wouldn't come back. But she was at the door again on Monday afternoon: I suppose she couldn't afford to risk losing her job.

I overheard my mother talking to her friend Polly Rocquier about Jack one afternoon. Polly often came over for coffee. I thought she must have very cold hands, because she used to wrap them both around her mug as if she was trying to warm them up.

"I don't know what I'm going to do," my mother said, "he's getting worse."

"I suppose he must be suffering terribly, poor man," Polly said.

"I know. That's what makes me feel so guilty. Like Tom says, we're all he's got. But I keep asking myself: is it fair to the kids?"

Polly didn't mean to make Jack fall over. It happened

a couple of days later: she was coming out of the bathroom and he was going too fast down the hall on his crutches. When he saw her he tried to turn at the last minute, but he swung one of the crutches a little too far and it slipped out from under him. He seemed to fall in slow motion. The sound when his stump hit the floor was sickening.

"Oh my God," Polly said, rushing over to him. He was lying on the floor, groping for the crutch which had fallen just out of reach, but he was embarrassed and kept trying to shrug her off. She hooked her arms under his shoulders, but she couldn't manage his weight and ended up dragging him along the floor like a sack of potatoes.

"I'm alright, really. It's okay. I can manage. *Please!*"

That's when my mother came out. She didn't try to lift Jack up or anything like that; she just walked up to him, held out her arm and stood waiting. Jack took it and, steadying himself against the wall with his other hand, slowly pushed himself up. My mother picked up his crutch and gave it to him. Neither of them said a word, but he gave her a look I didn't understand until years after.

"God, I'm so sorry," Polly started saying.

"It's alright, Polly," my mother said, holding Jack's gaze, "nothing to worry about."

That was my mother: she couldn't stand to see anyone humiliated.

A couple of nights after that my father took Jack out to the pub. They went to the Black Dog in Bouley Bay, a little harbour between the hills, not far from the house. Martin said the smugglers used to hide there, and I liked to imagine it the way it must have been then: a wooden ship on the water and the men rolling barrels onto the pier under cover of the dark, while the sound of singing spilled out of the pub. It wasn't much to look at from outside, but inside it was all wooden panelling, low ceilings and black beams, and you could see how it must have been with the smugglers smoking their pipes, their pistols lying on the tables. I didn't know how my father could stand to go there at night, though, because everyone knew the pub was named after the ghost dog that roamed the hills. Anyone who saw the Black Dog of Bouley Bay was supposed to go mad with fear, and I used to lie awake sometimes worrying it would come up through Egypt Wood to Tempest House. Martin said the dog didn't exist, it was just another story the smugglers had made up to scare people away, but I knew he was wrong, because the fishermen said you could still see it some nights, and when you did it meant a storm was coming.

There was a different type of storm when my father and Jack got back that night. I had long gone to bed, but the sound of the front door slamming woke me.

"Damn it, Jack, why do you have to be so difficult?" my father's voice came up the stairs.

"I'm in pain," Jack said.

"Ah, the hell with it, I've had enough. You can drink yourself to death for all I care. You've always been the same."

"What makes you think I care?"

There was the sound of another door and my mother's voice, whispering hoarsely, "Quiet! You'll wake the children!"

"Oh, I'm sorry for living," my father said. There were footsteps and a door closed. I thought they'd all gone: it was several minutes before I heard Jack's voice. He must have been standing alone in the hall.

"Me too," he said. "Me too."

That was when I realised I had to do something. It was obvious the reason Jack was being so difficult was that he was unhappy, and I couldn't understand why no one else seemed to see it. He'd lost his leg and it was hurting him so much it was driving him mad, but everybody seemed to be angry with him. When I decided to try to cheer him up, it wasn't just because I felt sorry for him: it was the only way I could see to stop my parents fighting and get life back to the way it used to be. The opportunity came one afternoon. I was reading in my favourite spot in the hall, in a little alcove where I could sit with my back to a radiator. Martin had stayed on after school for football practice, Roz was round at her friend Louise's and my mother was doing her marking upstairs. Annie wasn't due for another hour or so. Cigar smoke was drifting out from under Jack's door at the other end of the hall. I was reading some sort of Arabian Nights adventure, but I couldn't concentrate and the moonlit alleys of the desert city kept falling back to words on the page. Marking my place in the book, I got up and went over to his door. The smell of cigar smoke was stronger there. I knocked nervously. There was no answer and I was about to turn away when I heard a vague mumble from inside.

"Uncle Jack?"

When I opened the door, he was staring right at me, but he didn't seem to see me. It was as if he was watching something else again, some scene I couldn't see. He was sitting in the broken old armchair. The room was a mess: clothes and books strewn across the floor, a half-empty bottle lying on its side. He murmured something to himself, the word I'd heard him say before that sounded like "traffic".

"Uncle Jack?"

Slowly, he came back from wherever he'd been. He looked around the room, blinking as if he was surprised to be there.

"Ben?" he said in a distant voice.

"I just, um," I stammered, "wanted to see if you were okay."

He stared up at me. I began to think I'd made a mistake coming: he was even madder than I'd thought.

"I'm fine," he said after a long time, and turned

away as if the conversation was over.

"Um, would you like a cup of tea?" I couldn't think of anything else.

"Tea," he said in a far-off voice, "why not?"

He got up and dusted at the armchair with his shawl.

"Take a pew."

I didn't know what that meant, but he seemed to be pointing at the chair, so I picked my way through the books and clothes on the floor. There was a bottle of whisky in easy reach of the chair, and a cigar still lit and giving off a slow trail of smoke in an ashtray balanced on one of the arms. He tried to wave some of the smoke away from me, and opened the window to let in a breeze that sent the curtain billowing and cigar ash scurrying across the floor. I was surprised how easily he moved around the room: he hardly used his crutches; most of the time he leaned against the walls and desk instead.

On the bedside table I saw a packet of pills like the ones he'd taken the night he almost died. The air was cold, and I could smell the sea; the waves were breaking below.

I was wondering whether I should go to the kitchen to get some tea when he reached behind the portable television and pulled out a small electric kettle. He groped blindly for the electric socket, balancing on his good leg, and I braced for him to electrocute himself or knock the TV over, but somehow he managed it. He set two dirty mugs on the desk.

"Your mum set this up for me," he said. "Very kind, your mum. Milk and sugar?"

He put two tea-bags in his own mug, I noticed. I thought he would have to send me to the kitchen for milk, because there was no fridge in the room, but he swung over to the window, reached out with one hand and drew in a carton that must have been sitting outside.

"Old trick," he said when he saw me staring. "Keeps it fresh."

The room was getting pretty cold from the open window, but it didn't seem to bother him. When he passed me my tea I saw he had bright red sores running across his palms.

"What happened to your hands?" I asked.

"Crutches." He showed me how the handle had worn away the skin where he held them.

"Does it hurt?"

"Yes."

He rubbed his hands together and the hard dry skin made a scratching sound. He sat on the bed and drank his tea in silence.

"How's your leg?"

It was so long before he answered I thought he must have forgotten I was there.

"Not good," he said at last. I waited for more but it

seemed that was it. He'd started staring again, watching something in the empty air. I had to think of some other way to get him talking.

"I'm having a bad day," I tried.

"I know how you feel."

"Because of your leg?"

"Mmmm."

It wasn't going to be easy. The room was getting colder; through the open window I could hear the gulls out to sea.

"You're getting really good on your crutches," I said. "Fast, I mean."

"Hmm," he said. "Should just about have got the hang of them when they take them away."

"Are they going to give you a pathetic leg?"

He looked up, angry, and I thought I must have said something wrong, until he burst out laughing.

"Pathetic leg!" he said. "Out of the mouths of babes!" It was frightening the way he was laughing, like a maniac.

"Did I get it wrong?"

"No, no," he said, then stopped himself. "Well yes, but I prefer your version. Pathetic indeed: my pathetic leg."

He'd finished laughing, and looked like he was about to start staring at whatever it was again.

"I'm sorry," I said. "About your leg, I mean."

"Me too."

"It wasn't fair, what happened."

"No."

There was something so sad in his eyes I had to look away.

"I'm sorry about your day," he said.

"Oh, it's not important. Not like your leg."

"Hmm."

"It's just this other kid, Luke Pendell, broke my bag."

"Why?"

"He hates me."

"Why?"

"I don't know."

"Sounds like a pig."

"He is."

"Did you get him back?"

"He's bigger than me."

He nodded. I ran out of things to say after that, and we sat drinking our tea together in silence, but he didn't seem to mind me being there. All the same, I was grateful when my mother came for me.

"I've been looking all over for you," she said. "You know you're not supposed to disturb your uncle."

"It's alright," Jack said. "He's been cheering me up."

"Has he? That was nice of you, Ben."

"Uncle Jack's been telling me about his proleptic leg." I gave him a nervous look but he didn't tell her about my mistake. She sat and talked with him a little. When we got up to leave, I was sure he gave me a smile.

I wish I could say our chat changed things, but they went on the same as before: Jack stayed shut up in his room and my parents were still on edge. Annie kept coming and Jack kept shouting at her. A couple of times she looked close to tears when she left, and I thought it could only be a matter of time before she told us she wasn't coming back. When I heard her voice raised one afternoon, I thought her patience had run out at last. My mother reached the door ahead of me. Inside Jack and Annie stood facing each other, the rubber exercise mat in a tangle between them, as if it had been kicked away.

"I'm sorry about what happened to you, Jack," Annie said. "I can't imagine what it feels like. Nobody knows what you've been through. It's a terrible thing and there's nothing anyone can do about that."

He glared at her.

"I can't change what happened," she said. "But I can help you walk again. If you want."

For a moment I was afraid he would shout at her, but he lowered his eyes and nodded. Without a word, Annie took his crutches and helped him back to the floor. She straightened the exercise mat and laid his crutches within reach. My mother smiled and closed the door.

Chapter Nine

The Talk

IT ALL HAPPENED because Mrs Maudsley held me back after school. It never would have meant that much to me if she hadn't said what she did. Earlier that afternoon she'd told us she had a new project for us: she wanted our parents to come into school and talk about their work, so we could learn about the different things people did for a living. I was gathering my books up when she touched me on the shoulder, and called me over to her desk. She waited for the others to leave, but I could see some of them hanging back in the corridor, hoping to hear what it was all about.

"I just wanted to say that of course in your case, Aubin, there's no point asking your mother in to speak to the class," she said. "We all have a pretty good idea of life here at St Edward's."

I nodded and mumbled something. I didn't need her to tell me that. Nor did I need Luke Pendell, who was waiting for me outside with a look of delight.

"Going to bring your one-legged uncle in to tell

us about the war?" he called after me, to his friends' laughter. "Probably just some window cleaner who fell off his ladder."

I wasn't planning to ask my mother and I certainly wasn't going to let Uncle Jack anywhere near the class. I couldn't think of anything worse than having to sit there and listen while he told them all how it felt to be dead, or said his leg was still there but they just couldn't see it. I didn't need to worry about any of that because I was planning to ask my father, and I knew his job was more interesting than any of the other parents'. Holly Le Boutillier's father was a doctor, but he was only a GP, while my father was the head of a whole department at the hospital—and the cancer department at that. Everybody knew cancer was the most dangerous disease and the hardest to cure.

He didn't seem as keen on the idea as I'd hoped, but he agreed and we set a date a couple of weeks later. Some of the other parents began to come into class, and as I sat through their talks trying not to let my boredom show, I knew my father's was going to blow them all away. Matthew's father, who was a lawyer, was the dullest of the lot, but I didn't have the heart to say so and told Matthew he'd been so fascinating I was thinking of being a lawyer myself one day.

Matthew was delighted when I told him about my visit to Jack's room. He particularly liked the way Jack kept the milk on the windowsill, and said he was going to start doing the same outside his bedroom window. I didn't think that was such a good idea, since his room was upstairs. He didn't ask about Jack as much any more, which was something of a relief; I hadn't told him about the pills, but it was getting harder to hide the truth from him. He'd developed a new obsession, with a thing he called The Harvester.

It was something he'd seen in a film. I think his parents must have got lonely at night because they often let him stay up late and watch television, and he saw a lot of scary movies. In this one, a group of teenagers had done something wrong and they spent the whole film being chased around by a tall ghost in a monk's outfit with a hood that covered his face. Matthew called him The Harvester because he had one of those long sticks with a knife on the end that they used for harvesting the crops in the old days.

"Did he cut their heads off?" I asked.

"No, he doesn't need to," Matthew said. "He just touches you and you die."

"Then what does he need the knife-stick for?"

"I don't know. I'm just telling you what happened."

I laughed and told him I wasn't scared of a stupid old Harvester. A couple of days later we were on our way back from the school sports field. St Edward's was out in the country, and the path back led between two farmers' fields. Matthew and I had fallen behind the others when he clutched at my sleeve.

"It's him!" he said. "The Harvester!"

The light was fading and I couldn't see anything, but when he started running I followed him. I didn't dare look back all the way through the fields, down the steps to the school car park, into the main building and through the kitchen corridor where we weren't allowed, out to the playground where I knew we were safe because Mrs Maudsley was scowling down at us from the classroom window, and she was more than a match for any Harvester.

I counted the days to my father's talk. I should have reminded him, but I was looking forward to it so much I couldn't imagine he'd forget. It was the evening before when he asked me to remind him when he was coming.

"Half past eleven," I said.

"No, Ben, which day?"

"Tomorrow."

He put down the book and stared at me. "Are you sure?"

"Oh Tom," my mother said.

I looked from one of them to the other, trying not to believe it.

"It's just Irene Rogers' chemo starts tomorrow."

"Can't you change it?"

"I can try, but it's not going to be easy."

"You're still coming, aren't you?" I said.

He sighed. "It might be difficult. I've got this patient and she's really sick. She needs to start her treatment.

I'll see if we can change the time around."

"But I've told everybody."

"I'll do my best. "

"It's only for twenty minutes."

"I'll try. I promise."

The next morning, at breakfast, I didn't want to bring it up for fear of what the answer would be. It was my father who called me over and told me it wasn't looking good.

"I called the hospital and it's going to be tricky to move things around," he said. "I'm really sorry. Tell your teacher I'll come in next week, when things aren't so busy."

"You know your dad would come if he could," my mother told me on the way to school. "Mrs Rogers is very sick. Do you want me to come and explain to Mrs Maudsley?"

That would have made it worse. I told her I'd be fine.

"What're you looking so down for?" Martin said. "It's just stupid school work."

I could already imagine what Luke and his friends would say. I was hoping we'd get to school early so I could tell Mrs Maudsley before the others arrived, but we got stuck behind a tractor on the narrow country roads and I just made it to class on time. When I tried to tell Mrs Maudsley she waved me to my place and said it would have to wait.

"I know we're all looking forward to hearing from Aubin's father later this morning," she said, "in what promises to be one of our most interesting talks. But first we have work to do."

I thought of raising my hand and telling her, but I felt the others' eyes on me and I couldn't face it. I decided I'd tell her in the morning break when the others were outside. The morning passed slowly. Bored, I looked out the window. Keith, the school caretaker, was chasing leaves in the autumn wind. A taxi was pulling up outside the gates, and I wondered who would come to St Edward's in a taxi. I turned back to my books just in time before Mrs Maudsley looked round from the board and swept the classroom with her eyes. I tried to keep my head down, but the question of the taxi kept coming back to me. When she turned away again I risked another look and saw with astonishment Uncle Jack being helped out of the back of the taxi by the driver.

I wondered if Jack's madness was catching and I'd started seeing things, because he looked the way he was before the accident. Not completely: his leg was still missing, but in every other way he looked as if the last month had never happened. His beard was gone, and his hair wasn't hanging down the sides of his face any more but swept back, the way he used to wear it. There was no sign of his ratty old shawl; he was wearing a suit and tie, the empty trouser leg pinned neatly just below his stump.

"Aubin Merryweather!"

I whipped round to see Mrs Maudsley leaning over my desk. I could see the lines around the corners of her mouth, and where she'd smeared the lipstick to make her lips look thicker.

"I will not have daydreaming in my class," she said. "Daydreamers never amount to anything. They never get anything done. They dream their lives away. Well, if you want to waste your time, Aubin, that's your funeral. But you will not waste my time!"

I decided this wasn't the moment to tell her I'd just seen an apparition of my uncle crossing the playground.

"No, Mrs Maudsley. I'm s—sorry."

"Don't let me catch you looking out the window again."

I was so confused by what I'd seen that when the school bell rang I forgot to stay back and tell Mrs Maudsley about my father. Instead I went out with the others, wanting to see if it really was Jack or if I'd imagined the whole thing. He was in the middle of the playground, talking with Mr Wilson, who taught the older kids geography.

"Your uncle's just been telling me he's going to be talking to your class today," Mr Wilson told me. "Very good of you to step in at the last minute, Mr Merryweather."

"Pleasure," Jack said. Close up, he didn't took so

good. He'd shaved his beard off, but he was paler than ever without it, and sweat was gleaming on the sides of his face.

"I'd better let you get set up," Mr Wilson said. "Sure you don't need any help?"

"No, no," Jack said, waving one of his crutches in the air and narrowly missing a girl's head. "Get around fine on these. Ben can show me the way."

He was talking the way he used to before the accident, but as I led him towards the classrooms I could see his arms were shaking with the effort.

"Hope you don't mind me turning up like this," he said. "Thought I'd step in, since your dad can't make it. If that's alright with you."

"There are a lot of stairs," I said. I was too surprised to say anything else.

"We'll manage them between us."

I wasn't so sure. Images of him telling the class he was dead came back to me.

"Does my dad know you're here?"

"Didn't have a chance to speak to him. But he won't mind."

The hall was deserted. I thought he'd give up when he saw the stairs. He still hadn't managed to make it all the way up at home, and that was easy by comparison.

"Shall I get help?" I said.

"We'll manage."

He tucked one of his crutches under his arm and

started up the way my father had taught him, holding the rail with his free hand. He made it look easy at first, but after a few steps he began to get out of breath, and he had to stop and rest before we were halfway up. I was afraid he'd get stuck and I wouldn't be able to get him back down. The sound of the other kids in the playground seemed far away. He started up again, his arms shaking so much I thought he'd drop the crutches. With six steps to go he had to stop again. He had that look in his eyes, like he was staring at something no one else could see.

"Jack?" I said. "Are you okay?"

He didn't say anything, but started up again. I could see it was really hurting him; he looked like he might faint. Somehow he made it to the top, and slumped against the wall, exhausted. I stood watching him, wondering what I'd do if he collapsed. After what seemed a long time he wiped the sweat out of his face.

"Right. Which way now?" he said.

The classroom was empty, and he sat in Mrs Maudsley's chair. Under his jacket, his shirt was dark with sweat. He pushed his hair back where it had fallen into his face. He looked so unwell I was worried he might have a heart attack or something. Slowly, he got his breath back, but the climb seemed to have used up all his energy. When Mrs Maudsley came in with a mug of coffee and stopped at the sight of him, he didn't say anything, but sat staring into space. I began to dread his talk.

"Mrs M—Maudsley? This is my Uncle Jack," I said. "My father got stuck at work, so Jack's come instead."

"Hello Mr, uh," she said, holding out her hand.

He didn't say anything at first, and my heart sank. My fears were coming true. Outside the bell rang for the end of break. His eyes lost focus on whatever it was he was staring at, and he looked up at her and smiled.

"Jack Merryweather," he said, shaking her hand. "Forgive me not getting up, but as you can see..." He gestured towards the crutches.

"Not at all." She looked for somewhere to sit but our chairs were too small, so she leaned against one of the desks.

"My brother sends his apologies," Jack said. "He's detained at the hospital. You know, dying patients, weeping widows, that sort of thing. Thought I'd step in and take his place, if that's alright with you?"

"Well...yes, of course...I mean, that's very good of you. What will you be talking about, if you don't mind me asking?"

"Afghanistan mostly, I expect. That's where I lost this," he rubbed what was left of his bad leg. I'd never seen him so easy about it. The others were beginning to file back into the classroom, and fell silent when they saw Jack.

"Afghanistan?" Mrs Maudsley glanced at me and I saw her remember. "What took you there?"

"I'm a journalist."

"A journalist." Her eyes slipped towards his leg. "We haven't had a journalist yet. I don't suppose you write for the local paper then, if you're going to places like Afghanistan?"

"No, the *Informer.*"

That impressed her. The others were all staring at Jack, and she sent me and Matthew to the staff room to get another chair. When we got back, he'd moved to sit in front of the class. I heard whispering.

"Settle down," Mrs Maudsley said. "This is Aubin Merryweather's uncle, who has very kindly agreed to talk to us in place of Aubin's father, who couldn't make it because of an urgent case at the hospital."

The room fell silent as we waited for Jack to speak. He looked out at us, blinking. Someone shifted noisily in their seat.

"Hello everybody," he said at last. "Sorry Ben's father couldn't make it today. One of his patients isn't in a good way, so you'll have to make do with me. I can't tell you anything much about being a doctor, I'm afraid, though I've had a few let loose on me." He gestured to his leg. "I'm a journalist. I'm sure you all know what that is. There are lots of types of journalist: crime reporters, political correspondents, sports reporters... Well, I'm not any of them. What I do is, well, I suppose I'm what you'd call a war correspondent."

He had them hooked from there. He told the stories that had fascinated me as far back as I could remember, and I began to breathe more easily. He told them about Beirut and Berlin, Iraq and Iran, escaping from gun battles, running through streets of ruined buildings, getting arrested. And he told them about walking through the mountains of Afghanistan with the Mujahideen, and watching while they shot Russian helicopters out of the sky. About villages where there's no electricity, where the only light comes from hurricane lamps, and the only connection to the outside world is an old portable radio. He didn't say anything weird. He didn't mention his leg, but talked as if he had just dropped in to visit us between trips to the Middle East, and for a while I forgot the pale ghost of Tempest House.

When he finished, Mrs Maudsley asked if there were any questions, and of course someone wanted to know about Jack's leg. There was a long silence.

"I'm not sure we can ask Mr Merryweather—" Mrs Maudsley began.

"Got blown up," Jack said. "In Afghanistan, with the Mujahideen. We were in this village in the mountains, and we had to leave because the Russians were coming. We had to cross a minefield; it was the only way out."

I could see him reliving it in his mind, and wanted to tell him he didn't have to go on. I wanted Mrs Maudsley to stop him, tell him it was alright, but she said nothing. Everybody was waiting.

"The Afghans often walk through minefields," he said. "I mean, I wouldn't recommend it, but if you walk in single file and make sure you tread exactly where the man in front does, then you know you're okay. Of course, it's not so good for the man in front."

"Mr Merryweather," Mrs Maudsley said gingerly.

"We were unlucky, we ran into a mine. Those are terrible mountains. I don't know how they got me out."

"Was anyone else hurt?" one of the girls asked.

"Yes," Jack started to reply, but this time Mrs Maudsley cut him off.

"That was absolutely fascinating," she said, "and I'm sure we'd all like to thank Mr Merryweather for coming in at such short notice and giving such a fantastic talk." She started clapping, and everyone joined in. Jack sat looking down at the floor.

I felt bad: I'd been convinced he was going to say something weird and embarrass me, and instead he'd been amazing. All the others were staring at him, and I knew no one was ever going to laugh at my imaginary uncle again.

Mrs Maudsley sent me to help him back downstairs. I could see he was tired and had been trying not to show it. I'd thought it would be easier going downstairs, but he seemed to find it harder, and I was worried I'd have to go back for help, but we made it. The taxi was waiting for him outside the school gate. When we reached it, he leaned against the side of the car, exhausted.

"Thank you, Uncle Jack," I said.

"Pleasure. Hope the talk was okay."

"It was brilliant."

He smiled down at me. The driver helped him into the taxi. They had to turn round a little way up the road and come back, and I stood and waited to wave to them, but when they came past, Jack was sitting with his head thrown back, his face twisted with pain.

Chapter Ten

Corner Man

I SAT AND watched my mother sleep. The ward was even quieter than usual at this hour, the only sound the heart monitor as it kept vigil with me. It was past three in the morning, but I was used to wakeful nights—I might as well be here doing something useful. She had been asleep when I arrived, my father whispering in the corridor as he made me promise to stay with her and not go to sleep on the sofa in the staff room, even if the nurses offered it. He needn't have worried; I couldn't have slept if I'd tried.

There was something wrong with this reversal of roles, the child watching over the parent. I felt I was intruding on her privacy and sat back from the bed, by the window. I wasn't ready for this changing of the guard, as she and my father became the ones who needed us. I didn't want to watch them grow old and sick. All around, I could feel time carrying us forward, a tide that never turns but only quickens as it hurries you on to the dark.

She stirred in her sleep.

"Tom?"

"It's me, Mum," I said, "Ben. Everything's okay."

She murmured something I couldn't make out and settled again. She looked younger in her sleep, her face small like a child's. Once she had seemed impossibly beautiful to me. I wished I could tell her about Naomi, ask her advice. It would have been such a release to admit it all, but there was no way I could worry her with the collapse of my marriage now. The burden was mine alone, and I had to keep it from her the way she'd been keeping uncomfortable things from me all my life.

She turned in her sleep and I wondered what else she'd hidden from us. When Matt was born I promised myself I'd always be honest with him, but it hadn't taken long for me to understand how many lies children need. I'd been lying to Matt and Anna since they first learned to speak, and not just about Father Christmas. Naomi and I never fought; we discussed things. Anna's dog hadn't been put to sleep; it had gone to a retirement home. God was watching over them. Yes, of course I still loved Mummy.

Had my parents had secrets? I supposed they must have done. The only time I remembered them fighting was when Jack came. Had there been betrayals, unkindnesses? Had it truly been a happy marriage? I hoped it had. They were a part of each other in old age. I couldn't imagine one without the other. That was something

Naomi and I would never have. I wondered who I might have been if I hadn't fallen in love with her. Some one else, maybe even happy. But then Matt and Anna, the best of me, wouldn't have been born.

I was twenty-eight when I met Naomi. I saw her across the room at a party, one of those London evenings, cheap wine in plastic cups and a tiny flat so overcrowded it feels as if people are hanging out of the windows. I forget who the host was. I was just back from Afghanistan and still deep in my Uncle Jack phase, smoking a cigar I couldn't afford and telling war stories to anyone who'd listen, though the only real danger I'd been in was of freezing in the unheated guest house. I caught sight of her across the room, talking to someone I knew. Never trust a redhead, my grandmother used to say. But there was something about her and I couldn't help glancing across at her again. It wasn't just that she was beautiful; it was the way she held herself. I was wondering who she was when she turned and caught me looking. I can still see the laughter in her eyes. If I'd been more like the role I was trying to play, I'd have crossed the room to her, but I didn't have the nerve. The truth is I'm shy. When I looked over in that direction again she'd moved on: another opportunity gone. It was some time later when I saw her again, and this time I caught her watching me. She quickly looked away. I was still trying to summon up the courage to seek her out when I heard a voice at my elbow.

"Johnny tells me you've just got back from Afghanistan."

She was standing beside me, the same laughter in her eyes.

"I'm Naomi," she said.

"Ben. You know Johnny?"

"From work. I'm in marketing, he's a client. It's dull but it pays the rent. Not like Afghanistan. How was it? I can't imagine going somewhere like that."

"It was...cold, mostly," I said, too unsure of myself to come up with anything better. It was only after I said it that I realised it sounded like studied nonchalance.

"Don't be modest. I want to know."

"I was only in Kabul. It's actually quite calm there at the moment."

"Ah, well. If it's really that boring we can talk about client accounts or mortgages or whatever it is everyone else here seems to be so fascinated by," she said, smiling.

So I told her about the night I was woken by the sound of a rocket landing and was half dressed and ready to be evacuated from the guest house when one of the local staff emerged, blinking with sleep, to tell me it was nothing to worry about, it happened all the time and the rocket had landed on the other side of the city. And about the trip we'd made out of Kabul, up the Panjshir Valley, about the colours, the brilliant green ribbon of the valley as it cut through the barren mountains, the turquoise of the river and the flashes of flowers. She leaned in so close I could feel the heat from her body. Other men tried to get her attention, people she knew, but that evening she had eyes only for me. At the end of the party she scrawled her phone number on the back of someone else's business card—"I always forget to bring my own," she said, "but it's more personal this way. And you get two numbers for the price of one." The card was a man's, and I wondered if he was a business contact or someone who'd tried to pick her up.

She made me wait a full week to see her again. I wanted to take her to a quiet wine bar I knew, a place I thought was romantic and where I'd taken women in the past, but she insisted on meeting in the cellar bar at the Coal Hole pub on the Strand. It seemed a gloomy place, and I couldn't see the attraction until she explained it.

"You know this is where Edmund Kean used to drink. The actor," she said. "He used to come here straight off the stage. Macbeth and King Lear drank here. Byron called him 'the Sun's bright child'. I love places with a history."

She was quieter that evening, more cautious. I could see her watching me behind the playful manner, trying to make up her mind.

"Do you always play it so cool?" she said.

I looked at her in surprise.

"Making women come up to you? At the party

the other night. I thought you were never going to say hello."

"No, I—"

"It's alright. I like corner men."

"Corner men?"

"The ones who stand in corners, watching. I like to get them out of their corners."

We were still at an age when we were trying to be people we weren't. I was mesmerised by her confidence, the way she was the centre of attention the moment she entered the room. It wasn't until much later that I saw her self-assurance was as much of an act as mine; she was just better at it.

I wanted to impress her for our next date, so I took her to the Duke of York in Fitzrovia and told her it was where Anthony Burgess got the inspiration for *A Clockwork Orange* after he saw a razor gang tearing the place apart—though it was his wife who stopped them in their tracks by drinking three pints of beer in a row without spilling a drop.

"I hope you're not going to ask me to do that," she said.

"I don't think they get razor gangs in this part of London any more. Just estate agents."

"The place has gone down in the world."

I took her to Ye Olde Mitre, off Hatton Garden, which was legally part of Cambridgeshire even though it was in the heart of London, and she took me to the

Star, in Belgravia, where the Great Train Robbery was planned. She let me kiss her at the end of each evening but broke away when I tried to take it further, and resisted all my attempts to talk her back to my flat. I was beginning to fear she was a tease, and even think she might be a virgin, when she called one afternoon and asked if I could see her that evening. We'd always planned our dates a couple of days in advance. She wanted me to meet her in Islington, at a pub I'd never heard of, called the Turk's Head. I looked it up on the internet to see what its story was, but I couldn't find anything about it. It was a cold night when I emerged from the Tube at Angel, and it started snowing as I hunted the pub down through the back streets. It was so unlike her usual choices I passed it twice before I found it: it was a nondescript place, part of a big brewery chain, thick with the smell of bad cooking. She was sitting in the corner by the gas fireplace, looking vulnerable in a way I hadn't seen before.

"What's the story with this place?" I said, when we'd kissed and I'd bought a much-needed beer.

"Oh, nothing special," she replied, "just somewhere I like to come."

"So why the sudden urgency? Not that it isn't great to see you."

"I don't know," she said, pushing a beer mat in idle circles. "I just missed you, I suppose."

It was a couple of drinks later when she asked me

back to her flat. I thought it must be around the corner, and that's why she had chosen the pub, but she led me through the streets of Islington in the snow, which was falling thickly now, gathering on the barges moored in the canal and dancing in the yellow of the street lights.

"Don't you just love the snow," she said, huddling close to me. "Oh, you poor thing, you're shivering. Here, we're warmer together."

Actually I was trembling with desire, and the closeness of her body made it worse. I had wanted her for so long, and now I was finally going to be with her.

She lived on the fifth floor of an old Victorian terrace house with no lift, and by the time we reached the front door of her flat my legs were aching. We started tearing each other's clothes off before she'd even closed the door behind us, and made love on the living room floor, only moving to her bed after because of the cold. Inside, she was scalding hot, as hungry for me as I was her, pulling me to her as if she wanted to fuse our two bodies into one. Not a virgin then.

"I thought you'd never make a move," she said after, as I lay wound in her legs, watching the snow as it melted against the window panes, "my poor shy corner boy."

She found the scar on my ankle and asked what it was.

"Byron had a club foot," she said, running her fingers along the silvery scar tissue. "Does it hurt?"

I shook my head, but when she bent to kiss it I pulled away.

"What is it?"

"I'm ticklish," I explained, only realising my mistake as her eyes lit up.

"Here?" she asked "What about here? Oh, definitely here."

And we fell on each other's bodies again.

"What was the story with that pub?" I asked her later.

"What about it?"

"It just didn't seem your sort of place. No story to it."

"There is a story. Just not an obvious one."

We made love regularly after that. We called each other two or three times a day, and started giving each other the books and music we had loved most in our lives. I spent entire afternoons hunting down out-of-print books in the second-hand bookshops on Charing Cross Road, and she gave me old vinyl LPs though I didn't even have a record player. But still she held out against a formal relationship.

"It kills it if you give it a name," she said. "Why ruin something that's perfect?"

It wasn't perfect for me, though: I was in love and I wanted her to be mine. I'd had a couple of semi-serious girlfriends before, but I'd never thought of settling down. There seemed to be so much time left in those days. Naomi changed all that. When I had to go to the West Bank, a trip that would have excited me before, I was distraught at the idea of being apart from her for a week. I racked up such a large bill calling her every day Asylum thought the mobile phone company had made a mistake. I had to make up a story about a family crisis and offer to pay the money back.

When I got back to London I went straight to her flat from the airport and we fell into each other's arms.

"Don't ever go away from me again," she said.

"Then be mine."

"I can't live without you."

"So live with me."

She still held out but her resistance was weakening. I realised the absence had worked in my favour and forced myself to stay away a little. Eventually, in the same nondescript chain pub where she'd taken me the first night we made love, she agreed to be my girlfriend.

"What is the story with this pub?" I asked. "I've searched everywhere but I can't find anything."

"Oh, you wouldn't," she laughed. "It's where my parents met."

It was only much later, after we were married, that I learned the real reason she had held out so long. When I first met her, she was already seeing someone else. All those weeks, when she was keeping me hanging on, she was trying to choose between us. She never told me: I found out years later, from a friend of his. Apparently he was devastated when she left him: he'd been planning to ask her to marry him. I never let on that I knew. All marriages need their secrets.

Chapter Eleven

Waking Lazarus

JACK DIDN'T JUST come back from the darkness one day, like Lazarus or Rip Van Winkle: it wasn't as simple as that. When I got back from school after his talk, he was shut up in his room again, and he barely looked up when I went to thank him. At first I thought he was just tired from the effort, but in the days that followed he was as bad as ever. It was as if his visit to St Edward's had never happened: he spent most of his time in his room, and when he emerged it was to sweep past us in the hall without a word, or to sit picking at his shawl and muttering to himself. When I tried to speak to him he was gruff and short, or wouldn't answer at all. He was difficult with Annie and refused to do his exercises.

"You look nice without the beard," she said.

"What does it matter?" he said, refusing to meet her eyes.

All the same, I noticed he didn't let the beard grow back.

I'd been worried my father would be upset Jack had

given the talk instead of him, but he just seemed relieved that Jack had stopped feeling sorry for himself and done something, even if it was only for a day. My mother was pleased too: they both seemed to think it was all down to me for some reason; they kept telling me how well I'd done and how they were proud of me, when as far as I could see I hadn't done anything.

"See if you can get yourself another problem at school," Roz told me. "Seems to be the only thing that'll get him out of that room."

Roz was changing around that time. She would get angry for no reason, or sit staring moodily at nothing until I began to worry she'd caught Jack's madness. My mother said it was just a stage she was going through. Roz said it was because she was turning into a woman, which made me and Martin laugh, because she was only thirteen.

I was popular at school after Jack's visit. Kids I didn't know would come up to me in the playground to ask about my uncle the war correspondent, and let me go in front of them in the lunch queue just to hear about him. Martin said he was getting the same questions, and Matthew somehow managed to get in on it because he was my friend; I found him one afternoon telling a group of younger kids some nonsense about Jack stowing away on a nuclear submarine and escaping from Moscow with a gun hidden in one of his crutches. For some reason, Matthew was convinced Jack had a gun and slept with it under his pillow.

I felt bad for Jack: his visit to the school seemed to have made everyone else happy, but he was still miserable. I hoped it would cheer him up when my father took him to the hospital to be measured for his new leg, but when they got home he was grim and withdrawn, and went off to his room without a word.

"It's often like this at first," my father said. "It's one thing to sit dreaming about getting a new leg and being able to walk again. But the first time you try one on you can't even stand up on it. It hurts like hell."

He seemed almost pleased about it; I suppose it was something to do with being a doctor and seeing these things all the time. I'd thought Jack would come back with the leg, but it had just been a fitting. The leg had to be specially made and wouldn't be ready for a week or so. While he was waiting, Annie pushed him harder than ever at his exercises so he'd be ready for it. One afternoon I looked in through the sitting room door and saw her doing something weird. Jack was sitting up on the sofa with his bandages off and his stump showing, and Annie was tapping at the end of it with a cloth. It seemed cruel: poor Jack was wincing with the pain as the cloth pressed against the raw skin, but he didn't move away or ask her to stop. When I asked my father he told me Annie was trying to desensitise the stump, so the new leg wouldn't hurt too much when it pressed against Jack's skin. He said they had to teach the stump not to feel so much by getting it used to being touched. I tried it that night with my own bad leg, tapping at the scar with a cloth, but it didn't seem to make any difference. Perhaps I was already desensitised, I thought.

When Jack's leg arrived, it was worse than the day of the fitting. My father drove him down to the hospital to pick it up. We all waited for them to get back, and at first when Jack got out of the car he looked great. It was as if his leg had grown back: you couldn't tell that it was a fake leg at all. Everyone was telling him how amazing it was, but he didn't look happy. It was when he tried to walk that we saw the problem. Even with the crutches, he couldn't use it at all. The moment he tried to put his weight on it his face twisted with pain and he had to stop. He tried to move on the crutches the way he was used to, but the new leg dragged along the floor and nearly tripped him up. He almost fell three times before he even got inside the house. As soon as he did, he sat down on the hall chair and started scrabbling at his trouser leg to get at the leg and take it off.

"Hang on," my father said, "let me help you."

But Jack pushed him away.

"Get it...*off*!" he panted.

The leg was nothing like I'd imagined it. When he pulled his trousers up out of the way I saw it was just a thin metal rod with a shoe at one end and a sort of plastic cup that fitted over his stump at the other. He pulled at the complicated straps that kept it on, but he couldn't undo them. My father had to kneel down and undo them for him.

"It'll take time," my father said as he gently pulled the leg away and Jack gasped with relief. But as soon as he put it down on the floor, Jack kicked it away savagely with his good foot. It skidded across the hall and bounced off the wall, taking a chip of paint off the skirting board. I saw my parents look at each other. Jack heaved himself up on his crutches and swung down the hall to his room without speaking, slamming the door closed behind him. He looked close to tears.

"Do you think you should...?" my mother said.

"No," my father said. "Give him time."

Martin was staring at the leg lying on the floor. I could see he wanted to take it apart and find out how it worked: he loved tinkering with things and putting them back together. My father picked it up before he could get his hands on it. Jack's shoe and sock were still on the end of the metal pole; it looked funny, as if they'd somehow preserved his own foot and fixed it to the leg. The plastic cup at the top was padded, but even so it was painful to imagine it pressing against his raw stump. My father checked it to make sure it wasn't damaged, and put it carefully against the wall outside Jack's door the right way up, with the foot on the floor. There was something gentle in the way he touched it, as if it were his brother's real leg.

When I came down to breakfast the next morning,

it was gone, and I thought perhaps Jack hated it so much he had thrown it away in the night, but he was wearing it later that day when Annie came over for his exercises. From the sounds I heard coming from the sitting room, his exercises were even more painful than usual with the leg.

"It's going to be hard at first," Annie told him as he limped with her to the door, "but it will get better."

"What's the point?" he replied. "It'll never be like before."

"No. But it will be better than now."

That night, the leg was lying on the floor outside his room again. It became a ritual: every night Jack would leave the leg there, as if he didn't want it, and every morning he would take it back into the room before any of us were up. As my father went round locking up before he went to bed each night, he would pause outside Jack's room, pick the leg up and set it upright against the wall, until one evening Jack left the waste-paper bin from his room outside the door with the leg jammed down inside it, as if to make his intentions clear. My father just smiled, took the leg out of the bin and set it in its place as usual. The next morning it was gone again. As far as I know they never spoke about it; neither of them said anything to the rest of us.

Slowly, piece by piece, Jack came back to life. It was just small things at first. One afternoon he smiled at me as we passed in the hall. A couple of days later he wished me a good morning. He came to sit with us more often and once he even laughed at the television.

He started treating Annie better, and I heard them laughing together sometimes behind the sitting room door, when he wasn't gasping with pain. He let her use his first name, and called her "my torturer" as a joke. Though he still hated the exercises, he didn't hide away from them in his room any more, but would be ready with the leg strapped on when she arrived. He even started practising on his own in the hall when she wasn't there, trying to walk on the new leg without crutches. You had to give him a lot of space, because he wasn't very steady, and sometimes he'd lose his balance and clutch at the wall for support. More than once he fell, and I felt bad when I saw how it hurt him, but he would haul himself back up, and try again.

The change in Jack seemed to fix things between my parents: my mother wasn't on edge any more, and my father stopped giving her worried glances across the room when she wasn't looking. I heard them laughing together for the first time since Jack arrived, and through the kitchen door, I saw my father grabbing playfully at my mother while she pretended to swat him away with a tea towel, laughing and saying, "Tom, the kids will see!"

There was still a sadness in Jack, though: you could see it in his eyes. The old moods would come over him sometimes, and he'd stare at the empty air. I suppose he was thinking about what had happened, and his life before the accident. I wished there was some way we could desensitise him to that, but I didn't know where we'd have to tap. His soul, perhaps.

He and my father started going out to the pub again. Once, they woke me up coming in, but this time it was with laughter: Jack was singing something, and my mother came into the hall and told them to be quiet before they woke the whole house up, but she was laughing as she said it. Jack went to the Black Dog several times a week. My father would drive him down and stay for a drink, then leave him to make his own way home. Most of the time he managed to get a lift back with one of the regulars. Jack wasn't much good at being quiet, especially when he'd been drinking, and I often heard him coming in, but there was always the sound of my parents' voices to reassure me.

One night, though, I was woken by the sound of breaking glass. I listened for my parents, but there was nothing. Then I heard laughter. I sat up, my heart pounding. The sound of an unfamiliar voice whispering came from below, then someone said "Shhh".

I groped for the light. My alarm clock showed it was past midnight. My worst fears were coming true: someone was breaking in. I stared at my bedroom door, too frightened to move. I thought of calling out to my parents, but I was afraid the thieves might hear and get to me first. There was another noise from downstairs, as if something was being dragged along the floor, and more laughter. I heard my parents' bedroom door open.

"What the hell—?" my father's voice came, but it was cut off by the sound of a huge crash. I leapt from my bed in a panic, tore open the door and ran out onto the landing.

My father was standing at the top of the stairs, staring down at something and looking angrier than I'd ever seen him.

"Dad?"

But he ignored me and started down the stairs. Martin appeared across the landing, wide-eyed with shock, and I heard Roz's door opening. I ran to the banisters.

Below, Jack was lying on his back in the middle of the hall carpet, his crutches out of reach as if he'd fallen and a stupid grin on his face. A woman I'd never seen before was standing over him, swaying like she'd lost her balance and laughing. Beside Jack on the floor there was a broken bottle, and a puddle of whisky was spreading into the carpet. He'd spilled some sort of white powder on the floor, and he was trying to clear it up before my father could see it.

"What the hell do you think you're doing?" my father whispered furiously.

"Sorry, think I musht've tripped," Jack replied in the thick voice he got when he drank too much. "Thish's Erica, by th'way."

My mother came out onto the landing, tying her dressing gown around her.

"Do you realise what time it is?" my father said. "You've woken the whole house up. Don't you realise the kids are trying to sleep?"

"What's going on?" Roz asked, not coming out of her bedroom, but peering out from behind the door.

"It's alright, love," my mother told her, "it's just your Uncle Jack."

"You're scaring the kids," my father said downstairs, but at that moment I was much more scared of him than I was of Jack. He wasn't shouting, he was speaking softly, but somehow that made it worse. I was afraid he was going to hit Jack.

"I can't do this any more," he went on. "I have to think of the children first."

"Sorry," Jack muttered. He wasn't laughing any more.

I thought my father would help him up, instead he just stood and watched as Jack scrabbled for his crutches. He kept slipping over again and again. Erica tried to help but she wasn't strong enough to lift him. In the end my father had to pull him up, though not in his usual gentle way. Jack's face creased in pain, and more of the white powder spilled out of his hand.

"You can get that stuff out of my house. Right now," my father said.

My mother told us to stay where we were and went

down to clear up the broken bottle. Erica tried to help her, but for some reason my mother got angry when she started scooping up the white powder.

"Leave it," she said, "it's going in the bin."

"I'm sorry," Erica said. She kept apologising; you could see she was frightened. I thought my parents were being hard on her, but when she said she had no money for a taxi home my father gave her some.

I heard him talking with Jack long after my mother had sent us all back to bed. The wind was up that night, and the ghost was restless in my chimney, but he didn't frighten me. I just wished he'd quieten down so I could make out what they were saying.

Jack wasn't at breakfast the next morning. There was nothing unusual about that: he often slept in late, especially when he'd been to the pub. But when I asked about him my parents changed the subject, and I was afraid my father had thrown him out in the night. When I got back from school that afternoon, though, he was waiting for Annie in the hall with his leg strapped on, and there was a large bunch of flowers in the kitchen with a note addressed to my mother which read "Sorry!"

"Never underestimate the power of flowers over women, Ben," my father told me later.

"Don't go teaching the boy nonsense," my mother said.

Jack stopped going to the pub after that. He stopped practising with the leg as well. He fell back into one of his dark moods and took to his room again, only coming out for his exercises with Annie.

The storms of autumn gave way to the still of winter, and the ghost in my chimney fell silent. It was dark in the morning when I left for school, and dark when I got home, and the only daylight I saw was in break time when Matthew and I watched our breath turn to fog and pretended we were smoking. The trees outside my bedroom window were bare skeletons, and the ground was hard. The cold crept inside Tempest House and we had to light a fire in the evenings, but the change in the weather made no difference to my father, who still went around each morning opening windows: we needed the fresh air, he said. My mother used to close the windows as soon as he left for work, but I remember coming down to breakfast one morning to find snow blowing in and melting on the kitchen floor.

December came, and with it Martin's birthday. My parents gave him a new bike, and said that now he was eleven he could ride out alone to meet his friends, though I'm pretty sure they'd have changed their minds if they'd heard him and Harry planning what to do with their new freedom a couple of days later.

"We could go to Wolf's Caves," Martin said.

"What for?" Harry asked. "My dad says there's nothing down there, just a few small caves you can't even stand up in."

The caves lay at the bottom of the cliffs, a short drive

round the coast from Egypt Wood. They used to be a tourist attraction but no one had taken care of the path down to them in years, and it was so overgrown it had disappeared completely in places. Martin had wanted to see them since as far back as I remembered, partly because they were named after his favourite smuggler, but mainly, I think, because my parents said it was too dangerous.

"That's because you can't get down to the biggest one," he said. "There used to be a ladder but the Germans took it away during the war. Now the only way in is by sea."

"What's the point then?"

"Maybe we could get down with a rope."

Harry laughed. "No chance. What about the German watchtower, where we found the sleeping bag? We could go and see if that weirdo's been back."

"Yeah, that's not a bad idea. We could stake him out, make it a proper military operation, the way the army would do. Hide out in the undergrowth till he comes, and then disappear without leaving a trace, like snipers."

"Don't," I said, and they laughed.

"What are you worried about?" Martin said. "You won't even be there."

They made me swear not to say anything to my parents. When Saturday came Martin dressed in his camouflage fatigues and showed me a little tub with segments of what looked like brown and black shoe polish.

"It's camo cream," he said, "camouflage for your face. The army uses it."

He had it smeared over his face when he got back. My mother said if he stayed out that late again she'd take the bike away.

"What happened?" I asked. "Did you see him?"

"What do you care?" he replied. "I thought you were scared."

He was too excited to keep it from me for long. The tower was empty when they got there, but there were signs the owner of the sleeping bag had been back: empty food tins and the remains of a fresh fire. They'd hung around outside the tower for a time, hoping he would return and they could get a look at him. It was as they were leaving that Martin saw a lone figure in the distance, heading across the heath towards the tower. By then they were too far away to make out his face, but they were planning to go back the following week and keep watch for him.

I was terrified. Whoever the man was, I didn't think he'd be happy to find two kids spying on him. The idea came back to me that he could be hiding in the tower: why else would he choose to sleep out there with the ghosts? The tower would be freezing at this time of year, and the thought of a night out there with the sound of the wind crying out in the upper floors was enough to fill me with dread. Only a murderer on the run or a maniac would choose to stay out there, I told Martin, but he laughed at me. There was no one like that in Jersey, he said, it was just some crazy old guy. He made me repeat my promise not to say anything, and told me all sorts of terrible things that happened if you broke a solemn oath: that creatures came in the night and cut out your tongue, and that you couldn't be buried in holy ground. All week he and Harry were planning their next trip to the tower. Martin said he was going to "borrow" my parents' Polaroid camera so they could try to get a picture.

He didn't say anything about not telling Matthew, and we spent the breaks at school discussing who the man in the tower might be. Matthew wasn't convinced by my theory of a murderer on the run: he said we'd have heard about it if anyone had escaped from the Jersey prison. He was still convinced it was a Nazi who didn't know the war was over. I said it could be the ghost of a German soldier, returned to the tower to avenge his dead comrades, but Matthew said why would a ghost need a sleeping bag, and I had to admit he had a point.

I knew there was no way anyone could live on Jersey and not know the war was over: we weren't in the middle of the jungle. All the same, I couldn't get what Matthew had said out of my head. The man could be a Nazi who knew the war was over and his side had lost, but who had stayed on the island in secret, waiting for his chance for revenge. The tower was the perfect hiding place, where no one would even think of looking. I wondered if there were any Germans who'd stayed on the island or disappeared after the war. Normally I'd have asked my father, but he'd have wanted to know why I was asking, and I couldn't risk breaking my promise to Martin.

I don't know where I got the idea of speaking to Jack about it, but when it came to me it was perfect. If anyone would know the answer it was Jack, who was interested in wars and that sort of thing, plus he wasn't likely to be bothered why I was asking—he didn't seem to be bothered much about anything, which was another reason to talk to him. He'd been shut up in his room since what my father had started calling the Incident of the Almighty Crash in the Night, and this was an excuse to try to cheer him up.

Cigar smoke was drifting out from under his door when I knocked. "Uncle Jack? It's Ben."

There was a grunt from inside. I pushed the door open: the cigar smoke was hanging across the room in thick strands that made my eyes water.

"Ben," Jack said from the armchair. "Tea?"

He got up and reached for the kettle without waiting for an answer, knocking the ashtray from the arm of the chair where it had been balanced. I bent to pick it up, but he waved me away, scooping the ash in his hand and leaving a grey smudge where it had fallen on the carpet. I'd always liked the smell of his cigar smoke before, but it was so strong in the room that day it was making me feel sick, though I tried not to show it. His leg was lying on the floor next to the bed, his shoe still on the foot, neatly laced.

"Three sugars, wasn't it?" he said.

I tried to reply, but it came out as a cough. As soon as I gave in to the itch in my throat the coughing wouldn't stop.

"Sorry," Jack said, squashing his cigar in the ashtray, "I forgot. You should have said."

He opened the window and began wheeling his arms, trying to chase the smoke out. He looked funny balancing on one leg, both arms whirling, and I couldn't help laughing. I looked up, worried I'd hurt his feelings, but he didn't seem to have noticed. He showed me to the chair and handed me a mug of tea. The mug looked as if it hadn't been washed since my last visit. He sat on the bed, sipping his tea in silence. He hadn't even asked me why I was there.

"How's your synthetic leg?" I said.

"Closer," he said.

I waited for him to say more, but he didn't.

"Uncle Jack," I said, "can I ask you something?"

"Hmm."

"You know the Germans were here? In the war, I mean."

"Hmm."

"Well, do you think any might still be here?"

"Germans? I suppose there are some tourists, in the summer."

"No, I mean Nazis," I said.

"Nazis? Shouldn't think so."

"Only there was this Japanese soldier, in the jungle. He didn't know the war was over, and went on fighting for years."

"That's true," Jack said, leaning back against the wall and yawning. "Doubt there's anyone like that in Jersey, though."

"But what if a Nazi was still hiding here?"

"Why?"

"To get revenge."

He nodded, slowly.

"Where would he hide?"

I couldn't mention the tower without breaking my promise to Martin. "In one of the old bunkers."

"No chance. The British army cleared them all out at the end of the war."

"So they'd have checked everywhere? I mean, not just the bunkers but...the gun positions and the towers and everything?"

"Definitely."

I tried not to show my relief.

"Why do you ask?" he said, looking straight at me for the first time.

"It's just something Matthew and I were talking about."

"If you really wanted to hide," he said, leaning forward, "you wouldn't go and stay in one of those draughty old places. You'd change your name and identity, and pretend to be someone else."

"Really?"

"Lots of Nazis escaped at the end of the war. Most of them went to South America. They changed their names and everything. A few got caught, but plenty got away."

I stared at him in alarm. Could the owner of the sleeping bag be an old Nazi who'd changed his name and lived in hiding for years, and slipped out to the tower sometimes because he missed it?

"Do you think there's someone like that here?" I asked.

"No chance. It'd be too difficult in a little place like Jersey: they'd get noticed. Everyone knows each other. It's easier to disappear in a big city."

He sounded almost disappointed. We drank our tea in silence.

"Are you interested in the war?" he said after a time.

"I like to imagine the soldiers. How it was in the bunkers, listening for the bombers. Only sometimes it scares me."

"I'd forgotten about the bunkers. I should go and see some of them again."

"And I like to imagine I'm one of the British

commandos who came up here, through Egypt Wood."

"At the end of the war? I don't think there were any commandos in Jersey."

"No, the secret mission. In the middle of the war."

"Secret mission?"

I could see from the way he looked at me that he thought I was making it up, so I told him about Captain Ayton and how he'd led his team of commandos up through Egypt Wood one Christmas night. I was so carried away with the story I'd spilled out how Captain Ayton stepped on a landmine before I realised what I was saying. As I was describing it, I saw his leg lying there on the floor and stopped, looking up at him.

"It's alright," he said, after a silence that felt like for ever. "I know I'm not the first to get on the wrong side of a landmine. What happened to this Captain Ayton?"

"He...er..."

"I see."

I felt terrible. "There's a memory stone for him, at the bottom of the hill," I said.

"Right here, and I never knew it," he said to himself. "Do you think you could show me?"

"It's a bit far."

I'd expected him to be upset, but it was almost as if the story of Captain Ayton had brought him back to life. He kept asking me little details I didn't know, and wanted to go and see the memorial. I wasn't sure

my parents would be too happy with me if he started limping down through Egypt Wood, and said he should probably speak to my father about it.

"So you think Jersey's safe then?" I said as I was leaving.

"Huh?" He looked confused, then remembered our earlier conversation. "Oh yes. No old Nazis."

"And no escaped murderers, or anything like that?"

"Escaped murderers? God no," he said, the sleepy drawl returning to his voice, "there's nothing that exciting. Not in Jersey."

Chapter Twelve

Hidden Memories

MY MOTHER WAS discharged from hospital at the weekend. Dr Jenkins said she'd made an excellent recovery, and that keeping her in hospital any longer would only risk driving her insane with boredom. She'd been restless, chafing at my father's attempts to wrap her in cotton wool. So long as she kept taking her medication and avoided too much stress, Jenkins said, there was no reason she couldn't go back to a full and normal life.

My father was constantly coming up with ideas to make my mother's homecoming "easier", when I could see she wanted as little fuss as possible. At one point he even started talking about moving the fold-up bed down to the sitting room and setting up a sick room like the one they'd made for Jack all those years before, so she didn't have to climb the stairs.

"Don't be daft, Tom," she said. "What do I want to sleep in the living room for? I'm coming home to my own bed, thank you."

It was just as well she was coming home. It was a

long time since my father and I had shared a house, and things had started to get a little fraught between us. As long as we were both busy being worried about my mother it had been fine, but we'd been getting on each other's nerves since she was out of danger. My father, an early riser by nature, didn't like my habit of staying up late at night and said I kept him awake. I found his early-morning energy exhausting. I began taking long walks and spending as much time as possible out of the house. I went back to Egypt Wood and walked down to the memorial and the Wolf's Lair cottage. I thought of ringing the doorbell at Tempest House, explaining who I was and asking to have a look at the place, but decided I didn't want to see it with someone else's belongings lying around, someone else's life in progress.

My mother's return meant it was time for me to go home to the broken pieces of my own life. I'd spoken to Naomi every day on the phone but still hadn't said a word about Richard. My mother's illness had given me time to think. I missed Matt and Anna after just a few days apart: I couldn't face the thought of moving out permanently, and I wasn't going to put them through the hell of a custody battle. Perhaps I'd misunderstood what I'd seen that day in London, I reasoned with myself. It could have been an innocent meeting, Richard there to discuss work or drop off some documents. When she put her arms around him it could have been a sexless hug between friends.

Alright then, he had come to try to win her back. But what if she'd turned him down, that embrace the last farewell of former lovers, not the heat of rekindled passion? They hadn't kissed, after all. I decided I'd been too quick to judge, that I had to give our marriage the benefit of the doubt. I couldn't escape the absurd idea that my mother, who had spent much of her life rescuing me from my own mistakes, had contrived to do it one last time and save my marriage by having a heart attack at precisely the right moment. But I was still reluctant to go home. Though I longed to see Matt and Anna again, I wanted to stay in Jersey too, in the safety of my parents' house.

The morning before my mother came out of hospital, I drove out to Les Landes to see the old German watchtower. I hadn't been there in years, and it would be my last chance on this trip. It was hard to believe the place had frightened me so much as a child: the heath was blazing gold with gorse, and beyond the cliffs the sun was bronze on the shield of the sea. Bees grumbled in the undergrowth, the gorse was sweet on the air. There were a couple of paragliders in the distance, struggling to keep up in the light breeze, but aside from them the place was deserted. I was reminded how odd it was that Jersey, a small crowded island, had so many empty spots. There wasn't a house or building in sight—apart from the tower, which loomed black on the horizon where the land tumbled into the sea. The sun was warm on my back as I made my way down towards it. I passed an odd wooden frame I didn't remember from my childhood. It must have been something to do with the nature reserve, but it looked unsettlingly like a gallows. The last stretch of path to the tower was as steep and loose as I remembered. At one point I slipped, and in the instant before I regained my balance I had time to think how ironic it would have been to have survived all our recklessness there as children, only to fall to my death as a fully grown man. Below me the sea was calm, but the rocks looked as forbidding as ever.

The tower was locked: in the years since I had last visited it seemed someone had finally got round to replacing the padlock. The door had been freshly painted. Edging round, I found a notice saying the tower was being restored, and was to be opened as a museum the following year. I was pleased someone was finally taking care of the old place, but a part of me regretted the passing of its wildness. No one else would get to sit and listen to the ghosts calling inside. I stood looking out to the endless blue promise of the sea. I felt again that sense of dislocation from the past, as if it wasn't real and I'd imagined it. Did I invent my childhood or did my childhood invent me?

On the way back to the house, I made a diversion to Bouley Bay, down a series of steep switch-backs that cut through the wooded hills to the old smugglers' harbour at the bottom. I parked at the end of the stone pier and walked back up the road to the Black Dog pub, its entrance as uninspiring as I remembered. Inside, though, it still looked like a set from a pirate film. It was half empty in the middle of the afternoon: just a handful of regulars and a couple of tourists sitting by the window. I ordered a pint of the local Liberation ale.

"I know you, don't I?"

An old man was staring down the bar at me, a weathered face, his nose red with broken blood vessels from years of drinking.

"I don't think so—"

"Don't tell me," he said, "it'll come."

"I haven't lived on the island for years—"

"Jack Merryweather!"

I don't know why my blood went cold. "You knew Jack?"

"Can't be, you're too young. His son, are you?"

"He's my uncle. I haven't seen him in years."

"Your uncle? You must be Ben! You were this high when I last saw you."

He held his arm out at an absurdly low height that would have made me a dwarf even at eight years old.

"Norman Mauvoisin," he said. "You won't remember me. I was a friend of your uncle's. Used to come in here drinking, after he lost his leg in the war. What's become of him then? Years since I saw him."

"I don't know. We lost touch."

"Well, that was Jack for you. Wasn't the sort for

staying in touch. He left plenty of women behind over the years." He laughed beery breath at me. "He was a one. How's your dad? Dr Merryweather, isn't it, from the hospital? Took care of my Nettie when she was sick."

"He's well. Retired now."

"A real gentleman, your dad. Not like that brother of his," he said, breaking into hoarse laughter that turned into a fit of coughing and left him gasping for air. "We had some times, Jack and me," he continued when he'd got his breath back. "Was a time I thought he'd stay on the island, but he wasn't the sort to settle down. Always on the move."

"You don't have any idea where he went?"

"Me? No. He just upped and went. First I knew of it was when he stopped coming in for a drink. Speaking of which," he said, holding up his empty glass, "can I get you another?"

"No thanks, Norman, I'm driving. But let me get you one."

"Much obliged." He rolled a cigarette while the barmaid poured him another beer; he had a tremor in his hands and a gentle rain of tobacco leaves fell on the bar top. Did Jack look like this now, his golden years sacrificed to drink and hard living?

"What was it then, family row?"

"What's that?"

"How you lost touch."

"No, I—I don't know. I was a kid."

"He could be a dark one, that Jack. Used to mutter to himself when he'd had a few. I remember a couple of times he started talking about some terrible mistake he'd made, but he'd never say what it was. He was something on those crutches, though."

I looked at my watch: it was time I headed back to the house. I told Norman I'd remember him to my parents.

"Let me know if you ever hear anything of Jack," he said, raising his glass to me as I left.

When I got back to the house, my father was rearranging the furniture in the sitting room.

"I want to make sure there's no stress for your mother," he said, unscrewing a light fitting. "I thought I could set it up so she can lie down here if she's too tired to go upstairs."

Nothing was more likely to cause her stress than coming home to find the house turned upside down, I thought, but I could see it was no use arguing with him, so I offered to help. At least the two of us could get the place back in some sort of order by the time she arrived.

"You decided when you're heading back?" he said.

"Tomorrow, if I can get a flight."

"Don't leave it too late to book. They fill up fast this time of year."

"I expect you'll be glad to get me out of here and the place back to yourselves."

"No." He looked at me. "It's been a godsend you coming. I'm not sure I'd have…I don't know what I'll do if…" He trailed off, unable to say it.

"Nothing's going to happen, Dad. You heard Dr Jenkins."

"I thought I'd lost her."

I put an arm on his shoulder and we stood in silence. I remembered when he'd sat up with me and stilled the ghosts in Tempest House.

"Perhaps if we move the television here," he said, moving away.

"I met someone who knows you this afternoon, down in Bouley Bay. Norman Mauvoisin, said his wife was a patient of yours."

"Mauvoisin? Yes, Nettie Mauvoisin, I remember her. Nice woman. I wasn't that crazy about her husband."

"He said he was a friend of Jack's."

He stiffened. "That would fit."

It was more than he'd volunteered about Jack in years. I ventured a little further out over the ice. "What happened to Jack?"

"God alone knows. He always suited himself. Better off without him."

I felt the ice begin to crack beneath me and retreated, but it was too late. The moment of intimacy between us was gone.

He went to pick up my mother on his own. He said he didn't want to wear her out with a crowd, but I think he wanted the homecoming to be theirs alone, and I couldn't begrudge him that.

I opened my laptop to book a flight, and found a reply to my email had come from Uncle Jack's old newspaper. The foreign desk manager wrote to say she was afraid they'd lost touch with John Merryweather and had no contact details for him, but I could try Oliver Sharpe, a former foreign editor, who was retired but liked to keep in touch with some of the old correspondents who'd worked for him. She didn't have an email address for him—he was old school, apparently—but she gave me a telephone number. I called it while I had the house to myself. I got an answering machine and left a message asking him to call me back.

Roz came over with flowers for my mother. It was a warm evening and we opened the windows to fill the house with sea air, and set up the table on the patio so we could sit outside. There were a few people out with their dogs down on the beach, and the sound of children laughing.

"Let's not wait for an emergency to get together again," she said. "I was thinking, we should do something for Mum's birthday next month. Bring Naomi and the kids; it'll be a real family get-together."

We opened a bottle of wine and sat drinking in the sun until we heard my father's car pull up. My mother looked well: it was remarkable the difference just getting out of hospital made to her. You could see she was happy to be back in her own home. Relieved too.

"What have you done, you old fool?" she said when she saw what my father had done to the sitting room.

"I'm sorry for living," he said, but they were smiling, comfortable back in the old routines.

"What're you trying to do, finish me off?" she said when he poured her a large glass of wine.

"Doctor's orders," he replied, pushing it towards her.

We had a quiet family dinner, the four of us, sitting out by the beach to catch the last rays of the sun as the tide came in, only moving inside when it grew cold, to the dining room where our younger selves watched from the walls and mantelpiece.

"The nights are closing in," my mother said, "summer's all but over. In a couple of weeks we won't be able to sit out any more."

"I don't know," Roz said. "I think you two are due an Indian summer."

Watching them that evening, I saw how deeply they all cared for each other. Roz might complain about my father's anxieties, but she quietly tended to them, slipping reassurances into the conversation. My parents squabbled, but beneath it they were glad of one another. The next day I had to return to my own troubles; however, for an evening I felt at peace, while the waves broke outside.

My phone rang while we were sitting over the

remains of the meal. Thinking it was Naomi, I went out to the darkness of the patio, but when I answered a man's voice spoke.

"Oliver Sharpe," he said. "You called me earlier."

I didn't recognise the name.

"I used to be foreign editor at the *Informer*," he said. "You called about Jack Merryweather."

"Oh, yes. Thank you for calling me back," I said, closing the French windows so the others wouldn't hear.

He had no contact address for Jack and no idea where he was, but if I was trying to delve into my family history he was happy to help out in any way he could. We arranged to meet for lunch when I was back in London.

"Who was that?" Roz asked when I came back in.

"Just something for work."

It was while I was packing the next morning that I found them. I was looking for the jacket I'd worn on the way over and remembered I'd hung it up in the old heavy wardrobe from Tempest House, alongside my old school uniform and Martin's camouflage fatigues. As I reached inside for the hanger, my hand knocked against something and an old cardboard box fell, spilling its contents over the floor. I bent down to pick them up, and saw there were other memories besides Martin's and mine hidden away in that old wardrobe. Pictures of Jack: some I remembered from Tempest House before he and my father fell out; others I'd never seen before. Jack in a suede jacket, beside some expensive sports car he'd somehow managed to get his hands on. Jack in his beloved Afghanistan before he lost his leg, wearing Afghan clothes, standing with a ferocious-looking group of Kalashnikov-brandishing Mujahideen. Jack with both my parents, all three of them raising glasses to the camera, smiling out of the past. I was so busy looking through them I didn't hear my mother come in.

"What's that you've got?" she said, looking over my shoulder, and when she saw, "Where did you find those?"

"In the wardrobe."

"I thought your father threw them all out. Look at us, we were all so young."

"You look happy."

"I suppose we must have been."

"What happened with Jack? Why did he and Dad fall out?"

"I don't know. They drifted apart. It happens."

"It seems sad. They used to be so close."

"Jack was...a complicated man. Always running away, never facing up to things."

She seemed uncomfortable. I didn't push it.

"Put them back when you've finished, would you, love?" she said.

After she left, I found something else at the bottom of the box: a note with Jack's name on it, a telephone number and an address in Cornwall. And beneath that, yellowed and falling apart, an old letter I remembered from long ago, still folded in its original envelope, soft and frayed where it had been torn open. I recognised the colourful stamps and, partly hidden by the sticker redirecting it to Jersey, the original address written out in strange, childish handwriting.

Chapter Thirteen

The Man in the Tower

I WAS WORRIED my father would be upset with me for telling Jack about Captain Ayton and the land-mine, but he didn't seem all that bothered when Jack mentioned it at breakfast a couple of days later—at least not until Jack said he wanted to see the memorial. My father tried to put him off, telling him the path would be muddy after all the rain we'd had, and the stream would be too deep to cross, but Jack kept insisting until my father had to tell him the truth: he just didn't think Jack was good enough on his prosthetic leg yet.

"It's a steep path and it's pretty hard-going in a couple of places," he said. "Give it another month or so, then we'll go."

But Jack still wanted to try. "Want to come along, Ben?" he said. "It was your idea, after all."

I looked up in horror, convinced my father would blame me for the whole thing, but he gave me a smile.

"At least wait till the weather dries out," he told Jack. "The place'll be a sea of mud right now."

"If it's too muddy I'll just turn back," Jack replied,

getting up from the table. "No harm in trying."

My father sighed. "Sometimes I wonder if it's worth living," he said when Jack had left the room.

"At least he's cheerful about something for a change," my mother said.

"We'll see if he's still smiling when I have to carry him back in," my father said. "Come on then," he added to Martin, Roz and me. "If he's going we may as well go with him."

Jack brought his crutches along, but he was fine without them all the way to the end of the lane. He must have been practising in secret, when we were all out at school. When we got to the start of Egypt Wood, though, my father was right: it had rained heavily overnight and the path was like a bog. I couldn't have got down there in my wellingtons, but Jack plunged in all the same. Immediately the mud oozed up over the top of his good foot. He should have backed off then, but he'd made too much of it and wanted to show us he could do it.

"It's just a short patch, then it dries out," he said. He took another step further in, and the mud rose up over the foot of his artificial leg.

"Come on, Jack, this is nuts," my father said. "You've made your point."

Jack was having none of it. He put his weight on both crutches and tried to pull the prosthetic leg out of the mud, but it stuck and he swayed dangerously. My father reached forward to steady him, but Jack shook his arm off and managed to pull the leg out. He took a couple of steps further but made the mistake of pausing, and the leg sunk deeper into the mud. He'd got confident by then, and when he started up again he tried to take too big a step. The bad leg stuck and twisted underneath him as he fell. Jack gasped with pain and clutched at his stump. My father ran forward to help: I thought he'd be angry, but his doctor's calm had returned.

"Are you alright?" he said, pulling Jack's trouser leg out of the way so he could unfasten the leg.

Jack didn't say anything, but he was breathing hard as if he was trying not to cry out. My father's fingers worked quickly at the straps and he pulled the leg away. He passed it to Roz and helped Jack up. We made an odd procession, Jack leaning on my father's shoulder and limping along with one crutch, while Martin carried the other and Roz followed with his leg. It looked strange to see her carrying it with the shoe and sock still on the end, caked in mud.

When we got back to the house, Jack reached for the leg and began strapping it back on.

"Are you sure—" my father started.

"Get back on the horse," Jack said. "Or the wooden leg."

His face was twisted with pain as he pulled the leg tight but he made himself stand up on it, and walk a few steps.

"Just as long as you're not thinking of heading back down that path," my father said.

"Not today," Jack said. "But it gives me something to aim at."

When I got back from school that afternoon he was out in the rain, walking around the garden without his crutches. The rain was running down his face and my mother tried to get him to come in, but he refused, so she took out a hat, an old flat cap of my grandfather's no one had worn in years.

"I thought this was better than an umbrella," she said, "leaves your hands free." He put it on and she smiled. "It suits you."

He passed the window of the sitting room, and a few minutes later he came by again, walking in circles around the house until the cap had turned black with the rain. In the days that followed I saw him out there every day, pounding away on the leg and gritting his teeth against the pain. My parents seemed happy about it, and Annie was delighted with his progress, but I wondered why he was so hard on himself. It was as if he was punishing himself for something.

At the weekend Martin set off on his bicycle to meet Harry at the tower. He'd packed our parents' Polaroid camera. I didn't think my parents would have been too happy if they'd known he was taking it out to the heath, but I didn't say anything. I spent the day waiting for him to come home. By afternoon I'd already convinced myself he and Harry had stumbled in on the man in the tower and been taken prisoner, and I was trying to make up my mind whether I should break my solemn oath and tell my parents where they were, when Martin came in looking pleased with himself.

"Well?" I said. "Did you see him?"

He didn't say anything and just smiled, which made me sure they'd seen the owner of the sleeping bag. But when I pressed him he shook his head, and slipped into the dining room to put the camera back where he'd taken it from. He held out for an hour, refusing to answer any of my questions, before he gave in.

"Alright," he said, "but you've got to promise not to say anything to Mum and Dad."

He pulled a photo out of his rucksack and held it out to me. "Don't touch it like that, you'll spoil it," he said. "You have to hold the edges, like this."

It was of an old man with a hard, unfriendly look about him. The tower was in the background, and you could tell from the angle they'd taken the picture from low down, near the ground, where they were hiding in the bushes. The man's hair was cut very short. He was wearing a blue anorak and he had a sort of bag with him. There was nothing out of the ordinary about him, but I was sure I'd seen him somewhere before. I couldn't remember where, and I didn't say anything to Martin about it. I hoped he and Harry would lose interest now they'd seen the old man and got his photograph, but

Martin said they were planning to go back the next week and try to find out what he was up to in the tower. I looked at the photograph again. I didn't like the idea of Martin following the old man around, whoever he was.

When I told Matthew, he was convinced it proved his theory that an old Nazi was camped out in the tower.

"He's the right age," he said, "and he's got short hair, like a soldier."

"Why wasn't he wearing a uniform then?"

"He could be undercover."

"A Nazi in a blue anorak?"

"Why not? That's what you'd wear if you didn't want to be noticed."

I didn't tell him what Uncle Jack had said about there being no Nazis on Jersey. I didn't think it would make much difference to Matthew, and I was too worried that he could be right. But the next weekend brought good news: Martin came back looking disappointed, and told me that when he and Harry went back to the tower the sleeping bag was gone and there was no sign of the old man.

"He's probably gone on his Christmas holidays," Matthew said when I told him.

"Nazis don't go on Christmas holidays."

"I thought you said he wasn't a Nazi."

It was more likely he had found somewhere warmer

to stay for the winter months, I thought. The nights were cold, and there was a white frost on the lawn at Tempest House in the mornings. Out at the tower it would have been freezing. But the important thing was it meant that Martin and Harry couldn't follow the old man about any more. I'd been lying awake at night thinking of what might happen if he caught them.

The cold did nothing to stop Jack: he was out practising with his leg every afternoon. He went out in the dark, and once in the fog. He'd made it all the way down the lane to the main road, but he hadn't tried the path down into Egypt Wood again. He was learning to drive with one leg, as well. My mother's car was an automatic, which meant he was allowed to drive it. At first, he only took it up and down the lane while he got used to it, but my father said if he could manage that narrow lane, he was ready for anything.

It was strange when he started going out after so long: I'd got used to having him around the house. He started driving down to the hospital for his appointments with Annie, and she didn't come up to the house any more. The last day she came she gave me a hug to say goodbye.

"I'll miss you the most," she said.

I stood waving at the window as she drove away down the lane.

But I couldn't be sad for long, because the cold meant Christmas was coming. You could feel it in the air, in the way the exhaust from the cars hung smokily in the school car park, and in the clear nights when you could see all the stars spread out, glittering dust across the night sky. Time crawled towards the school holidays, and Mrs Maudsley kept saying "Don't jump the gun" whenever any of us got excited. When the last day finally came, she wished us all a merry Christmas, though it was hard to imagine her having a merry anything. I pictured her in a Christmas hat, holding one end of a cracker while Mr Maudsley held the other, looking at her watch and warning him not to jump the gun.

As surely as it brought Santa and magic snowmen who took you out flying in the night, Christmas drew two other visitors to Tempest House: my grandmother and her dog, Colin. Granny Merryweather wasn't your sweet old lady type of grandmother, though she some-times fooled people with her packet of mint humbugs and her handkerchief stuffed up her sleeve, and Martin and I loved to watch when someone made the mistake of talking down to her or trying to push her around.

My parents told us we had to be careful around Granny that year, because she might be upset about Uncle Jack's leg—I always forgot Jack was her son too. She didn't seem all that upset when she arrived, though: the first thing she said to him was, "Where's your peg leg, then?"

"Right here, Ma," he said, tapping it with his crutch.

"They've made it look like a real one. What's the point of that?"

"That's the way they make em."

"You'd be better off with a wooden one," she said. "Then people would know to stay out of your way."

It seemed a mean thing to say to me, but Jack laughed and put his arm around her shoulders.

"Don't ever change, Ma," he said.

"Don't you think Colin would be better off outside?" my father suggested.

"You leave him alone," Granny snapped.

This was an argument they had every year. It wasn't that my father didn't like dogs—it was hard to imagine anyone not liking Colin, who was old and deaf and didn't jump up or bark but sat staring at you like a wise old man. Even when a stranger came to the door, he just lifted his head and gave a token bark, more out of pride than anything. But my father didn't believe dogs should be allowed inside the house. He said it was unhygienic.

"I just think he'd be happier where he can run around," he persisted. It didn't seem likely: Colin had made himself at home and was snoring, head on paws, by the fire.

"What do you want to send him out there in the rain for?" Granny said.

"He's designed for it, that's why he's got a coat of fur."

Granny refused to go anywhere without Colin. She

even let him sleep in the bedroom with her at night, and my father spent her visits picking imaginary dog hairs off the furniture.

"At least you're not going back to any of those dreadful places any more," she said to Jack. "Afghanistan with its mad hatters, or whatever they're called."

"Yes, I am, just as soon as I get the hang of this leg."

"Don't be stupid."

"Half the people there are missing an arm or a leg. Someone's got to tell their story."

"Oh, you make me so *angry*. You always were a stubborn child." The firelight reflected from her eyes and she started blinking. "Now I've got something in my eye," she said.

She told him he was doing his exercises all wrong, and that Annie was an idiot, but you could see she was upset about Jack, whatever she said. I saw her with his filthy old shawl one evening. He'd left it thrown over a chair in the sitting room, and there was something in the way she folded and smoothed it, running her hands over the dark stains. Jack started taking Colin with him on his walks, and since they were both pretty slow they got along fine. He seemed determined to prove the leg wasn't going to hold him back: when Martin wanted to put Christmas lights up outside the house, he said he'd help, and my father had to stop them going up on the roof.

On Christmas Eve, Granny said she was going into town for some last-minute shopping and asked if any of us wanted to come. The others all said they were busy but I felt bad for her and said I'd go. She was a very slow driver—my father said her eyesight was going and she shouldn't really still be driving, but she told him to mind his own business—and a long line of traffic began to build up behind us. The driver of the next car tried flashing his lights a couple of times but Granny just ignored him. She was telling me how they'd spent Christmas in London during the war: she was supposed to be evacuated but her mother had hidden her and kept her at home. Every time they heard the bombs coming, Granny had to go and hide under the stairs.

There was the sound of a horn from behind. Granny broke off from her story and looked in the mirror.

"What's he on about, hooting and flashing his lights like it's the *end of the world*?" she said.

I turned in my seat. The driver behind looked really angry: he was waving his arm and shouting something. Granny pulled over to the side to let him pass, but as he came level she held her hand out of the window to tell him to stop.

"Where's the fire?" she said.

"What?"

"Don't you 'what?' me! What have you got, ants in your pants?"

The man looked embarrassed. You could see he

didn't want to get in a fight with an old lady with all the other drivers watching.

"Flashing your lights and blasting your horn like a maniac!"

"I—I'm sorry—I just—"

"Well, go on then, I thought you were in a hurry!" Granny said. "Or do you want to keep me waiting all day?"

When we got to town, she took ages to park the car. In King Street, a fat man was dressed up as Father Christmas, ringing a bell, and a brass band was playing "God Rest Ye Merry Gentlemen". Granny wanted to buy Jack a walking stick, so he could get around without his crutches. We looked at some with handles like the heads of dogs and deer, and even a lion, but in the end she chose a simpler one. It was black with a curved silver handle and looked like the sort of thing men in top hats carried in old movies.

After a while Granny was tired and said she wanted to sit down. I thought she meant on one of the benches in the street, but she stopped outside an estate agent's office and peered in through the window.

"Come on," she said, pushing open the door. I thought perhaps she wanted to buy a house in Jersey, but she ignored the woman who looked up from her desk as we came in. She led me to the sofa in the waiting area, where she sat down and started looking through the magazines.

"Good afternoon, madam," the estate agent said from behind her desk.

"Hello," Granny said.

"Can I help you?"

"No, I'm just resting my legs, thank you."

The estate agent looked as if she was about to say something, but changed her mind. I looked out the window. Just across the street was the old covered market, where they sold fresh meat and vegetables, and there was also a goldfish pond. A little down the street there was a second-hand bookshop I'd been in a couple of times, an eerie old place called Twentieth Century Books, full of dark corners and shelves piled to the ceiling with musty books. There was a stand full of tattered paperbacks outside, and I wondered why the owner trusted people not to steal them. A lot of them looked in pretty bad shape and I supposed he thought no one would bother. He didn't seem to be trying particularly hard to sell anything: the lights weren't even on inside.

It was then, looking out the window of the estate agent, that I remembered where I'd seen the old man in Martin's photo before. He was the owner of the bookshop, and I'd seen him sitting behind the cash register inside watching sourly as I searched the shelves.

"No children's books here," he'd said to me. "Run along."

There had, though, been a lot of books about the

war. Some of them even had swastikas on them, and I wondered if he could be an old Nazi. The bookshop was the perfect place to hide: hardly anyone went inside.

Granny took so long getting the car out of the parking space that a policeman came and told her she was blocking the road. She told him that was no way to speak to a lady and he apologised and offered to move the car for her. When she replied that she was perfectly capable he sighed and stopped the traffic in both directions so she could reverse out.

When we got back the house was full of Christmas smells: my mother was making mulled wine and heating mince pies. My father had put carols on the record player, and Roz was lighting candles. I decided not to tell Martin about the bookseller: I was afraid he'd go to the bookshop looking for him after Christmas. I thought the best thing to do was tell Uncle Jack. The post had come while Granny and I were out, and among all the last Christmas cards there was a letter for Jack. You could tell it wasn't a card because the envelope was very light, made of a sort of paper so thin it felt like it might tear in your hands. It had been sent to Jack's flat in London first, and then on to Tempest House, but you could still see the original address in big, careful letters, like those of a child. It had been crossed out once where whoever had sent it had made a mistake, and they'd misspelled Britain as Britun. The stamps were unlike any I'd seen before, from Pakistan. I took the letter to

Jack's room, thinking it would give me an excuse to go in and tell him about the bookseller, but I found the door open and no sign of him. My mother said he'd gone out to do some last-minute shopping.

"I doubt it," my father said. "More likely he's gone to the pub."

I put the letter on the mantelpiece and forgot about it in the excitement of getting ready for Christmas. My parents had said I was old enough to go to midnight mass with them that year. It was the only time any of us went to church. Martin started it, not that he was religious or anything like that. I don't think he even believed in God; he just liked to sit at the back with Harry and sing the carols really loud. We asked Granny if she wanted to come but she said she wasn't about to start going to church at her age, and what did they want, holding services in the middle of the night? As the evening wore on and Jack didn't return she started to get worried.

"What if he's had an accident?" she said as we set off for church.

"He'll be back," my father told her, "when the pubs close. You'll see."

But when we got home there was still no sign of him. It was past midnight and Christmas Day already, except it wasn't because we had to go to bed and sleep before we could open our presents, and Granny was sitting up waiting by the fire, with Colin curled at her feet.

"The pubs have been closed a good hour," she said.

"Something must have happened."

"Nothing's happened," my father replied. "He's probably just gone off with a...friend."

"You don't know. Anything could have happened to him. He could have got drunk and fallen in a ditch for all you care."

"Come on, Ma, you're scaring the children. Nothing's happened. He's been to Russia and Afghanistan, and crossed the Berlin Wall Lord knows how many times. I think he can take care of himself in a tiny little place like Jersey."

"Afghanistan? And what happened there? He lost his leg and nearly died! And now he's out there with a peg leg on this wretched island where they don't even light the streets! I told him not to go out drinking, but does he listen? Yes, Ma, no, Ma, he says, but he does what he likes. And where did that get him the last time? Crippled before he's thirty-five! I *don't know*!"

"It's alright, Ma," my father said, putting his arms around her, "he'll be fine. You know what he's like. Remember when we were kids and he tried to run away to France? He thought he'd go and see what it was like, he said."

"Your pa wasn't half furious," Granny said, her voice softer, smiling at the memory. "Gave us the fright of our lives."

My mother sent us up to bed, but I lay awake worrying about Jack long after I heard my father lock up and come upstairs. He might have got drunk and fallen into the sea, I thought, or tried to walk home from the pub, and run into the Black Dog.

I decided I couldn't sleep that night, and would stay up and wait for morning. After a time I felt myself floating: I was out on the dark waters off Bouley Bay, looking up at the lights of the pub on the shore, and Jack was running with the Black Dog on his heels, dragging its chain after it. I tried to call out to him but he couldn't hear me, and the dog had turned into Colin, who couldn't keep up and was knocking his head against the door of the pub so he could lie down next to the fire, until I realised it was Martin hammering on my door and telling me to wake up because it was Christmas Day.

"Uncle Jack's not back," he told me. "I checked his room."

I thought I was late but it turned out everyone else was still asleep and Martin had just woken me because he was bored. I was looking at the presents under the tree and trying to guess what was inside when Granny came downstairs in her dressing gown, Colin padding behind. She went straight to Jack's room and, when she saw it was empty, stood at the bottom of the stairs and called out, "Tom! He's not back! Tom! Wake up!"

"Well, that's one way of getting everybody up," Martin said.

"Jesus wept," my father groaned, coming down rubbing sleep from his eyes. "I expect the kids to wake us early at Christmas, Ma, not you."

"He's not back."

"He's just stayed over...somewhere. He was always doing it when we were teenagers."

"He was *not*. I wouldn't have allowed him back in the house. Call the police."

"Are you crazy? He'll be back any minute."

"He's probably fallen in the sea and *drowned*."

Roz and my mother came downstairs, and my father said that since we were all up we may as well open the presents, but Granny sat looking out the window and fretting.

"There's a car coming!" she called out. "No wait. It's stopped and it's turning. Must be a wrong—No, it's him! It's him!"

"What did I tell you?" my father said, going to the door.

I ran after him, wondering why the car had stopped halfway down the lane instead of turning at our door, where it was easier, and got there just in time to see Jack leaning in through the driver's window to kiss Annie on the mouth.

"Annie!" I called out, running towards them before my father could stop me.

"Hello, Ben. Happy Christmas." She was blushing for some reason.

"Merry Christmas," my father said to Jack, with a strange sort of smile.

"Ah, yes, and you," Jack looked embarrassed. "You know Annie."

"Of course."

"Happy Christmas, Tom," she said.

"You'd better come in. Sarah won't be happy if I let you go without a Christmas drink."

Jack and Annie looked at each other. "Okay," she answered, "thanks."

"We were going to wait to tell you," Jack told my father while she parked the car.

I had no idea what they were talking about, but Granny came out and cut them off, telling Jack he'd given her the fright of her life.

"Come and have a drink," my father said.

"At least let the kids open their presents first," Jack suggested.

"They already have. Sorry, they couldn't wait."

"No, I mean, I forgot to put these under the tree," he announced, disappearing into his room and coming back with three packages wrapped in newspaper. "Sorry. Forgot to get wrapping paper too."

He'd given me a book about the Second World War, with pictures of Hitler and Churchill, and the bombing of London. He gave Roz a skipper's hat for sailing, and Martin a football shirt in the colours of his team.

Everyone seemed very happy about Jack and Annie, who stood blushing and smiling while my father made jokes and my mother told him he was drunk already.

Even Granny seemed back to her usual self. She sniffed at the glass my father had poured for her, and leaned down to tell me, "They call it champagne, but I think it's *horrible*!"

Everything was going perfectly, until I remembered the letter on the mantelpiece that had come for Jack.

"This came for you," I said, taking it down and handing it to him. "I think it's from Pakistan."

He stopped smiling and stared at me. He took the letter and read the writing on the outside, but didn't open it. He went over to the sofa and sat down, turning it over and over in his hands. They were shaking.

"Who's it from?" Annie asked.

But Jack didn't say anything.

"What is it? What's the matter?"

He got up from the sofa and walked out of the room. Down the hall, I heard the door to his room close. Annie looked at us.

"Perhaps I'd better go to him," my father said.

"No," she said. "I'll go."

A little later Jack came out of his room and he and Annie joined us for lunch. He did his best to smile and join in, pulling crackers and wearing a paper crown. But the mood of the morning was gone, and at times I caught him staring into the fireplace as if he could see something there, and muttering to himself, the way he had when he first arrived. Something about that letter had really bothered him.

Chapter Fourteen

The Letter

AND I HAD never found out what it was. Now, over thirty years later, I held the letter in my hands. The old-fashioned air mail paper was so light it was almost transparent, and I was afraid it would fall apart. Granny Merryweather, dead these ten years, watched over my shoulder. I saw my parents young again, full of hope for a future that was now long past. Jack, lost somewhere along the way, reached out across the years. And Annie, smiling Annie, what had become of her? I stared at the letter. I had no right to read it, but after so long I had to know. The paper fluttered in my shaking hand as I reached inside and slid it from the envelope. It had split along the folds and almost came apart as I opened it out. It was written on the same flimsy air mail paper, in the same round childish letters, as the address on the envelope, the spelling wrong in several places. "My dear Mr Jack," it read,

How are you my frend? I hope that inshala you have come to your home safely. I went to look for you at the hospitul but the doctoors told me you had gone back to your contry. I am writing to send you gretings from your brothers here. Al your brothers are sorry at you lose your leg. You were brave to leve the peace of your contry and be with us in the place of blood and martyrs. You have suffared with us in our struggle.

Al your brothers are now safe in Pakistan, alham-dulila. Inshala we will stay in the camp here for the Wintr, and go back to Afghanistan to continue our srtuggle in the Spring.

I miss you my friend. I send you gretings from the camps of the martyrs.

Your friend,
Ahmad

I turned the letter over in my hand; there was nothing more. I felt a sense of anti-climax: after all these years, there was nothing in it to explain Jack's sudden melancholy, or the moods of darkness that would grip him from time to time, before his strange disappearance from our lives. It was clear the letter was from one of his friends in the Mujahideen, and it must have brought back to him the horror of the minefield. But somehow I felt that wasn't all: he had been happy that Christmas Day with Annie, he had begun to accept the accident and put it behind him. The letter wasn't enough to explain the way he fell back to a place where none of us could reach him.

I folded it carefully and slid it back into the envelope. I was about to put the box away when, on a whim as much as anything, I copied out the Cornwall address and telephone number. Perhaps I'd see if I could find Jack there.

I finished my packing. It was time to leave for the airport, and I looked at the room, stripped of the possessions that had made it mine for a few days. My parents were waiting downstairs.

"Got everything?" my father said. "Ticket? Passport?"

"They don't ask for a passport between Jersey and England. Not yet."

"You know the way? You won't get lost?"

"I think I've got the hang of it."

"Just follow the coast road into town then through the tunnel—"

"It's okay, Dad," I said, hugging him, "I'll find it." I turned to my mother and put my arms around her. I wanted that heart to go on beating.

"It was good of you to come," she said.

"I'm just happy to see you looking better. You take it easy, Mum."

"Ah, don't worry, I'm fine. Give my love to Naomi and the kids."

The car was parked a little way down the road and I turned at the door to look back at them, one hand raised in farewell. Then I was out in the evening sun, the feeling of safety already falling away.

The flight was on time. I took the train in from the airport and caught the Tube, walking the last stretch to avoid the memory of that last time in the taxi, when I'd seen Naomi with Richard. I told myself to put it aside: whatever had been was past, and I had a marriage to save.

As I approached the front door, I saw Anna watching for me, standing on the back of the sofa to see out of the window, and love chased all other thoughts from my mind. How could I ever have thought of leaving? When she caught sight of me she smiled and waved. She ran around while I was fumbling with my keys and was there when I opened the door.

"Daddy!" She threw her arms around me, and I bent down and picked her up.

"Alright, Dad." Matt stood, awkward, at the end of the hallway, too grown up to come and hug me.

And beyond them, framed in the evening light spilling in through the windows, Naomi.

"I missed you," she said.

"Me too."

And it was true, I thought, taking her in my arms: in spite of everything I'd missed her. The smell of her skin, the laughter in her eyes, the feel of her body through her clothes. I kissed her. "Ugh," Matt said from the doorway. "You two are gross."

As I sat and ate with them, I felt the crisis was past.

That night, I made love to Naomi for the first time in weeks. After, while she slept, I got up to open the window, and looking back at her face in the moonlight, I saw no shadow hanging over our lives.

I was late waking up the next morning, and when I got downstairs the kids were ready for school.

"Don't worry, I'll take them," Naomi said. "I didn't like to wake you; you looked like you needed the sleep." She gave me a conspiratorial smile.

"Thanks. I'd better get a move on, or I'll be late for work."

"Tell them your flight was delayed. And you got waylaid by a wild woman." She leaned in to kiss me.

"Mum!" Matt complained.

"See you later," she said with a smile.

I ate a hurried breakfast and set off for the Tube, giddy as a teenager. I didn't know what had come over me, but it felt good. I was alive again. I checked my emails on my phone while I waited for the train. There were more messages from work about the Syria report. I shouldn't have left them unanswered while I was in Jersey. I'd been on compassionate leave; no one would object, but it had been a tactical error to leave the others to deal with it in my absence, and now the thought I might have to live with the consequences began to cloud my mood.

Asylum had moved into new offices in the rejuvenated and frantically hip East End of London a few years before, and I had to negotiate my way through crowds of young people with strange haircuts. They looked alarming with their nose piercings and tattoos, but they moved aside politely when they saw my jacket and tie. I looked like their fathers, I realised; it made me feel older than I was. Running into Nigel in the office lifts didn't help: our executive director was ten years my junior, dressed in jeans and an Asylum T-shirt, carrying his laptop in a backpack as if he might be called upon to trek into the mountains at any moment in central London.

"Ben," he said, pulling one white earphone out of his ear and sending tinny music spilling into the lift, "good to see you back. How's your dad?"

"My mum," I said. "She's fine. A lot better, thanks."

"Good, that's good. And great to have you back. Look, I know you're going to want to get back up to speed and all that, but could you drop by for a quick chat this morning? We need to talk about the Syria report. In an hour or so? Give you time to get your feet under the desk."

My colleagues were kind and solicitous about my mother, and it took me a few minutes to get across the open-plan office to my desk. I hung my jacket over the back of my chair and took my tie off, wondering why I wore one. Hardly anyone else in the office did. I was clinging to some idea of professional attire from another generation: my father had never gone into work at the hospital without a tie. And yet I'd only started wearing one regularly a few years ago: as a field researcher I'd revelled in the informality of the role, turning up to meetings in a fleece jacket and boots caked with the mud of a refugee camp. I was turning into my father, an old man railing at a world that had the nerve to move on while he wasn't paying attention.

I opened my email and read through the messages I'd been avoiding about the Syria report. It didn't look good. I could see my colleagues were inclined to agree to the minister's request and tone it down. They'd been seduced by the access to power, and who could blame them? If you want to be pure, you can stand with a placard in the rain, but don't fool yourself it'll make a difference. If you want to get anything done you need to be on the other side of the barricades.

Nigel was on the phone in his glass-walled office, with its vanity view of the towers of the City, but he waved me in and to a chair. I sat and waited while he wound up his conversation.

"...I say we go for it, park our tanks on Amnesty's front lawn," he was saying, "there's nothing wrong with being first...it's win-win...Anyway, Jeff, I've got to go, got a meeting. We'll talk later. Okay." He hung up without saying goodbye, I noticed. "Ben, thanks for dropping by," he said, crossing the office to close the door. "Listen, I wanted to have a word with you about the Syria report. We had to move things along a little while you were away, and the feeling is we're going to go with the government on this one."

"I think that's a mistake—"

"Hold on, Ben. We're not going to take out anything. I'm not censoring a report at the beck and call of the government. It'll all be in there, in black and white. All we're changing is our recommendations. We're just not going to call too much attention to that particular group at the moment."

"But—"

"You made your case and a part of me still wants to side with you. But we, that is, the board, felt we'd be doing the wrong thing if we brought out a report that could scupper the chances of the West finally going in and doing something about this mess. We don't want to be the ones who stopped it. It's not as if we're going to give these guys a free pass. We're still going to be calling for them to face justice when all this is over."

"We'll be tainted because we didn't say it now."

"I'm sorry, Ben, the decision's been taken and I need you to get on side with it. I need you to speak with the minister and explain what we're doing and what we're not."

I couldn't be bothered to argue the question further: I could see his mind was made up, and it wouldn't have done any good. I called the Foreign Office for an appointment. The minister, it seemed, was eager to see me: his appointments secretary said he could fit me in the day after next. This was what I had amounted to, a messenger boy carrying the news that we'd decided to sell out. I thought for a moment of going back to Nigel's office and resigning, walking out of the building in a glorious moment of vindication, and then I thought of the next mortgage payment, the children's school fees. I was forty years old and only employable in a narrow field: I was in no position to make heroic gestures. I had sold out, I realised, a long time ago.

There was no point making too much of it. I had enough to be thankful for, with the rekindling of my marriage and my mother's recovery. I spent the rest of the day dealing with unanswered emails. Jack's old foreign editor called to confirm we were meeting for lunch the next day, and there were several documents to read through, but I couldn't keep my mind off Naomi and the evening ahead. I even left early, in a small act of rebellion I doubt Nigel as much as noticed.

She was cooking when I got home. I couldn't remember a time she'd cooked two nights in a row. "Just something special for my loving man," she said. "How was work?"

"The usual. The Syria report."

"Glass of wine'll make you feel better. My treat."

She held out a bottle, French, expensive-looking. I knew the name from somewhere. I poured a glass and took a long drink.

"Easy," she said, drawing the glass from my lips and kissing the wine from them. "I know how to cheer you up. Later. Now go and sit down while I finish in here."

It was a warm evening and I sat in the garden. Matt was practising with a football, making it dance from his feet in a way I never could. He reminded me of Martin. The trees I'd planted when we moved in were growing strong. I ran my hand along the smooth bark, grateful for something that made me feel rooted. An aircraft passed overhead, on its way to Heathrow. A wasp landed on the edge of my wine glass. I went to swat it away and it fell in. Cursing, I tried to fish it out with a piece of rolled-up paper.

"Dad! Dad! Look at this!"

I looked up. Matt was showing off a new trick I hadn't seen before, flicking the ball up in the air and catching it on the back of his neck.

"That's neat," I said, "where'd you learn that?"

"Richard showed me."

"Richard?" Probably some friend at school.

"Mum's friend. From work."

My blood turned cold. I kept my voice even. "When did you see him?"

"He came over for dinner. While you were away. He showed me some tricks while Mum was cooking. Look at this."

I looked back at Naomi through the kitchen window,

singing along to the radio as she worked. Had she made him the same meal, held onto his body the way she had mine? While I was at my sick mother's bedside, she had brought another man into my house and let him play with my son, teach him things I couldn't do.

"Richard said he can get tickets for Arsenal," Matt said. "Can I go? Please."

"Yes, sure," I said. I was good at hiding my feelings. He went on practising his tricks and I didn't say a word. You can't, when you have children: you have to go on smiling, keeping their world together while yours falls apart. When Naomi came out to say dinner was ready, I went and ate and told her how wonderful it was. Later, after the children were asleep, we made love again. She mistook my anger for desire, said I hadn't been that passionate in years. I said nothing. How could I, when it would have meant tearing my family apart? I lay awake beside her, watching her sleep in the light from the street lamps, and the next morning I set out from my empty marriage to my empty job.

I didn't feel much like lunch with Jack's old foreign editor, but it was too late to call and cancel. We had arranged to meet in a pub on Fleet Street, a relic of his life as a journalist, I supposed, though all the newspapers had long departed the area and left it to the lawyers. The place was crowded, and I was wondering how I would pick him out when a large weathered man raised his arm to me from a table in the corner.

"Oliver Sharpe," he said, getting up to meet me. "You must be young Merryweather. Recognised you the moment you came in. Took me back twenty years. You look just like him, you know."

"Thank you for agreeing to see me," I said when I'd fought through the crowds and back to get us a couple of beers and order some food. "It's good of you."

"Oh, it's a pleasure. I so rarely get the excuse these days," he said. "Used to come in here for lunch every day, put it on expenses. The place was one of Jack's favourite watering holes, you know. When he was in town, that is. I should tell you now, I've no idea where he is or what's become of him. But I thought it was the least I could do, to meet you. I've always felt a little bad where Jack's concerned, you see."

"Because of his leg?" I asked, fearing the lunch was going to be a waste of time. Sharpe, it seemed, just wanted an excuse to revisit memories.

"No, not that, though of course I did feel dreadful when it happened. Worst thing that can happen to a foreign editor, short of one of your corrs getting killed. I remember when the news came in. We didn't know anything about it till they got him to the hospital in Pakistan. Then I got a message, Jack's been injured, might not make it. None of us went home; we sat up all night trying to get through to someone in Pakistan. The British High Commission was no use, they never are. The Islamabad correspondent managed to get hold of some brigadier in the government and he arranged everything. Got Jack on a flight to London. I was going to fly out to get him but this brigadier fixed everything. I think they wanted him off their hands, to be honest.

"But no, that's not why I feel bad. It was later, you see. When he came to me looking for his job back. I couldn't do it. I wanted to; he was the best I had. But there was no way we could send him back out into the field with a peg leg. We couldn't get the insurance, and anyway the editor wasn't having it. And he was right, though Jack couldn't see it, of course. He'd been pushing himself up and down some hill in the Channel Islands to prove to himself he could do it. And I daresay he could have done, but what position would we have been in if that leg got him killed somewhere and we'd sent him out there? I had to tell him and he didn't take it well. It was in here, at that table over there. We offered him a job, of course. On the desk in London at first, and then maybe a nice easy posting in a couple of years, when he was up to it: Paris or Washington. But he was having none of it—he wanted to go back out to the field. He wanted me to send him back to Afghanistan, for Christ's sake. Can you imagine? He said if I couldn't give him that he didn't want anything. It turned ugly, he stormed out on me. It was the last time I ever saw him."

"When was this?"

"A few months after it happened. He went to recover

in the Channel Islands over Christmas; it would have been after that."

"And you don't know what happened to him after that?"

He shook his head. "He'd have been alright. Financially, I mean. He got a big insurance pay-out because of the accident, enough to live off. He never needed to work again, but Jack wasn't the type to sit at home. I thought he'd get a job on another paper, but he never did. I always wondered what became of him."

Our food had arrived and we sat and ate in silence for a while.

"It was guilt, you see." he said.

"You don't have anything to feel guilty for," I said. "What could you have done?"

"No, I mean Jack. It was guilt that made him want to go back out. Not that he had anything to feel guilty for either," he added hurriedly, "but he felt responsible. For the kid who died. Felt he had to pay something back somehow."

"The kid who died?"

"In the accident, when the landmine went off. Didn't you know? It wasn't Jack who stepped on it. Those things, they didn't just blow a leg off. He didn't get the full force of the blast, you see. He was supposed to go first, he told me it was his turn. But there was this kid who said Jack couldn't go first because he was a guest and volunteered to go instead. Jack talked about him so much I can still remember his name. Shafiq, it was. He was the one who stepped on the mine. Killed instantly. And only fourteen years old."

Shafiq. That was the word Jack had mumbled to himself as he stared at the empty air. I had thought it was shuffle or traffic. I never imagined it could be someone's name.

"Jack was still wrapped in the boy's shawl when we got him back from Pakistan," Oliver went on. "The thing stank, it was covered in the poor kid's blood but he wouldn't let us take it off him."

Jack's shawl. Noble stains.

"The kid's father was one of the ones who got him out. He could've blamed Jack for his son's death: he was supposed to be in front that day. But instead he carried Jack out of the mountains in his own arms. He'd just lost his son. That's the Afghans for you, I suppose. Jack told me the guy sent him a letter all the way from Pakistan, from one of the refugee camps. He'd got a professional letter-writer to do it for him because he couldn't write in English. They have these people out there: you tell them what you want to say and they write the letter for you, for a few rupees. And he didn't even mention his son in this letter. All he does is ask how Jack is and tell him he hopes he's well. Christ. No wonder Jack felt guilty. So he thought he had to go back, you see. He had to go back and pay his debt."

The letter. That was why it had sent Jack back into

the darkness on Christmas Day. That was why it took Annie so long to bring him back. And, I supposed, it explained why he'd been the way he had with me, why he let me in when he shut out everyone else, why he'd dragged himself out of his room and up the stairs at school to save me the humiliation of going in with no one to give my father's talk. He was paying his debt to the child he couldn't save, in Afghanistan.

"And of course I suppose this Shafiq reminded him of his son," Oliver said.

I stared at him. "His son?"

"Yes, didn't you know? Well, I suppose you wouldn't; he kept it pretty quiet. Told me when he was drunk one night. Swore me to secrecy. I shouldn't be telling you now, but I don't suppose it matters after so long. Jack had a son, but it was a big secret. He wasn't married to the mother, you see. Some fling when he was young, and he'd never acknowledged the kid. He felt really bad about it; he knew he'd done the wrong thing. He hadn't been there for his child. I can't imagine how that must feel. I don't know why he didn't come forward. It's never too late, I told him, but he said it was complicated. Said he couldn't do it now, it wouldn't be fair. Apparently the kid had grown up thinking someone else was his father."

Chapter Fifteen

Gone

IT WAS DAYS before I managed to get to the bookshop. I didn't want Martin to find out about it, so I waited until I was over at Matthew's one afternoon, and got him to talk his mother into taking us into town. "Twentieth Century Books" was painted over the door in peeling letters that looked as if they hadn't been freshened up in years, and I thought the name was hopelessly grand for such a run-down old place. The stall of tattered paperbacks was still outside. As far as I could see they were the same books, and I wondered whether the owner ever sold any, or if the place was just a cover to hide his secret.

"What do you want to go into that dingy old place for?" Matthew's mother said when we asked to look inside. "They won't have anything for kids. Come on, I'll take you to De Gruchy's."

But Matthew persuaded her to let us take a look. Up close, the windows were dirty, and there was a crack in one of the panes. There was an old-fashioned bell on the door that rang when I pushed it open, but there was no reaction from inside the shop. I stepped in. Immediately I was surrounded by the smell of old books. The place was dark and gloomy, and it took a little time for my eyes to adjust to the light. There were books everywhere: on the bookshelves that ran from floor to ceiling, piled in leaning towers on the floor, stacked along the bottoms of the windows. On the shelves, I saw, they were two rows deep, with more jammed in flat above. It was the sort of place you could trip over books and fall into more books. In another situation I'd have loved it, but that day it gave me the creeps. It was cold, as if there was no heating.

Matthew ran his finger along the shelves. I scanned the books' titles. Some, with names like *Passion's End* and *A Woman Betrayed*, sounded like the sort of dreadful romantic story where the hero spends all his time worrying about the girl instead of doing anything. But it wasn't long before I found something more interesting: a whole alcove full of books about the war, away from the windows so you wouldn't see it from outside. Some of them were even in German, the titles written in funny letters like the names of newspapers. I pointed them out to Matthew and he nodded silently. Off to one side, I saw, there was a half-open door that led to a staircase. I was peering through it when Matthew's mother stopped me.

"Come away from there, Ben, that's private. It's

the way up to the owner's flat."

So that was where he stayed in the winter months, in a flat over the bookshop. I looked at the carpet on the stairs: it was stained, and had worn out in places. There was another door at the top of the stairs.

"Over here," Matthew called. He was staring wide-eyed from the back of the shop. I followed him to an old glass-fronted cabinet. There was an old dagger lying on the green velvet shelf inside, and with a clutch at my heart, I saw there was a large metal swastika where the handle should have been. Beside it was a grenade. Pinned to the back of the cabinet was a sign in German with a skull and crossbones on it, next to a picture of Jersey during the occupation, with Nazi soldiers standing in the harbour.

"Alright, that's enough," a man's voice came from behind. "Go on, out of here with the pair of you."

I turned to see the man from the tower standing right behind us, looking anything but friendly. He must have come down the private staircase.

"Come on," he said, "or do I have to throw you out?"

"Excuse me," Matthew's mother said, coming up behind him, angry, "that's no way to talk to them."

He wheeled round in surprise. "I beg your pardon, madam. I didn't realise you were with them. Thought they were just kids messing about. I get a lot of that, you see. Can't stand messing about."

He didn't sound German, but I supposed he must have learned to disguise his voice after so many years in hiding.

"Actually, my son wanted a book."

"Of course. Anything in particular?"

"No, I don't think I want to buy anything here," she said. "We'll go somewhere we're more welcome."

I felt his eyes on me all the way to the door as she led us out. It was a relief to be back outside, in the clean air and sunlight. Matthew gave me a questioning look.

"It was him," I said, "the same as in the picture."

"Well, that proves it then," he said. "Only a Nazi would keep that dagger."

I felt betrayed. Books had been my refuge all my life, and that crammed bookshop should have been a place of wonder for me. Instead I'd found a Nazi hiding inside, and I was too scared to go near it again. I decided not to say anything about it to anyone. The last thing I wanted was to encourage Martin. He hadn't mentioned the tower since the last time he and Harry had been there, and I hoped he'd forgotten about it. They'd started hanging out near the airport instead, at the end of the runway where you could watch the planes pass right over your head as they came in to land.

I'd have asked Uncle Jack about the bookshop, if it hadn't been for the way he'd been since the letter arrived at Christmas. He'd gone back to spending long periods alone in his room, and staring into the air, muttering to himself. He was worried about what he was going to do for work when he got better: I heard him talking with my father about it. He didn't need help washing or changing his bandages any more, but my father still went to his room to talk with him most evenings, and I listened through the door.

"Who am I kidding?" Jack said. "No one's going to send me to Afghanistan with this leg."

"I should think you'd have had enough of places like that."

"That life's all I ever wanted, Tom. I wanted to make a difference."

"And you have done. At least the newspaper said they'll have you back."

"As what, some crippled old has-been at a desk, correcting other people's copy?"

"It's a start, Jack. One step at a time."

"Easy for you to say."

"It's the only way to walk."

It was Annie who brought him back out of the darkness. She came round almost every day to see him. She didn't make him do his exercises any more; they went for walks together, out on the road. He was getting better on the leg, and didn't need his crutches any more, but just used the stick Granny gave him for Christmas.

Roz said that Annie was Jack's girlfriend now. I thought that was good news, but my parents didn't seem all that happy. I heard my mother telling her friend

Polly about it one afternoon, as they sat drinking coffee in the kitchen.

"I just hope he's not messing her about," she said. "He's got a history, that one. I know I shouldn't say it, with him being Tom's brother, but he can be a bit of an S-O-B with women."

"What's an S-O-B?" I asked.

"Never you mind, just eat your soup."

I overheard my father talking to Jack about it. "I hope you're going to treat that girl right," he said, "she's not one of your wild women."

"You think I don't know? This one's different, Tom. Trust me."

"I've heard that before."

"Let us work things out at our own pace."

"Just be straight with her, that's all I'm asking. Don't go pulling one of your disappearing acts."

But Annie kept coming, and slowly, day by day, she brought the old Jack back. I would come home from school to find them sitting in his room together, laughing like children. And when Martin and I went to play in Egypt Wood, I would see them out walking. Jack was still determined to make it down to Captain Ayton's memorial, and Annie took him a little further down the path each day. I was amazed how strong he'd got: even on the path, he didn't need his crutches; he just leaned a little heavier on the stick. I noticed Annie never made a fuss of his leg, but was always there when he needed her. She didn't make a show of it; she'd just reach out a hand for him to steady himself, or cover for him by talking while he got his breath back.

She used to bring me little presents: a badge from the hospital, a pen with the name of some medical company on it. They seemed happy together, and I began to hope Jack might stay in Jersey after all instead of going back to London. He and Annie could get a house, I thought.

And then, just when things seemed to be going well, Jack disappeared. There was no warning; he didn't say anything. My mother sent me to his room to see if he was coming for breakfast, but when I pushed open the door I knew he was gone. The room was emptier than I had ever known it. The books that used to lie strewn across the room, the half-empty bottles, the cigar ash scattered on the floor, all gone. Even the smell of him was gone: he'd left the window open and the sea air had blown every trace of him away. The sheets were neatly folded on the bed, beside them a handwritten note that just said "Thank you".

"He's gone," I said, running to my mother in tears, "he's gone." She told me not to worry, that he was probably at Annie's. But when we called Annie she had no idea where he was, and was as confused as we were. My mother rang the pub, but they hadn't seen him. My father looked grim.

"I knew this would happen," he said.

He drove over to the airport in case Jack was

waiting for a flight, even though it meant he would be late for work. The airlines wouldn't tell him if Jack had been on any of the flights to London that morning, but a taxi driver remembered picking up a man with a limp and a walking stick from an address near our house. We tried the number of his flat in London, but no one answered. Granny Merryweather hadn't heard from him. We even tried his newspaper, but they didn't know anything either.

When Annie called back, my mother told her not to worry, but you could see from her face she didn't believe what she was saying. My father asked for the phone, but my mother shook her head.

"She's a real mess," she said. "He didn't say a thing to her, just upped and went, without so much as a goodbye."

"He's always been the same. If anyone starts to get too close, he cuts and runs. I really thought he'd be different this time. I thought he'd changed after...well, you know."

"That poor girl. It was bad enough with the others, but at least they knew what they were letting themselves in for."

We searched for a letter or a note, but there was nothing apart from that simple scrawled message: "Thank you". Every time the phone rang, I thought it would be Jack, explaining everything, but it never was. Everyone talked about Annie, but no one thought of me. I couldn't understand why he'd left without saying goodbye to me. I'd thought there was something special between us: I was the one who had talked to him when everyone else gave up; I'd got him out of his room. And I understood him, I knew how he felt, because my leg didn't work properly either. None of them knew what it was like to watch while others ran. I didn't believe it. Something must have happened to him. They were hiding it from me, I was sure. He'd died in the night, taken too many pills again, and they'd got his body out while we slept. Or he'd gone to London to see his news-paper, but his plane had crashed on the way, and they weren't telling me.

When Annie came round I hoped she might give me some clue as to what had happened, but she just sat there crying and saying she couldn't believe it. I thought they must be hiding it from her too.

"I'd understand if we'd had a row or something," she said, "but everything was going well. We were even talking about getting *married*. He was *happy*. To leave like this, without saying anything, I don't understand. I just don't understand."

Maybe none of them knew what had really happened. Perhaps he'd gone for a walk and had slipped on his bad leg, and was lying in a ditch, or had fallen into the sea where his body would never be found. Every time the phone rang I jumped up, hoping to hear his voice.

My parents took his fold-out bed out of the study

and moved my father's things back in. After a while Annie stopped coming over. I remember the last time she came: I found her in the sitting room, looking at the carpet where Jack used to do his exercises in the early days, when he was so hard on her. She'd changed her hair.

"When's Uncle Jack coming back?" I said.

"He's gone," she said. "He's not coming back."

"Why?"

"He got scared."

"Why?"

"I don't know."

The weeks became months, and there was no word, no explanation. Only silence.

Chapter Sixteen

Betrayal

I WALKED THE streets of London, reeling. I had no idea where I was, or how I'd got there; I didn't even know how long I'd been walking. People looked at me in alarm; women hurried to the other side of the street. All I knew was I had to keep going; there was something unspeakable on my trail. I felt it getting closer, ducked into a doorway, out of sight, pressing myself back against the stonework. I saw eyes on me from the window opposite and bent, pretending I'd stopped to tie my shoe.

My mind raced. Images flashed before me: a child's body, the head missing; a woman screaming; men closed in, their eyes accusing. I heard a voice cry out, people were running; I braced myself for an impact that never came, an eternity of waiting. And then it came, again and again with every step I took, an explosion that kept repeating itself madly in my head. I gripped the wrought-iron fence of a house. I had to slow my mind, get my thoughts under control. This had happened before. Post-traumatic stress disorder: the therapist said it might return, triggered by new stress, but you can always get it under control. Breathe.

The rocket had been in Afghanistan. We'd all scrambled for cover but it never hit, a false alarm. The men had been in Afghanistan too, a village where a wedding was hit by an air strike. The dead child had been in Gaza. I didn't remember where the woman had been. But they were all safely in the past. None of them could reach me now.

I remembered Oliver Sharpe in the pub, shock in his face as I started out of my chair, said I had to leave.

"I hope I didn't say something wrong," he said.

"Not at all, a crisis at work," I lied, too late now to fake a phone call. "Thank you so much, you've been a great help. I'll be in touch."

His words playing over in my mind, I'd stumbled into the street like a drunk, while people stared. Jack had a son, he'd said. As far as I could make out I was in the docklands, an area I didn't know. I wondered how to get back to the office. I'd been walking for two hours: I'd have to plead my mother's illness, more bad news from Jersey. Jack had a son but who was that son?

It couldn't be, could it? It was ridiculous even to think it. I was overreacting, imagining things. Mrs Maudsley would have said I was daydreaming, making things up. And yet it would explain a lot. It would answer every question that had been lying unanswered for the past thirty-odd years.

Could I be Jack's son? I'd always wondered what could have happened that was so terrible it would undo a relationship like my father's with Jack. They'd been more than just brothers. I'd never been able to think what might have driven them apart. But this would. Had my father found out when Jack was with us in Jersey? It would explain, too, why my mother had been so reluctant for him to stay after his accident: for fear that, with the morphine and the pain and despair, his secret, their secret, would spill out.

I remembered my mother a few days before in the heart ward, bedclothes drawn up to her chin. She would never have done such a thing, never have betrayed my father. What was I thinking? I was confusing her with Naomi. The previous night's revelation had been too much; I was losing my mind.

And yet. It would explain why Jack had come out of the darkness for me alone all those years before at Tempest House, fighting his way up every step of that school staircase to give a talk because my father couldn't be there. Perhaps my father had been there. People had kept telling me I looked like Jack, even my own sister. Had I been blind to something everyone else could see? Was it written on my face?

But it was nonsense, it must be. Why would they have kept it hidden from me for so long? My father, the one I'd known all my life, had never changed towards me, never wavered in his love. And Jack had disappeared from my life. It was crazy to think I could be his son.

I forced myself to stop going over it in my head, found a Tube station. I felt eyes on me in the carriage: I must have looked wild. I stopped off at a pub to wash my face in the gents', and after, drank a double whisky at the bar to calm my nerves.

"You alright, Ben?" someone said when I got back to the office.

"Delivery van nearly hit me," I lied. "Came out of nowhere."

"Did you get the number? Those drivers are lethal."

"You want to sit down for a bit, mate, you look really shaken."

"Streets are a death trap round here."

"You want a glass of water or something?"

I sat at my desk but I couldn't get the thoughts out of my head. Matt and Richard playing football together. Roz telling me I looked like Jack. Naomi smiling up at me, her hair spilling over the bed. Jack staring into air, seeing things that weren't there. I didn't want to be his son; I wanted to be me.

Stop this, I told myself, you're making a fool of yourself. I caught people looking at me across the office. But they would think it was just the shock of my mother's illness. Nothing had been revealed.

When I got home Naomi was busy at her computer. She called out that she'd be with me in a minute. She was probably chatting with Richard, I told myself, but who was I to complain? I was an impostor, another man's son. She must never know. The children were watching television in the living room. I slipped past to the kitchen. Naomi's brief enthusiasm for cooking was over, it appeared. It was my turn to prepare the evening meal and I looked in the fridge to see what we had. The empty wine bottle from the previous night was standing on the counter. It was when I went to put it with the recycling that the name hit me. I remembered where I'd heard it before: it was the wine Richard had recommended.

"Hi, my love," she said from the doorway. "How was your da—" She froze when she saw my face.

"Did you sleep with him?" It was out before I realised, but it was a relief to say it at last.

"What?"

"I know he was here."

"What are you talking about?"

"Richard. Did you sleep with him?"

"Why would Richard—"

"Matt told me. He showed him some football tricks."

"It's not what you think."

"What is it then?" The bottle was still in my hand, and I put it down on the counter. I didn't trust myself with it. "Did you cook the same meal for him?"

"It was a mistake, Ben, okay? I messed up."

"He was here, playing football with *my son*."

"It was just the one evening. He wanted to see me. I didn't think it would do any harm."

"With my son."

"Quiet," she said, glancing through to the living room at the kids. "It won't happen again. I promise."

"Did you sleep with him?"

"No."

"Don't lie to me."

"It was just dinner. Nothing happened."

"You let him be with my son."

"Stop going on about that. What does it matter? All he did was show him some stupid tricks."

"While I was at my mother's bedside."

I wanted to hurt her. I wanted to take hold of her and smash her head against the elegant granite work surface we'd chosen together, pound it again and again until I heard the bone crack. But I did nothing.

"Look, I made a mistake. I should have told you, I'm sorry."

"Did you sleep with him?"

"No! I told you. It was the first time I've seen him in a year, and nothing happened. I swear."

I stared at her. "What about last week?"

"What?"

"The restaurant round the corner. I saw you."

"You were spying on me?"

"I got back early. I saw you from the taxi."

"It was work. We were discussing a project, we had a coffee. That's all."

"Swear it, do you?"

"Fuck you, Ben! You know what? Fuck you! Yes, I slept with him. Do you know what it's been like living with you? Watching you come home from work like a beaten dog every day? Listening to you whine about how you messed up your life? If I hear one more word about your fucking Syria report! I'm sorry you hate your life, I'm sorry you have to be with me instead of being whoever it is you think you are. But if you hate it all so much, why are you fighting for it? What is it you want, Ben? Christ, you're such a *loser*! You've spent half your life trying to live up to some ideal that doesn't exist. Go on then, run off back to some war zone to prove you're a man! We built a life together and you throw it back in my face, and you're surprised I go off with someone else? When are you going to grow up? You have children—"

"*Don't talk to me about my children—*"

"Mum? Dad?" Anna was standing in the doorway, looking from one of us to the other.

"It's okay, love," I said, snatching her up while Naomi turned to hide her tears. "Your mum and I were just talking, that's all. Come on, why don't you show me the flowers?"

I wanted to scream at Naomi and storm out, but I couldn't, not in front of the children. I cooked pasta and we all ate together, a happy family. I watched television with them. After they went to bed Naomi wanted to talk, but there was no point. I slept in the guest room. When the kids asked about it in the morning I told them I'd had a headache. I walked them to school and watched from the gate as they went in. Anna turned to wave and smile from the door as she always did. And then I went home and packed a bag. I didn't leave a note; I didn't say anything.

I ran away.

Chapter Seventeen

The Storm

JACK HAUNTED EVERY corner of Tempest House: on the stairs in the morning, I saw his ghost climbing in the other direction, hands shaking on his crutches. When we sat watching television at night, I saw him sitting in his empty chair in the corner, picking at his shawl. I passed him in the hall, on his way to the bathroom. I saw him behind my father as he worked in his reclaimed study, sitting in the green chair that wasn't there any more. As I walked through Egypt Wood, past the new leaves trembling in the March winds, he was there, struggling to reach the memorial to Captain Ayton. Had he ever made it? He'd never said, and I couldn't ask him now. He was gone from our lives, Annie too. She stopped coming. My mother said it was only to be expected: the house had too many memories for her, and the poor girl had to get on with her life. But nobody told me how to get on with my life, nobody even asked how I felt. One day he was gone, and that was all there was.

"Do you miss him?" I asked my father. We were

standing in Egypt Wood, on the same spot where he'd told me how Jack lost his leg.

"Wha—miss who?"

"Uncle Jack."

"I suppose so. He's my brother."

"I miss him."

"I know, Ben." He ruffled my hair. "But your Uncle Jack was always a wild one. Here today and gone tomorrow. He'll be back some day."

Soon I had other things to worry about, because that was when Martin went missing. I suppose it was my fault in a way. It all started when Charlie Hill pushed in front of me in the lunch queue. Charlie was in Martin's year and he was big for his age, a head taller than Martin. He was always throwing his weight around; no one liked him.

"Thanks for saving us a place," he said, barging me out of the way. I shouldn't have said anything; but Matthew and I had been queuing for fifteen minutes.

"We didn't."

"What's that?"

"We didn't save you a place."

He towered over me, menacing. "Got a problem?"

"No."

He flicked me in the forehead with his finger. "Got a problem now?"

"No."

"I didn't think so."

But Martin had seen it, and he did have a problem. "Leave him alone," he said, charging down the length of the queue.

"This is nothing to do with you, Merryweather."

"That's my brother."

"Yeah? What you going to do about it?"

"Touch him again and you'll find out."

They were staring at each other like they wanted to have it out there and then, but to my relief one of the teachers came to see what the noise was about.

"Don't ever let anyone push you around like that," Martin said later.

"What am I supposed to do about it?"

"Punch him one."

That was his solution to everything. He thought that was the end of it, but the way I saw Charlie looking at me across the playground, I wasn't so sure. It happened a couple of weeks later. Charlie lay in wait with a couple of his friends on the path to the sports ground and ambushed Martin on his way back from football practice. They only planned a small beating, but they didn't reckon with Martin, who came after them in a wild rage. Charlie never saw him coming. One minute he was standing there, the next he was on the ground with Martin's fists flying at him. It was Mr Wilson who pulled Martin off. There was blood all down Charlie's shirt, and his nose was pushed up on one side: Martin hadn't just punched him one, he'd punched him several.

He didn't say a word about Charlie and his friends attacking him on the path back from the football field; it would have gone against his sense of honour. It came out anyway when some of the other kids were asked what had happened, but it didn't help: the headmaster said Martin should have come to him, not taken matters into his own hands. I don't think he understood kids.

Martin and Charlie were both suspended for a week. My mother had to come out of class to take Martin home, but it was my father who lost his temper with him that evening.

"What were you thinking?" he shouted. "That boy could have been seriously hurt. What if he'd ended up in hospital? Then you'd be answering to the police instead of me."

"You always told us we should take care of our own problems."

"I didn't mean with your fists, you fool. Something like this could jeopardise your entire future. And what about your mother? She has to go into work tomorrow and face the other teachers knowing her son is suspended."

"Alright," my mother said, "leave it."

"I'm just trying to get some sense into him."

But Martin wasn't backing down. He was supposed to write a letter of apology to the headmaster, but he refused; as far as he was concerned, he'd done nothing wrong. I think he thought being suspended would be alright till he found out he wasn't allowed to play the next football match. My parents sent him to his room without supper, and wouldn't let me see him. I couldn't sleep for a long time that night. When my mother came upstairs, I heard her hesitate outside Martin's room, then move on. Outside, the wind was getting up. The sea was breaking on the rocks below, and eventually I fell asleep to dream that I was drowning. I kept calling but nobody heard. I was thrown up and down, dragged out into the black water, further and further from the shore. And as I looked back at Tempest House far out of reach, I saw a giant black dog on the hill, howling into the storm.

When I woke in the morning he was already gone, though none of us knew it. At breakfast, my father said a storm was coming: through the window, I could see the trees moving at the end of the garden, clouds racing across the sky. My mother told me to go and see if Martin wanted something to eat, but when I ran up to his room he wasn't there. The duvet lay kicked off at the end of his bed, his clothes strewn across the floor. I checked the bathroom, but it was empty too.

"Mum," I called down the stairs, "he's not here."

"What?"

"He's not in his room or the bathroom."

"Well, look for him then."

I thought he might be hiding, and looked behind the curtains and under the bed, but there was no sign of him.

"Have you found him?" my mother called.

"No, he's gone!"

"He hasn't gone," my father said. "You just can't find him."

But they couldn't find him either, even when we searched the entire house.

"Martin!" my mother called out. "That's enough! We haven't got time for this."

But the only answer was silence.

"He's run away from home," I said.

"Don't talk rubbish," Roz said, her arms hugged to her chest.

"Calm down," my mother said. "It's just Martin playing the devil as usual. Doesn't like being told what to do so he's decided to show us what's what."

"But what if something's happened?"

"Nothing's happened," my father said.

"Something'll happen when I get my hands on him," my mother said. She searched the garden while my father went down to look in Egypt Wood.

"He's run away," I told Roz.

"Shut up," she said.

His bike was missing, his sleeping bag and rucksack too. My father came back to say there was no sign of him in the wood.

"You'd better take the kids to school," he told my mother. "I'll look for him."

"He'll show up soon enough when he gets hungry,"

she told us in the car. "Where's he going to go on Jersey?" She was trying to sound calm but I could tell she was worried.

I couldn't concentrate in class. All I could think of was Martin. At break, I looked for my mother to ask if there was news, but I couldn't find her. She was outside my classroom at the end of school. Roz was waiting in the car.

"We're still looking for your brother," my mother said. "It's nothing to worry about, but we called the police, just to be on the safe side."

The wind was picking up. The trees were swaying alarmingly; the new leaves, torn off before their time, span in the air.

"Will he be alright?"

"Of course he will. It's just Martin being Martin."

When we got home there was a police car parked outside, and an older man with a moustache sitting in the kitchen with my father. He didn't have a uniform, but you could tell he was a policeman from the way he spoke.

"This is Barry Falle, the local centenier," my father said. "He's helping us find Martin, and he needs to ask some questions."

He spoke to Roz first, while I waited in the other room with my mother, who kept getting up to look out the window as if she thought she'd seen Martin coming. I could see she was frightened now, though she was trying not to show it. She put the television on for me, but I didn't want to watch. After a time, my father called me through.

"This the young man then, is it?" Centenier Falle said. "Nothing to worry about, my boy, your brother'll be fine. See cases like this all the time. Wouldn't even bother looking for him if there wasn't a storm on the way. But we can't have him getting soaked through, can we?" He smiled and patted a chair for me to sit down. "Now, can you think of anywhere he might be?" There were brown flecks in the green of his eyes.

"No."

"Nowhere he likes to go when he doesn't want to be found? A favourite hiding place? Or just a spot he liked? You won't get in any trouble."

"He's always trying to get in the Wolf's Lair."

"The Wolf's Lair?"

"The abandoned smuggler's cottage at the bottom of the wood," my father said.

"Worth a look."

"I'll go."

"Anywhere else?" Centenier Falle asked after he'd gone. "Somewhere you wouldn't tell your parents? No one's going to get in any trouble, Ben, but we need to get Martin in out of this storm."

I shook my head. Outside the rain had started up. The wind was rattling the windows in their frames.

"Is there anyone he talked to? A grown-up your parents don't know about?"

I shook my head.

"We don't need to tell your mum and dad. It can be our secret."

"No one."

My father returned, hair streaming with rain, to say the Wolf's Lair was locked and empty. Two more policemen arrived, this time in uniforms.

"We'll take charge of this investigation from here on," the older one, who introduced himself as Sergeant Nicholson, said. "We're liaising with the Honorary Police in each parish, so we've got all thirteen forces out looking for your son. Don't worry. We'll find him."

I remember thinking Jersey had a lot of police for such a small island. Centenier Falle was from our local Honorary Police, who took care of everyday problems. My father said the two in uniform were States police, who dealt with serious crimes. I didn't want to ask what serious crime they thought might have been committed.

Sergeant Nicholson asked Roz and me all the same questions again. His partner searched the house, but he didn't find anything: it was my mother who saw some food was missing, a packet of biscuits and some ham. The rain was beating against the windows now, and the ghost was howling down the chimney so loud we could hear him in the kitchen. Through all this, Centenier Falle sat on his own, drinking his tea. I felt bad for him: Sergeant Nicholson had taken over and there was nothing for him to do. While the others were looking over a map of the island, he leaned across to me.

"Sure there's nowhere else your brother likes to go?" he said.

"We've asked him," Sergeant Nicholson said.

"It's always the kid brother who knows."

That's when it came to me. I could only imagine what it must be like, out there on the cliffs, where the wind blew right through you on a normal day. I could hear the wind screaming in the tower. I saw Martin huddled inside, the ghosts closing in. Outside, on the heath, I saw the old bookseller coming, the Nazi dagger in his hand.

"The tower," I said.

Centenier Falle smiled. "Which tower?"

"The German tower. At Les Landes. He kept going out there, trying to see the Nazi. There's this old German soldier who stays out there sometimes, in a sleeping bag."

"This is no time to let your imagination get the better of you, Ben," my father said.

"I'm not."

"The boy's very imaginative," he told the others, "always making things up."

"I'm not making it up. Ask Matthew. Or Harry."

Centenier Falle held his hand up. "Never mind this German soldier for now. Are you saying your brother likes to hang around the old tower at Les Landes?"

"Yes."

"He's been there on his own?"

"With his friend Harry. They went on their bikes."

He looked at the others. "What are we waiting for?"

Sergeant Nicholson spoke into his radio. "I'm going to need back-up at Les Landes," he said. "Everything we've got. Blues and twos. Get the fire brigade out and call the coastguard. We've got a runaway child on the cliffs."

Chapter Eighteen

Fathers

I RAN AWAY to Cornwall, to the address I had found with the photographs of Jack in my parents' wardrobe. I couldn't think where else to go. I didn't trust myself in the same house as Naomi. I felt as if everything I'd ever known or trusted in my life was falling away. I wasn't even sure who my father was any more: was it the man I'd grown up with, or the one who'd walked away and never looked back—a man, in the end, I barely knew at all. In the rage and despair of that London morning, I knew I had to find out the truth about Uncle Jack, because it was the only way I could unravel the mystery of myself. I tried the telephone number I found with the address first, but it was no longer in use. All I got was a recorded message from the phone company, a metaphor for my identity: Sorry, the person you are trying to reach does not exist.

By any standards, my childhood had been happy. I had been loved, protected. Had it all been a lie? In the safety of my parents' home I'd believed I could save my marriage, but that safety was out of reach now.

The traffic was slow getting out of London, plenty of opportunities to turn back. I thought of Matt and Anna coming home from school to find me gone. Would Naomi call *him* when she saw I was gone, I wondered, ask him to play with the kids while she cooked? But I couldn't go back to more lies, to another day of pretending as my world fell around me. I'd spent my life trying to be Jack, long before I ever imagined he might be my father, and now I'd finally succeeded in becoming him, only it was the one part of him I'd always despised: the part that ran away.

I had a meeting with a government minister in a little over three hours and I was driving hundreds of miles in the other direction. There was a missed call from his office, but I didn't care. My job was another lie. It was a long drive to Cornwall, but the miles slipped by in my new BMW, another trapping of the comfortable life Naomi said I hated. Was I such a hypocrite? I'd always told myself I'd made sacrifices for the children, but mine had been gilded sacrifices: I'd surrendered myself to a life of money and respect. I might as well cast it all on the bonfire now. If Ben Merryweather didn't exist, neither did his job or his marriage.

Somewhere around Stonehenge I had a panic attack and had to stop. I pulled over and got out of the car to breathe, a stabbing pain near my heart. Someone once told me the thing about heart attacks is you don't feel them in your heart; you feel the pain somewhere else. When it's your heart that hurts, it's just heartbreak. Whatever it was, I wanted to be sick. I sat by the side of the road and watched the cars passing, until I noticed people staring and realised I should move on before some busybody called the police. If I turned back now, I could be home before anyone knew I'd gone. I put it from my mind and drove on towards Cornwall.

When I passed Exeter I was already late for the minister. There was another call from his office, and several from Asylum, but I ignored them all, my mind made up. There was nothing they could do to me now.

When I reached Cornwall and turned off the dual carriageway, my back hurt from too long behind the wheel. The GPS took me along the local roads to a small coastal village. It had a look of Jersey about it, the low painted houses and the granite cliffs either side. A gull swept low over the car, keening as if for the lost past. It seemed appropriate that Jack should end up here: I could have been around the corner from Egypt Wood.

The house was a white-painted cottage in a street that ran down to the beach. I parked and sat looking at it. I wondered what I'd say if he opened the door. I walked slowly down the street, as nervous as I'd been in my first war zone, or on that first evening with Naomi.

It wasn't Jack who answered; it was a bigger man, shaven-headed and tattooed. He was suspicious at first, menacing, but the threat receded when he realised he wasn't the man I was looking for.

"Merryweather? No one of that name here," he said. "Sure you want Number 14?"

I looked down at my notebook. "The address could be out of date."

"Could be. We only moved in a couple of years back. Maybe he knew the tenant who was here before. Marie," he called to someone inside, "what was her name who lived here before?"

"What?" a voice came back.

"The woman who lived here before us."

"Val!"

"I know that, what was her surname?"

"I'm not sure," the woman said, coming to the door. She was younger than him, a child in her arms. "Something like Swan, wasn't it?"

"That's it. Val Swann. Two ns. If anyone knew this friend of yours, it'd be her. Thirty years, she was here."

"Do you have a contact number for her? Or an email?"

"No, but the landlord might. I'll get you his number." He stepped inside the house.

"Looking for someone?" the woman asked me.

"My...uncle. We lost touch. This is the last address I had for him."

"Don't think there was any man living here. Val was a single mum, what I heard." Her husband came back with a dog-eared business card for the landlord.

"You could ask her at Number 12, Irene. Been here for years."

The next-door house looked uncared for, the paint peeling, dirty net curtains in the windows. When I rang, an elderly woman opened the door almost immediately, as if she'd been watching me with her neighbours.

"Wasn't a man at Number 14 since Geoff Wharton got locked up," she said. "Sent to prison, he was. That was Val Swann's house."

"Could my uncle have been a friend of hers?"

"Val had a lot of friends, but I don't remember one called Merryweather."

I showed her the telephone number.

"That's Val's old number. From before they changed them all round here. Change everything, they do. I don't see the point, things were fine the way they were. What was he like, this uncle of yours?"

"He's only got one leg. He wears a false one, a prosthetic, you know?"

She shook her head. "A one-legged man? Then he definitely wasn't here. I'd've remembered a thing like that."

I thanked her and walked to the end of the street. There was a pub on the next corner and I asked in there, but no one had heard of a one-legged man called Merryweather. The barman suggested I came back in the evening, when the regulars started to come in.

"If he was ever here, one of them'll know," he said.

"Can't move through a small place like this without getting noticed. Where you staying?"

"I don't know, I just got here. Drove down from London."

"Long way to come for an uncle. There's a B&B a couple of streets over."

I went to take a look: it seemed the sort of place a man on the run from his life would end up. I walked around the rest of the village, but there was nothing more to see, except some empty tourist shops. I wandered down to the beach and sat on a rock looking out to sea; a cold wind was blowing in and the clouds were casting dark shadows on the water.

Jack remained elusive. Perhaps he'd moved on, and the address on the scrap of paper was out of date. Or maybe he'd never been here. I thought back to the time he'd disappeared from Tempest House, leaving nothing but another scrap of paper with "Thank you" scrawled on it. I remembered how I'd missed him, the sense I'd had that he'd abandoned me. He could have sent a post-card or made a phone call, something to let me know he was still alive, but there'd been nothing. He'd just left. I wondered what I was doing here, hundreds of miles from home, trying to find a father who would do that.

And I thought of my other father, the one I'd known all my life. I remembered how when I couldn't sleep, he would sit for hours in my room and silence the ghost with his presence. He must have been tired: he'd been working all day in the hospital, but he still found the energy to sit patiently with me. And I remembered how, when my leg slowed me down or stopped me doing something, he would find a way to make me feel better. He would sit for hours imagining with me, dreaming up scenarios where we were space explorers and his car was our starship, or spies on a mission behind enemy lines. I'd thought that I'd invented those games, but now I saw that he'd invented them for me, to give me something I could do while the other kids ran and played football. He was the one who'd pored over his big old-fashioned atlas of the world with me, tracing places with his finger, and first filled me with the desire to travel, not Jack, who had only told stories about himself. He had sat and listened when I poured out my first heartbreak at the age of sixteen and, smiling sadly, told me there would be more to come, but none of them would kill me. He was the one who'd told me to follow my heart and go to Afghanistan, when everyone else was saying it was too dangerous. His own brother had lost his leg there, but he didn't try to stop me. He'd joked with me down a scratchy satellite phone line from Jersey, and not let on he was worried, though he must have been terrified for me. He was the one who'd lent me the money so I could get married, and never mentioned it to anyone. He'd been the first to offer whenever I had money troubles, and the last to ask for any of it back. He'd cried tears of joy when Matt and Anna were born, held them in his arms, walked hand in hand with them, told them the same stories he'd told me, read them the same books, stilled their fears the way he once stilled mine. In all my life, I realised, he had never let me down.

What is a father: a few minutes of biology, or a lifetime of love and patience? We do not carry our children within us, as women do; we are not one with them before they are born. A woman is a mother from the moment she conceives; a father is made later. It is love alone that makes a father of a man.

I thought of Matt and Anna. What if I wasn't their father: would I love them any less? I was their father; Naomi could not unmake that, could not take away the times I had sat up with Anna, the way her hand took strength from mine, the trust in Matt's eyes, his need for my approval before all others'. And she could not take away my love for them, the one untainted, undamaged, unchanging truth in my life.

I knew I would never abandon them as Jack had abandoned me. I looked back across the beach to the pub. I wasn't going to wait for evening to ask the locals about Jack. He had made his choice a long time ago, and I was making mine. I was going back where I belonged. It was at least five hours' drive back to London, more if the traffic was heavy, but if I left now I could just get home before they went to bed. I sent Naomi a text message to say I was held up at work and would be back late, but to tell the kids I'd be there in time to tuck them in. There were more messages from work but I ignored them. I got in the car and drove, watching Cornwall and Jack recede in my rear-view mirror, until they were just a glint of sun on the sea in the distance.

When I got back, Naomi was waiting.

"Change your mind?" she said.

"What?"

"You took the suitcase. And since when have you taken the car to work?"

"Just something I had to take care of. Where're the kids?"

"In bed, but they're still awake. They wanted to wait for you. Listen," she said, coming close to me, "let's put this behind us."

"I don't know if I can do that."

She fell back, anger in her eyes. "Then why are you here?"

"Because of what I am."

"What," she said, mocking, "because you're a *man*?"

"No. A father."

Chapter Nineteen

Twentieth Century Books

I'VE HEARD OF hurricanes and typhoons, but I reckon when the wind really makes up its mind to blow in Jersey, it's a match for any of them. Jersey storms don't come along that often, but when they do, people talk about them for years. When the wind comes in off the sea in a fury, it's a living thing that can lift you up and knock you down and throw you over and blow the breath out of you. As we raced out to Les Landes in Sergeant Nicholson's car, the trees were already bending at crazy angles and the full force of the storm hadn't arrived yet. The streets were almost empty; everybody knew what was coming—everybody except Martin who'd run away without checking the weather reports.

I'd always wanted to ride in a police car with the siren on and the blue lights flashing, but there was nothing fun about the mad drive out to the tower that evening, huddled against my father on the back seat as Sergeant Nicholson's partner took the corners fast and the rain hammered at the windscreen.

Out at Les Landes, the storm was coming in. Huge ghost-figures of spray rose hundreds of feet in the air as the waves broke against the cliffs. Great towers of cloud were massing in the eerie yellow light; the sound immense, wind screaming across the sky and the sea thundering in reply. When Sergeant Nicholson opened the car door, the wind tore it out of his hand and slammed it against the side of the car. In the distance the tower stood, black and motionless.

We started down the path, crouched against the wind as it tore across the heath, the rain knives in our faces. Our voices were lost in the wind.

"...crazy....the boy..."

"...now we're here...gets worse..."

I was afraid I'd be blown away. I slipped on the stretch of loose dirt that led to the entrance, saw the long drop to the rocks, but my father held on and pulled me back to him. I looked over the edge: no hope if you fell there.

The tower door was jammed shut, and Sergeant Nicholson and his partner had a hard time getting it open. From the sound when we got inside, I thought the ghosts of all the soldiers who'd ever served there must have returned. The sea spray was blowing in through the gun slit.

"Where would he be?" Sergeant Nicholson said, his voice suddenly loud and clear in the tower.

"Could be anywhere," I said. "He liked to sit upstairs, but the sleeping bag was down there."

We followed him down to the lower level while his partner guarded the door. The room was empty, the sleeping bag gone. Sergeant Nicholson saw me shivering, and said I could wait with my father at the entrance while he and his partner searched the upper levels. I could feel the ghosts moving around us.

"Nothing," he said, coming back down. "The place is empty. We'll get a search party out."

My father nodded, solemn. On the way back I watched the spray breaking against the cliffs. No one could stay out there for long.

The light was fading by the time we made it back to the road. There was a second police car beside ours, and a shadowy figure waiting at the top of the path.

"... luck...?" Centenier Falle said, pushing back his hood to reveal his face. He opened the back of his car and gestured for me to get in; "...out of the cold..." he said. My father nodded. I watched from the back seat as they talked, huddled together to make themselves heard. In my mind I could see Martin slipping where I had on the path, with no one to hold onto him, and the long fall down into the mad fury of the sea.

"Don't worry, Ben, we'll find him," Centenier Falle said, getting into the front seat. My father was still talking with the others outside. "I'm going to run you and your dad home so Sergeant Nicholson can get on with the search. Now, I wanted to ask about this Nazi of yours."

"The bookseller?"

"Bookseller?"

"Yes, he's got a bookshop. That's where he hides out."

"What's that?" my father asked, getting in beside me.

"The Nazi," I replied.

"Don't start all that again."

"No, it's alright," Centenier Falle interrupted, starting the car. "Tell me about this bookshop."

"It's just his imagination."

"Still. No harm in it."

So I told him about Twentieth Century Books.

"That's not a Nazi," Centenier Falle said, "that's Joe Ronez."

"It was him. I saw him."

"Perhaps we should make a little detour. See if Joe knows anything."

"You're taking this seriously?" my father asked.

"Joe's no Nazi. Quite the opposite, in fact, but I can believe he was out at the tower."

"He's got a Nazi dagger in his shop," I said, "with one of those crooked crosses on it."

"I know he has, but not because he's a Nazi. Very interested in the occupation, Joe; sells a lot of books about it. Trying to work through his own past, if you ask me."

"You think he might be mixed up in what's happened to my son?"

"Not directly, no. But if your boy's been hanging around that old tower, Joe might have seen him."

"You mean—"

"Nothing like that. Joe's an old friend. He might have seen the boy, that's all."

The storm hadn't reached St Helier yet, but the streets were deserted. Some bins had blown over in the wind, and rubbish was scattering along the pavements. Twentieth Century Books was closed, the metal shutters pulled down over the windows. I hung back as we drew close, but my father put his arm around me.

"Don't worry," he said. "We've got the police with us."

Centenier Falle's small figure didn't look so reassuring to me. He didn't even have a uniform, and I was pretty sure the Honorary Police didn't have guns. He rang the bell at a small side door, and there was the sound of a window opening above. I looked up to see the old bookseller staring down at us, looking anything but friendly.

"Evening, Joe," Centenier Falle said. "Can we come up?"

"Not a great time, Barry."

"It's important."

Joe nodded and ducked back inside.

"He can be a little cranky at times," Centenier Falle whispered to us.

There was a sound of bolts being drawn, and the door opened.

"What brings you out on a night like this?" Joe asked Centenier Falle, giving my father and me a suspicious look. "Just sat down to my dinner."

"This is Dr Merryweather from the hospital and his son, Ben. His other son's missing, and we think he may have been in the old watchtower at Les Landes."

"It's not a watchtower; it's a range-finding tower."

"That's the one."

"You'd better come up then."

He led us up the staircase I'd seen from the bookshop; even here, I noticed, there were books piled along the walls. He showed us into a small sitting room. On a table in the corner was a half-eaten plate of food.

"A boy, is it?" he said. "Dark hair, green anorak?"

"Yes, that's him," my father said, starting forward. "You know where he is?"

He shook his head. "Saw him this morning and told him to clear off home. I don't know where he went after."

"Where was this?" Centenier Falle asked.

"Out at the tower. I thought he was just messing about. Kids are always getting up to no good in there. I found a couple of teenagers camping last year; they'd made a fire and everything. I've told the States, but nothing's been done. That place needs to be locked up,"

"What about my son?"

"I told you, I found him in there and told him to clear off."

"What time was this?" Centenier Falle said.

"Around ten."

"Did you see which way he was headed?"

Joe shook his head. "He had a bicycle with him. Last I saw he was on his way back to the road."

"You just let him go?" my father said. "Why didn't you do something, tell someone?"

"I thought he was going home. You should be grateful to me; he could've broken his neck in there."

"He could be anywhere."

"What do you want me to do, call the police every time I see some stray kid wandering about the island?"

"It might have been an idea," Centenier Falle said, putting himself between them. "Alright, Joe. You'll have to make a statement and everything."

"What about the dagger?" I whispered to my father, but Joe heard me.

"That's not a dagger, it's a bayonet," he said. "My brother stole it during the occupation. Stupid thing to do; could have got himself killed. I keep it to remind people how it was."

He didn't know any more about Martin, and Centenier Falle said he'd drive us home.

"It's not a lot but it helps," Centenier Falle said in the car afterwards. "We know the boy wasn't in the tower when the storm hit, because Joe chased him off in the morning. And he probably wasn't out on the cliffs there either, because Joe saw him leave on his bicycle."

"Do you trust him?"

"Joe? I've known him for years. Don't let his manner put you off—he's had a hard life. His mother was sent to a concentration camp."

"He was the last person to see Martin," my father said.

Their eyes met in the rear-view mirror, but neither of them said anything. Night had fallen. The rain was coming on hard now, and the wind was getting stronger by the minute. Except for police cars, no one else was on the road. A small branch came off a tree and whipped past the windscreen.

When we got home, my mother was alone; she'd sent Roz to stay the night with a friend. She looked hopeful at first, but when my father told her there was no news her face collapsed.

"It's alright," my father said, holding her in his arms. "We'll find him."

"Don't worry, my love," Centenier Falle said. "We've got teams combing the whole island. Chances are he's holed up somewhere out of the rain, but with the people we've got on this now we'll find him."

After he left my mother started crying. "How did we let this happen?" she said. "How did we let him go?"

I'd never seen my mother cry before, and I didn't

know what to do. My father reached out and pulled me in, holding both of us in his arms. When he spoke, he sounded like he was crying too. "We'll find him," he said. "Whatever it takes, we'll find him."

That was when Jack walked in.

Chapter Twenty

The Cliffs

"WHAT'S GOING ON?" he said. "Did something happen?" Apart from his suitcase he looked like he'd just come in from an evening at the pub.

"Jack?" my father said, bewildered. "What are you doing here? Where did you come from?"

"Never mind that now. What's *happening*?"

He listened in silence as my father told him about Martin, only interrupting to say things like "Christ!" and "The fool!" He sat down with his head in his hands, shaking it from time to time. When my father had finished he looked up. "What can I do to help?" he asked.

"I don't know what any of us can do," my father said. "We've got half the island out looking for him as it is. I wouldn't be so worried if it weren't for the storm. When did you get in anyway?"

"This afternoon. Flight was pretty rough, I doubt anything's coming in now. I went round to Annie's first. I had no idea."

"You wouldn't. So you came back?"

"Yes. Well, can't keep running all my life."

"How's Annie?"

"It'll take time."

"I'm not surprised," my mother said. "You can't just walk back into her life."

"I know."

I think they were grateful for something else to talk about for a moment, but you could see they were still thinking about Martin. Outside, the storm was coming in for real now; I could hear trees creaking as if they were about to fall.

My father got up. "I can't sit around like this," he said. "I'm going out to look for him."

"I'll come with you," my mother said.

"There's no point in us both risking our necks."

"If you're going, I'm coming."

They stood looking at each other.

"Go," Jack said. "Both of you. I'll take care of Ben."

"Are you sure?"

"Yes. Now get out there and find him."

When they opened the door the wind blew into the house. The trees were making a tremendous noise, and things were being thrown about in the dark. I remember thinking I wouldn't have wanted to go out into that.

"Be careful," I told my mother.

"Of course, love," she said. "Be good for your Uncle Jack."

I watched the car all the way to the end of the road, until the storm swallowed them. They were all leaving. Now it was just Jack and me.

"You eaten anything?" he said.

"I'm not hungry."

"Never miss a meal. Learned that in my first war. You never know when you'll get the chance to eat again."

While he made us something to eat, I asked where he'd been to take my mind off Martin and the storm. He'd gone to London first, he said, to ask his newspaper for his old job back. After that, he'd been in Wales, where he made himself walk in the mountains every day, just to prove to himself he could.

"It was agony," he said. "After a while I thought, what am I doing here when I could be back in Jersey?"

"Are you going to stay now?"

"I don't know. Annie's pretty angry with me. I don't know if she wants me to stay."

"I want you to."

Outside it sounded like the world was coming to an end. Whole trees were falling now, with a noise that shook the ground, and I kept away from the windows, frightened one might come into the house. There was a huge oak tree next to my bedroom: if that fell, I thought, it would come through the wall.

I told him about Joe Ronez, and how I'd thought he was a Nazi, and about the tower and how terrifying it had been in the storm.

"Don't worry, Martin'll be alright," he said. "He's a tough kid." But he didn't sound like he believed it any more than the others.

Tempest House lived up to its name that night. The windows and doors were shaking and the chimneys were roaring as if the storm was trying to force its way in. It sounded as if the trees had been uprooted and were marching on the house, closing in all around and hurling themselves to the ground. Soon I was sure one would hit us. I was too frightened to leave the room, even to go to the bathroom, and stayed close to Jack. I thought of my parents out in the midst of all that. I wished they'd left it to the police to search.

It was about an hour later when the lights went out. Jack flicked on his lighter.

"Power lines must be down," he said. "Do you know if your parents have got any candles?"

We went and looked in the kitchen. We hadn't thought to close the curtains in there, and the room was filled with a strange light. Outside I could see the trees moving impossibly, great oaks bending like rubber. Jack found my father's electric torch, but said we should look for candles as well in case the battery ran out. When we found them we lit several in the sitting room, but the wind coming down the chimney blew them out. Jack blocked it with a piece of board and that was enough to stop them going out, though they still flickered and sent our shadows moving across the wall.

The phone lines were down too. My parents had probably already found Martin and were safe at the police station, Jack said; they just couldn't get through to tell us.

One of the windows flew open with a crash, and blew all the candles out again. I leapt up in fear. Jack put the torch on and tried to close the window. It wouldn't stay shut, and he said we needed a piece of string or rope. There was an old length of rope that used to hang by the coat hooks just inside the back door, but when I led him there it was gone. I looked to see if it had fallen on the floor, and felt the wind rushing in under the door. But there was no sign of it there either. I looked to see if someone had moved it to one of the other hooks. I saw the hook where Martin's anorak usually hung and thought how this must have been the last place he stood before he ran away, in the silence of the early morning, the rest of us still asleep upstairs. He would have reached up, as I was doing now, and his hand would have brushed against the rope—

"I know where he is," I told Jack. "I know where Martin is."

"What?"

"Wolf's Caves. He's in Wolf's Caves."

"Where? How do you know?"

I tried to explain, but the thoughts were racing through my head too fast, and the words came out in a jumble. Jack had to put his hands on my shoulders and tell me to take a deep breath and start again. I'd seen it, standing there by the coat hooks. He'd had it all planned out, he wasn't just going to the tower but on a tour of all the places he wanted to see. He'd started at the tower, where he'd finally met the man he'd been staking out, only to find out it was Joe Ronez who told him to clear off. But he wasn't planning to stay at the tower anyway. He was going on to Wolf's Caves, which my parents had never let him visit, and where even Harry had refused to go with him. He was going to prove he could get down there. That was why he'd taken the rope: I remembered him telling Harry the Germans had taken away the ladder to the big cave, but he thought they could still reach it with a rope. It was the perfect plan. He would hide in the same caves where his favourite smuggler, the Wolf, had once hidden, and none of us would think of finding him there. When he'd given my parents a good fright, he would come home, probably refusing to say where he'd been. But he'd made one mistake: he'd forgotten to check the weather forecast. I thought of the sea out at Les Landes. I could only imagine what it would be like at the caves.

"Where are these caves?" Jack said, when I'd explained it all.

"Not far from here, just around the coast. We've got to tell the police."

"There's no phone."

I stared at him.

"Are you sure he's there?"

"Yes."

"Then we'll have to go."

I looked out the window, at the trees dancing in the wind. "Out there?"

"There's no other way. You'll have to come with me; I can't leave you here alone. We'll find a search team and get them to radio it in. They can send the coastguard."

He left a note for my parents on the kitchen table, and another in the window in case the police came over, saying "URGENT! MARTIN IN WOLF'S CAVES! SEND HELP QUICK! GONE TO FIND POLICE!" I was shaking as he fastened my anorak around me. The house had felt like the only safety I had left.

"Don't be scared," he said. "We're just going to find the police. They're probably at the end of the road."

He had a look I recognised in his eyes, the same one he'd had the day he came to talk to my class at St Edward's and I'd thought he wouldn't make it up the stairs. I felt the wind as soon as he opened the door, blowing so hard I could hardly breathe. My eyes streamed. I couldn't walk against it, and he had to take me by the shoulders and pull me with him. His car was rocking in the wind and I started to panic, thinking it would be blown over.

"Nothing to worry about, I've seen worse," he said, but I think he just said it to calm me down, because he told me later he'd never seen a storm like it. He pulled out a map of Jersey and found the caves on them. "Christ!" he said. "It'll be lethal out there tonight. Let's hope we find someone quick."

We could hardly see anything for the rain, even with the wipers on full speed. There were things blowing around us, tiles torn from the roofs of houses, and branches from the trees, and I thought something was bound to hit us at any moment. When something large and white hit the windscreen full on, I closed my eyes and waited for the glass to shatter, but it was just an empty plastic bag.

"You're doing great, Ben," he said. "Just a little further."

Our little lane through Egypt was a terrible place that night, things came flying low across the fields and hit the sides of the car. A couple of trees had blown over, but they'd fallen into the fields and left the road clear, though we had to inch our way over the debris. When we got to the main road there was no sign of the police. A big tree had fallen and blocked the left-hand turn, which would have led to town and the police station. The only way open was to the right, back towards the coast. Jack said we had to keep going. I don't know how he managed to stay calm, but it helped. He behaved as if he did this sort of thing all the time. There were no other cars about; you had to be mad or desperate to be out that night. We had to go slowly, watching for fallen trees and things in the road. Once, a huge branch came out of the sky towards us, and I was sure it was going to kill us, but Jack slammed on the brakes and it hit the road in front of us. I didn't think he'd go on after that, but he drove around the branch and continued down the road. I began to think I could have been wrong about the caves: my father could have moved the rope a few days before, and I would have brought us out for nothing. There were trees down all over the place, but somehow Jack managed to find a way through. At one point he got out of the car to push one of the smaller trees out of the way. He couldn't move it very far, and there was a scraping sound from the side of the car as we passed. We still hadn't seen anyone, and I was beginning to think they must have called off the search because of the storm.

"Don't think I'm getting my deposit back," he said when something big hit the side of the car. "We need to find a working phone."

There was a house ahead, candle light flickering in the windows. He pulled up outside and banged on the door until someone answered. When he came back he said the phones were down there too.

It was only when I saw the sign for Wolf's Caves that I knew we were going all the way. We hadn't seen anyone since we left the house, so I suppose we didn't have much choice. The road ended in a car park, where the trees were swaying dangerously. Jack didn't want to leave me there alone, so we set out together for the cliffs.

"I'm sorry I've got you into this, Ben," he said. "Just hold onto me and don't let go."

I don't know how he managed on his leg, with the wind blowing the way it was. Out on the cliffs, the sound was terror itself. When the moon broke from behind the clouds, white wraiths of sea spray towered hundreds of feet over our heads, but a moment later they would slip into the dark again, and it was hard to see where the land ended and the long drop into nothing began.

There was something blowing around, making strange metallic noises. Jack shone the torch in the direction the sound was coming from and I saw Martin's bicycle chained to an old wooden bench, bent out of shape from being tossed around in the storm. I was right: he had come here. But there was nothing we could do for him. The cliffs weren't sheer there the way they were at Les Landes; there was a slope of heather and gorse, but it would have been too steep for a one-legged cripple and an eight-year-old even on a clear summer's day. There was no one else around. We had come so far, I thought, only to stand helpless as he lay somewhere in the dark below.

But Jack wasn't giving up. He led me to the start of the path, inching his way down the wet heather and grass. I was sure he would slip and we'd both go down into that deafening sound, and I forgot about Martin. Fear had taken hold of me and all I wanted was to go back. Jack crouched down and shone the torch at the bottom of a wooden post that must have been part of the old handrail. Tied to it, I saw, was the rope that had been missing from the coat hooks at home.

"Martin!" he shouted. "Martin!"

But the wind drove his voice straight back. He shone the torch down the path: it was so overgrown it disappeared after a few feet. He took me back to the bench and, kneeling beside me on his good knee, told me to wait there.

"Keep this pointed at the path," he said, giving me the torch, "and whatever happens, hold onto that bench and don't let go!"

He said something else as he left me, but I couldn't hear it in the wind. I kept the torch trained at the top of the path for him as he made his way back down. He stuck his walking stick into the ground, so it wouldn't blow away, took the rope in his hands and started making his way down. It was madness: you couldn't get down there with two legs on a night like that, and I knew it was only a matter of time until I saw him slip and fall into the vast sound below. I kept the torch pointing at him, hoping it would help, but after a time he was too far away and all I could make out was the faint glitter of the rain. I stared into the darkness, but there was nothing. I tried calling his name a couple of times, but no sound came back, and I couldn't tell if he'd heard me.

I don't know how long I was alone there in the

darkness. After a time the torch began to fade. The battery was failing and I switched it off. Jack was gone, I was sure; he'd fallen down to join Martin in the raging sea. I cried into the wind for my dead uncle and brother. I held Martin's bicycle, all I had left of him now. The rain drove into my face and my hands turned numb from clinging onto the iron leg of the bench. I could feel it stirring in the wind, and wondered what I'd do if it was ripped up and blown away. I wept for myself. No one knew where I was. I didn't even know if my mother and father were still alive. By the end it was all too much, and I thought it would all just stop: the wind, the storm, the sea, the cliff, the world, everything: that it would be unable to go on.

I have no idea what state I was in when he found me; all I remember is a hand on my shoulder, and looking up to see Centenier Falle leaning down. I must have been in a bad way, because he took me in his arms and said, "Alright, boy. You're safe now."

He asked where Jack was and I pointed down to the seething fury below. I remember that I hurt all over, except my hands; I couldn't feel my hands. There were others with him, searching the top of the cliffs with torches. They found the rope, and I told Centenier Falle Jack had gone down after Martin. They shone their torches down into the darkness, but there was nothing but the empty gorse and heather. When I heard my mother's voice I thought I must be dreaming. She took me from Centenier Falle. I couldn't speak; I just clung to her and wept. My father was there too, kneeling over the bicycle.

"Says his uncle's gone down," Centenier Falle said, shining his torch over at the rope. My father rushed to the top of the path and looked down. I wanted to speak, but everything was gone from me. When I tried to talk, all that came was wailing for the dead. We had been too late. Martin and Jack were dead, lost down there in the sea and the storm. All I'd done was send Jack to die.

"Let's get him in out of the wind," my mother said. I wanted to argue, but I didn't have it left in me. The cliffs were behind us when there was a shout from below. I couldn't make it out, but my father touched my mother's arm and she stopped and turned. Another shout, and my father started back. I turned, trying to see what was going on. The police were all gathered at the top of the rope, shining their torches together on a single point. Centenier Falle turned and looked back at us.

"*He's coming*!" he shouted. "*He's coming up, and he's got the boy*!"

Chapter Twenty-One

After the Storm

"IS HE?" my father said. "Is he?"

The wind was dying a little and I could hear. My mother took me back to the cliff top and put me down so she could see what was happening. Picked out in the beams of the police torches, I could see Jack slowly dragging himself back up the rope. There was something I couldn't make out at first on his back, but as he got closer I saw it was Martin, clinging to his neck with both arms. Jack's prosthetic leg was missing, and one of his trouser legs was flapping empty in the wind. The police called out to him to keep going, telling him he could do it, but I was sure he would slip at any moment and they'd both fall back into the sea.

"Come on, Jack!" my father shouted. As they got closer, I saw Jack was in a bad way, gritting his teeth against the pain. My father started down the path to help, but Centenier Falle held him back.

"That rope's treacherous enough for one," he said. "You're more use here. You're the only doctor we've got."

My father nodded, seeing the truth of it. Jack inched his way up. I could see Martin clearly now, pale and limp. When they got close enough, two police officers reached down and took Jack by his shoulders, pulling him the rest of the way. Centenier Falle couldn't hold my father back any more. I ran to hug Martin, but his skin was cold and my father pushed me away, taking him in his arms. Jack was gasping for air. The police cleared a space and my father went to work on Martin.

"We need to get him out of this wind," he said, taking his coat off and wrapping it around Martin. I felt bad for Jack who just lay there, fighting to get his breath back. His hands were bleeding.

Centenier Falle called for an ambulance on his radio, but my father said we couldn't wait. They sent two policemen on ahead. My father carried Martin and the rest of us followed. Someone must have helped Jack, but my memories of the rest of that night are broken up, as if my mind had taken in all it could and there was no room for any more. There was a house; I don't know how we got there, but I can see Centenier Falle knocking at the door and the next thing I remember is sitting by a gas heater and the feeling coming back to my hands. The power was out and the glow of the heater was the only light in the room. I remember thinking Martin had died and they weren't telling me, and crying until my mother came and told me he was going to be alright. At some point there were blue lights and an ambulance, and my father must have gone to the hospital with Martin, because after that it was just my mother and me. And Jack, because I have a memory of him sitting drinking whisky, and someone telling him that might not be such a good idea after what he'd been through, and him smiling and saying it was the safest thing he'd done all night.

And then the storm was over, it was morning and we were leaving. The quiet hurt and it was strange having no wind to lean into. Everything was out of place, fallen trees everywhere, and even seaweed, which must have blown all the way up the cliffs. Jack was leaning on someone's shoulder because his leg was missing and he didn't have his crutches, and I remember my mother holding onto me and saying we were going home.

After that, I recall waking up at Tempest House, thinking, of course, I'd dreamed the whole thing until I opened the curtains and saw the wreckage. I ran to Martin's room in a panic, sure he was dead, calling his name until my mother came and told me they were just keeping him in the hospital for a while. Roz was there, shaken and quiet, and Polly, helping my mother clear up. In our rush to get to Martin, it turned out Jack and I had never got round to closing the sitting room window, and half the island seemed to have blown in. Jack was sitting in a litter of leaves and pine cones, wrapped in his Afghan shawl.

"You saved Martin," I said.

"No, *we* saved Martin. Couldn't have done it without you. We make quite a team—we should do it again some day."

I wasn't at all keen on the thought of that, but I didn't say anything. When he reached for his tea, his hands were bloody and torn up from the rope, but he said he was alright. "Can't say the same for my hire car. I don't think they'll ever let me have another."

"What happened to your leg?"

"Had to leave it behind."

"Can't the police get it for you?"

"I should think it's long gone. With any luck it'll get washed up on a beach somewhere and people'll think it belonged to someone who was swallowed by a whale."

"Whales don't eat people."

"Are you sure?"

"What'll you do?"

"Your dad says he's sending a pair of crutches from the hospital. And in the meantime, it's not all bad. Thank you," he said, as Polly brought him a plate of food and smiled down at him.

"You brave man," she said.

It turned out the note Jack left behind had saved us. When the search parties had no luck finding Martin, Centenier Falle had come round to check on my parents and see if they'd heard anything. He saw the note in the window, radioed it in and rushed over to find me on the cliffs. A little later my parents had got home to find the same note, and followed him.

It was Annie who brought round Jack's crutches that afternoon.

"Well," she said, standing in the doorway, "seems you're the hero of the hour."

"I don't know," he said. "The way I heard it, the hero gets the girl."

"You fool, you stupid fool. All that work getting you used to that leg and you went and bloody lost it."

"Never mind the damn leg. I can get another one."

"Come on," my mother said to me, "let's give them some privacy."

She closed the door. I tried to listen, the way I had when Jack did his exercises in there, but for once I couldn't hear anything and I wondered if the storm had damaged my hearing.

They kept Martin in the hospital another night. My father brought him home the next morning but said we had to leave him alone for a bit, because he was exhausted. Roz and I had to go back to school, which was a cruel blow, because I'd been sure it would be closed because of the fallen trees. The other kids were telling their stories of the storm. None of them came close to mine, but I didn't feel like telling it. Mrs Maudsley would probably have said I'd made it up. I told Matthew, though: he was disappointed Joe Ronez wasn't a Nazi, but the rest of the story made up for it.

When I got home, Martin was lying on the sofa with

a duvet over him. I knew he was feeling better because he was making the most of it, eating soup and watching a video. He thanked me for finding him in his own way, by making space for me under the duvet.

"I told them about the tower," I said. "Sorry."

"That's okay, I forgive you. Just this once."

He didn't tell me the whole story right away; it came out in bits and pieces over the next few days. After he got suspended from school, he'd decided to teach our parents a lesson. His original plan, as I'd guessed, was to spend the day at the tower and head to the caves for the night. If he'd stuck to it, he'd have seen the storm coming, but when Joe Ronez told him to clear off, he'd gone to the caves early. It had started to go wrong from the start: he'd taken the rope to get down to the big cave at the bottom, but the path was so slippery he had to use it just to get down the cliffs. By the time he got to the bottom, he decided to forget the big cave and set up in one of the smaller ones, but it didn't offer as much shelter as he thought it would, and what with the wind and the rain and the sea spray, he got very cold. After a bit he thought the best way to keep warm would be to move around. He explored a little, and found the place where the steps down to the big cave must have been before they were removed, but there was no way of getting down, even with a rope.

He was hungry and ate most of the food he'd brought. The weather turned bad and he huddled in the cave, trying to keep out of the rain. After a while it got so bad he decided to head back up. But it was harder going up than it had been coming down, and he'd left it too late: the wind blew him off course, and the rain made the path treacherous. He lost his footing a couple of times and almost fell. The last time he twisted his ankle. He slid back down to the cave to wait the storm out, but the wind kept getting worse. It was desperately cold and he ate the rest of his food to try to keep warm. When it started to get dark, he said, he got scared. He remembered sitting hunched in his cave with his hands in his pockets and his hood pulled low, thinking that he was going to die and we'd never know what had happened to him. He'd imagined some other kids one day finding his skeleton in the cave. He'd taken a torch with him, and when it got dark he switched it on. The waves were crashing over his cave by then, and he was afraid he'd be washed out to sea. He stopped feeling the cold after a time. He began to imagine things as if he were dreaming: he heard the voices of smugglers around him, discussing what they were going to do with the boy who was hiding in their cave, and how they were going to throw him into the sea. He became convinced there were real wolves out on the hillside, hunting for him, and they were getting closer. After that he didn't remember anything until he heard a voice calling his name. A torch shone in on him, and Uncle Jack was pulling him up out of the cave. All he remembered of the journey was Jack's leg coming off, and watching as it tumbled down into the sea.

My father told us Martin had hypothermia and was in serious danger by the time Jack got to him. "You've got a lot to thank your uncle for," he said, "and your brother too."

"I didn't do anything," I said.

"There's time enough for false modesty when you're older."

My parents offered to set up the fold-up bed in my father's study again for Jack, but he said he could manage the stairs now. He moved out a couple of nights later anyway, and went to stay with Annie who, it seemed, had forgiven him. They came over to visit fairly regularly. My mother bought Jack a large box of cigars, and told him he could smoke them in the house, but I noticed he went and sat outside, the way he used to before his accident. The evenings were growing warmer, and my father sometimes went to sit with him, and they drank whisky together. They talked about going swimming together in the summer, the way they had when they were children.

"We might find my old leg out there," Jack said, "you never know."

"I don't think those things float."

"You're telling me. Try wearing one."

"What are your plans," my father asked him, "longer term?"

"I don't know. Thought I'd stick around for a bit. I've got plenty of money left from the insurance, and things are good. With Annie, I mean. I don't want to mess this up."

"Settling down at last?"

"I can't run away all my life."

But a couple of months later he disappeared from our lives again, and this time Annie went with him. I never knew what happened. All I remember is being woken by the sound of my father and Jack arguing in the night, and the sound of a door slamming. It was a windy night, and I couldn't make out what they were saying.

Chapter Twenty-Two

Family Reunion

WHEN WE FLEW into Jersey for my mother's birthday, it was my brother Martin who came out to meet us at the airport. Something about his appearance had changed, and I couldn't work out what it was until Matt tugged at my sleeve and said, "Look, Dad, Uncle Martin's grown a moustache!"

"You grow that for charity?" I asked him.

"Nice to see you too, little brother," he said, taking the suitcase from my hand. "Come on, kids, car's out here. Sorry to hear about Naomi," he added to me under his breath as they ran ahead to the revolving door.

I've always been a little intimidated by my brother. He seemed to grow up quicker than I did, joined the army straight out of school, and was serving in Northern Ireland while I was still drinking in student bars. The tour of duty in Afghanistan, of all places, that had prevented him from coming home when my mother had her heart attack didn't seem to have done him any harm—if anything, he'd put on weight. I always wondered if there was a rank in the army where they let you stop exercising; if there was, Martin had reached it some time ago. He was a lieutenant-colonel now, with five hundred men under his command, and it was a little hard at times to believe he was the same Martin who'd got stuck in Wolf's Caves and had to be rescued in the middle of the worst storm in years when we were children.

Afghanistan hadn't played much of a role in his life. It was Iraq where he'd won his medal for bravery ten years before, personally leading a mission to rescue some of his troops who were pinned down under heavy fire. He'd seen combat before I ever got near a war zone. Our paths had crossed in Kosovo, but Martin made it clear he didn't have much time for human rights campaigners back then. We'd avoided any serious disagreements, but a part of me had never been able to escape the suspicion that he was right: he was the professional and I was a reckless amateur who had no business playing the tough guy. When I took the safe route into advocacy, he'd stayed on as the wars grew bigger and more dangerous. I'd asked him if he ever had any doubts about leaving his children behind, but he'd just shrugged and said he didn't see the point of starting something if you weren't prepared to see it through. He'd mellowed over the years, though, and even as I grew disillusioned with my work, he'd come to see a place for it.

His family life intimidated me too. He'd got married when he was only twenty-two, and the eldest of his three daughters, Marianne, was already eighteen. His wife, Jane, was a lawyer who'd made his life easier by taking on the role of army wife and running the family in his absence. Like my parents and sister, he'd made a success of his marriage while mine was over.

It had been a relief to have it finally in the open. Naomi and I had agreed to a trial separation, and to remain on friendly terms for the sake of the children. They seemed to be taking it as well as could be hoped, and though it had been a heavy day when I moved out of the house, it was only then that I realised the impossible pressure I'd been living under. I'd rented a small flat not too far away, and I saw the children every day, often staying for dinner. Naomi had been cooperative about them coming to Jersey for my mother's birthday: it would give her a chance to get away for the weekend, she said. I didn't ask where she was going. It was strange how much easier things were between me and Naomi with no more secrets. She'd stopped seeing Richard almost as soon as I moved out: whatever she was looking for, it seemed it wasn't him. I suspected his main attraction had been as a way of getting back at me for not being the man she'd wanted me to be. There were times, over dinner, when I had the impression she was trying to get me back, but I didn't want that. I'd met someone new: a soft-spoken Indian woman who reminded me of Annie.

I didn't lose my job. It turned out the missed calls

from the minister's office on the way to Cornwall had been his appointments secretary trying to let me know he couldn't make our meeting and would have to reschedule. My absence from the office that day had been easily explained away by my mother's illness. All the same, I'd sought out Nigel a few days later and told him I didn't think the role in advocacy was working for me any more. He'd heard me out and asked whether I'd consider moving back to my old department. The current head of research was leaving to join a rival organisation, and if I wanted it, the job was mine. It would involve travel to some of the world's less alluring spots, but as head of department I'd spend most of my time coordinating the team from London. I told him I'd think about it, but I already knew I was going to take it. I'm too old for a more drastic change of career, and it was a way back into a life I'd missed.

They were all waiting at my parents' house: Martin's wife Jane, and their three daughters; Roz, Neil and their children; and my parents themselves. My mother was back to her old self, the pallor of the previous month gone. My father insisted on carrying my case upstairs over Martin's and my protests about his bad back. "My back's fine," he said, "never been better. Christ! What have you got in here, the kitchen sink? I thought you were only coming for the weekend!"

He'd been making the same speech pretty much every time I visited for the last twenty years, but the kids loved it. I could see my mother was happy surrounded by her grandchildren, my father too, though he grumbled and pretended to be much put upon. It was too cold to sit out now, the beach given up to the wind for another year, so we ate inside. My father had put in the extra leaves from Tempest House's old dining table, which filled the little dining room in their new house so that Martin had to sit with his chair legs in the doorway to the kitchen, and Matt was jammed up against the wall at the far side of the room and had to crawl under the table to get out.

"What did you want putting all those leaves in?" my mother protested. "There isn't room to breathe."

"How else can we all sit together?"

"We'd have been fine a little closer. The kids don't need so much space."

"Oh, I might as well jump out the window."

"You can if you like. We're on the ground floor."

I remembered the last evening I had spent with my parents and Roz here on my previous visit, and the safety I had felt with them just before the storm broke in my life.

But everything felt different now. The call came when we were eating dessert. I slipped out to the patio to take it, as I had done before, though I felt the chill through my thin jacket. I kept the conversation brief, and made the arrangements for the following day. By the time I stepped back inside, my father and Martin were both a little drunk, and I decided to join them.

Martin and his family were staying at Roz's house, while the kids and I shared my parents' guest room. My father had put out the fold-out bed, and Matt of course insisted on taking it. I wondered if it was the same one Jack had slept in all those years ago. Probably not, I thought: the chances were that one was long broken and thrown out. Later, while they slept, I lay awake and listened to the waves. I had not, in the end, travelled so far in my life, I thought. I'd been out to the wilds of Afghanistan and around the world, but this was still where I belonged, by the sound of the sea. Anna stirred in her sleep and I pulled the duvet close around her. There was a lot to live for.

The next morning, while Matt and Anna were playing with their cousins, I asked my father if he wanted to go and take a look at Tempest House, for old times' sake. Martin was looking over Neil's new motorbike, and Roz and my mother were busy in the kitchen with another meal. I offered to drive, and he was as nervous a passenger as ever, telling me I was getting too close to the verge on the narrow lane. He looked through the gates and sighed.

"They've ruined it," he said. "Such a beautiful house."

"Nothing lasts for ever," I said.

"That's no reason to change things that don't need to be changed."

"Why did you leave here? You loved the place."

"It was getting too much for your mother, a big place like that. And it was impossible to heat in the winters. You feel the cold when you get to our age."

We walked down through Egypt Wood. The leaves had started falling again, and muffled our footsteps on the path. All around me, I felt the memories pressing in.

"This place hasn't changed," I said.

"No. Some things last."

We stood at the bottom looking out to sea together, the way we had the day after Jack arrived.

On the way back, I took the turning down to Bouley Bay.

"What're you going down here for?" he said.

"I thought we could get a quick drink before lunch."

The Black Dog was crowded with the Sunday lunchtime crowd, and it was a moment before I saw the man I'd brought my father to see, sitting alone at a table in the corner.

"Dad," I said, "there's someone you should meet."

"It's not your uncle, is it?" he said, stopping in the doorway. "Because I don't want to see him. I know you've been digging around the past, trying to find him, but I'm not interested. I was done with him a long time ago."

"No," I said, "it's not Uncle Jack. It's his son. Your

nephew. Dad, this is my cousin, Alex."

The man I'd brought him to meet stepped forward out of the shadows.

Chapter Twenty-Three

Sons

I WASN'T JACK'S son. I had discovered this some weeks before, in the immediate aftermath of my return from Cornwall. In my obsession with finding out everything about Jack, I'd spent hours poring over his old newspaper articles, searching for clues. When the small selection available online didn't prove sufficient, Oliver Sharpe arranged for me to visit the newspaper's archive. In the ill-lit basement of its plate-glass offices, in yellowing newsprint clippings stuck to pieces of card from the pre-digital age, I'd found incontrovertible proof that I couldn't be Jack's son. In the months when I was conceived he was in Vietnam, covering the final stages of the war. He couldn't have been Martin's father either—I checked, just to be sure—because he was in the Middle East during the relevant months.

The first effect of this was a burden lifted from my shoulders. I returned from the bowels of the building to the sunlit streets above, and to the knowledge that I was who I had always believed myself to be, my father's son. It was an end to the madness that had taken hold of me since I found out about Naomi's infidelity, and I saw that it had been absurd even to think Jack might be my father. It was only later that I understood it wasn't the end of my quest for him—or for his son. I was clearing away the extensive notes I'd made when I found the page where I'd copied down the Cornwall address from my parents' wardrobe. I'd thought it was where Jack was living, but I realised there could be another reason my father had written Jack's name by it. It could have been an address he was intending to pass on to Jack.

I called the number the new occupants of the house had given me for their landlord and, after a little initial reluctance, he gave me a number for his former tenant, Valerie Swann. The lady who answered my next call told me Ms Swann had passed away a few months ago, but that if I wanted she could give me an email address for her son. And that was when I knew I'd found him: the address she gave me was alex@alexmerryweather. co.uk.

I sent a message explaining who I was and that I was looking for my long-lost uncle, and got a reply within the hour. Alex replied to say that Jack was indeed his father. He said he could answer my questions; he was living in London, and asked if we could meet.

I met my cousin for the first time in a pub off the Tottenham Court Road. I recognised him immediately: though much taller than Jack, he had a familiar look about him, flowing hair and intense eyes. He also, unlike me, had Jack's old knack of striking an effortlessly languid pose.

Alex was friendly, but reserved. There was something withheld in his manner, which I came to understand as he told me his story. He was born, he told me, in the Cornish fishing village I had visited a few weeks earlier, a little under a year before I would be born in Jersey. He had no brothers or sisters. For the first seven years of his life, he lived with his mother and the man he thought was his father, Geoff, a violent drunk who often came home in a rage and beat his mother. Sometimes he beat Alex too. One evening, when his mother and Geoff fought, Alex learned from the insults they screamed at each other that he wasn't Geoff's son. He lay awake in his tiny room at the back of the cottage that night, wondering who his real father was. He tried to ask his mother the next day, when Geoff was out at work, but she flew into a rage. After that he didn't ask again. It was around a year later when Geoff beat his mother so badly she had to go to hospital. A couple of days later the police came and took Geoff away. Alex never saw him again. Alex's mother had been sad, but Alex had been relieved it was just the two of them now. He had no idea who his real father was.

It was another couple of years before Jack came into his life. During that time his mother had other boyfriends but none of them, thankfully, came to live

with them. Alex was playing in the garden one afternoon when she brought a stranger out to meet him, a
man with long, flowing hair who walked with a stick.
He told Alex he was his father. He said he was sorry he
hadn't come before, that he'd made a lot of mistakes,
but now he wanted to put them right. He wanted to be
a part of Alex's life.

Alex knew his mother wasn't happy about it at first:
she only let his father spend a couple of hours with him
a week, and didn't let them leave the house. But in time
she got involved with a new lover—another drunk, but
thankfully not a violent one—and started letting Jack
take Alex out so she could have a few hours alone with
him at home. Meeting his father, Alex said, had trans-
formed his life. It wasn't that he hadn't loved his mother,
he said, but it had been a lonely childhood.

"Do you have any idea where Jack is now?" I
asked.

"Of course. He knows I'm meeting you today.
He'd like to see you." He looked away, shifted in his
seat. "The thing is, he was pretty badly hurt by what
happened with your family."

"Whatever happened, it wasn't me, Alex. I was only
a child."

He nodded, reassured. "I know. I just wanted to
make sure. They live in Dorset. I thought perhaps we
could go and visit them at the weekend."

"They?"

"Oh, I thought you knew. My dad and his wife. Annie."

It turned out I had passed not far from the village where Jack was living on my way to Cornwall. Alex and I drove down together, and on the way he told me a little more about his life. He'd moved in with his father and Annie when he was sixteen, after one too many clashes with one of his mother's lovers. He'd never turned his back on his mother, had visited her every weekend and had been at her bedside when she died a few months before. For a long time she had resented Jack's involvement in his life, but in her later years they'd become reconciled, and she'd even spent a couple of Christmases at Jack and Annie's house, along with Alex and his wife. Alex's brother and sister were also there: Jack and Annie had had two children together. They were called Tom and Sarah, after my parents. Alex was an architect, and his wife was a musician. They'd been unable to have children of their own, and had adopted a daughter.

"You know, it's strange, but I can't quite believe you're real," Alex told me. "All these years my father's been talking about you, all of your family. I don't know if you realised what it meant to him, the way you took care of him when he lost his leg."

The village where Jack lived wasn't by the sea; he told me later he never felt easy with the sound of the waves after that night he went down the cliffs for

Martin. Alex led me to an old stone building with a small restaurant on the ground floor; its name, I was amused to see, was the One-Legged Man.

Jack was waiting for us outside. He hadn't changed much, except the still thick-flowing hair had turned white, and he'd finally put a little weight on.

"Ben," he said, "is it really you?"

"Uncle Jack."

"After all these years. I'm so glad to see you." His cheeks were damp when he embraced me. "Come on up. Annie's dying to see you." His voice sounded old. He still had the silver-headed stick, I saw. The limp had got much worse. He led me through a dining room of low beams and mismatched chairs. He'd bought the restaurant with the insurance money for his leg, he told me, and he and Annie had been running it ever since. "It's a nice little business, but it was back-breaking work starting it up." There were old photographs of him from his time as a war correspondent in Afghanistan and Vietnam on the walls. "We get a lot of the old war hacks in, looking for a discount. I tell the buggers they can pay double." He had to stop for breath on the staircase.

"How's your leg?" I asked.

"My pathetic leg, as you used to call it? Less trouble than the real one, these days. I'd get them to chop that off too if I could."

Annie was waiting in their private flat on the floor above and for a moment it looked as if she hadn't aged at all but had remained miraculously as she was in 1983, until she stepped forward into the light and I saw her hair had turned grey. There were tears in her eyes.

"Oh Ben," she said, "it's good to see you."

They showed me into a sitting room with pictures of their children on the mantelpiece. "You must meet them, you'd get along with young Tom," Jack said. "He's a dreamer, just like you were."

I saw a photograph of Jack in his golden youth on a side-table, his hair swept back, smiling challengingly out at the world. "Look at you then," I said.

"That's not me, that's your father," Jack said, "from before he lost his hair. You know, you look just like him."

Annie made tea and Jack asked if I'd like something a little stronger in mine, topping his up from a whisky bottle.

"Dad," Alex said, "remember what the doctor said."

"What does he know, the old quack? You hear how my children boss me around?"

"I'm just the same with my dad. Martin and Roz too."

"I always knew if anyone came it would be you, Ben. You were the one who came to cheer me up when everyone else had given up. I'll never forget that, you know."

We talked over old times. I told him about the

letter I'd found in my parents' wardrobe, from Ahmad, the Afghan whose son had died in the minefield, and his face clouded. He got up and went out of the room, and I was worried I'd offended him, but he came back with the old shawl I remembered, still filthy and unwashed.

"It was his," he said, "Shafiq's. Poor kid. He'd have been older than you are now, if he'd lived. Probably already a grandfather, in Afghanistan. It wasn't his turn to go first. We were walking single file, you see. That's how they do it, the Afghans, to get through the mine-fields. If you're not sure where the mines are, you go single file, one man at a time, so if one of you steps on a mine, the rest don't get hit." Annie moved to sit beside him, and took his hand in hers.

"It was my turn to go first, but Shafiq said I couldn't because I was a guest. 'You can't let a guest go first,' he said. Poor kid was showing off to the others. He was only fourteen; he wanted to show them all how brave he was. Of course, I argued, said I had to take my turn like everyone else, but I was relieved when they let him go first. I wasn't even second—one of the others insisted on that. They were all happy, protecting their guest.

"I tried to reach him, after it happened. The others were all shouting and waving, but I couldn't hear a word; my ears had gone with the blast. I tried to walk but my leg just wasn't there. So I crawled. All I knew was that I had to get to Shafiq. I must have blacked out, because the next thing I remember they were carrying me through the mountains.

"Ahmad didn't make a big thing about it. That's the way the Afghans are. He just told me Shafiq was killed, it was God's will. He carried me in his arms for days through the mountains, and he wouldn't even let me thank him. And all the time, his son was dead and it was my fault."

"It wasn't your fault," I said.

"It was. I was the only reason we were in that mine-field in the first place. The Mujahideen I was with were local tribesmen. The Russians couldn't tell them apart from the villagers; they could have melted away. I was the problem. If the Russians had found me, they'd have known we were Mujahideen. Why else would they have a foreigner with them? I told them I'd give myself up, the Russians wouldn't have done anything to me. But the Afghans said that was no good, because the Russians would have known why I was there, and come for them. Shafiq wasn't even scared. He used to make the tea, because he was the youngest. I remember him laughing when I tried to speak the language."

Later, I asked him what had happened between him and my father.

"It was Alex," he said. "Your dad tracked him down. I'd lost touch with his mother in those days, you see, and I didn't know where they were living, but Tom found them. It must have taken him weeks, there was no internet or anything like that in those days. He didn't tell me at first, because of my leg. He didn't want to say anything until he thought I could handle it, so he kept it to himself all those months while I was staying with you. It wasn't until after we rescued Martin that he told me. I suppose he thought I was ready. Well, I'm not proud of it, but I flew into a rage. Told him he had no business sneaking around behind my back and hiding my own son from me. Said if that was how he was going to behave I didn't want to be his brother any more. We both said things we shouldn't have, things we didn't mean. It got out of hand. When I left that night, I had no idea it was for the last time."

He looked bereft. I told him that was all in the past, that they had to get back in touch. Whatever had been said in the heat of anger, I felt sure it would be forgotten when they saw one another again, and when my father heard how Jack had followed up on the address he'd tracked down for him, and taken on a responsible role in his son's life.

"That's what I've been telling him," Alex said,

But Jack was reluctant. "I don't know," he said. "It's complicated." Annie gave me a warning look and I didn't push it any further. Outside the light was fading: it was time for Alex and me to return to London. They walked with us to the car, the scent of a bonfire in the air.

"Thank you for coming," Annie said. "It means so

much to him. Next time, bring your children."

On the drive back, Alex and I talked about the rift between our fathers. "I've been trying to get my dad to get back in touch for years," he said. "Annie too, but he won't listen. It's always the same, he just shuts the idea down. I thought, with you coming, maybe we could change his mind. But no."

I knew we had to find a way to repair the break. But not long after Alex had dropped me home, I got a phone call from Jack. He sounded agitated.

"You haven't spoken to your father about what I told you this afternoon?" he asked.

"No, I—"

"I suppose I'd better tell you. You'll hear it from Tom, sooner or later.

"The thing is, it didn't happen quite the way I said it did. Our falling out, I mean. I couldn't bring myself to tell you this afternoon." He sighed. "I hadn't lost touch with Alex's mother, you see. I knew where they were living. But she didn't want me in his life and I...well, I didn't do anything about it. She was with someone in those days, you see: a terrible drunk. And Alex had grown up thinking he was his father and I...I let him.

"Your father had gone to so much trouble finding Alex and when I told him I'd known all along, well, he was the one who lost his temper. Threw me out of the house. Told me he was ashamed of me. Said I was no brother of his if I wouldn't acknowledge my own son.

"I got angry then. Said if it wasn't for me he would have lost one of his sons. Told him it was his fault Martin had run away and nearly died, and that he had no right to lecture anyone on being a father. And that wasn't the worst of it: I said some terrible things that night, things I wouldn't repeat to you even now.

"The thing was, deep down, I knew he was right. Of course he was. But I'd just got back together with Annie, and I thought if I told her I had a son…"

I heard Annie in the background, reassuring him.

"Well, some time after that I told her, and of course she was the one who put everything right. Told me I had to be a part of Alex's life. But by then the damage was done with your father."

"But then, surely if he knew about you and Alex—"

"No, you don't understand. Some of what I said that night, it was unforgivable. After everything he did for me. When I lost my leg, if it hadn't been for him… he saved my life. I have no right. Some things are best left in the past."

These new details only made me more determined to bring them back together while there was still time. My mother's illness had made me all too aware of my parents' mortality. Alex, I felt sure, was the key: my father still believed Jack had abandoned him, and I thought that, more than anything Jack might have said, was the real source of his anger. All I had to do was get him to see how Jack had taken care of his son. I called Alex the next day, and together we made a plan.

He flew to Jersey on the same flight I took with Matt and Anna. We didn't risk telling the children; we nodded to each other like business acquaintances at the airport, before he took a taxi to his hotel and I met Martin.

In the bar at the Black Dog, Alex told his story while my father listened in bewilderment.

"I can't believe it," he said. "All these years and I never even knew. Why didn't he tell me? I lost my own brother for half my life."

Alex held out his mobile phone. "Do you want to speak to him?"

We went out to the pier. Alex called Jack and explained where he was, then put my father on. We stood some way off to give him some privacy. When we returned, there were tears in his eyes.

"It was good to hear his voice," he said. "I missed him."

Alex came back to the house with us and I introduced him to the others. We set an extra place at lunch for him. "There's room enough on that table of yours," my mother told my father. When the others had finally finished asking him questions, and the children had stopped staring at him, my father leaned across.

"Welcome to the family," he said.

"Thank you," my father said to me later that

evening, when we were alone. "You know, I always tried to protect you from Jack. I could see the effect he had on you when you were a kid. But I was afraid he'd let you down the way he let everybody down. I didn't want you to get hurt."

Jack and Annie flew to Jersey a week later. Neither Alex nor I were present for the reunion: we felt our fathers had earned their moment of reconciliation alone. But my mother told me later it couldn't have gone better: they were a little awkward with each other at first, she said, but once they'd got over their initial reserve it was like they'd never been apart.

Afterwards, they'd all gone to visit Tempest House together and, in fulfilment at last of the promise he had made to himself thirty-two years before, Jack had walked down amid the falling leaves and laid flowers for Captain Ayton at his memorial in Egypt Wood.

Author Q&A

1) Tell us about what inspired The Return Home

I think we all sometimes wonder what it would be like to go back in time and see ourselves as children. The troubling question, though, is what our childhood selves would make of what we've become. *The Return Home* came out of that.

I was the kid who grew up on a tiny island and spent my days dreaming of the world beyond the sea. And then I grew up and got to travel to places like Afghanistan and Iraq and witness extraordinary events.

I wanted to bring those two worlds together: to take someone who'd lived that adventurous life and throw him into the quiet, sheltered sort of home where I'd grown up, and see what happened. I wanted a sense of the distance we travel in a life, only to end up back where we started.

And so Uncle Jack was born. The first image that came to me was of a child watching from the top of the stairs as this broken, wounded man comes in.

I didn't want Jack to get away with being a detached observer, in the way journalists pretend to be: I wanted him to have been a victim of the violence he covered, I wanted him to be involved.

I felt the discovery waiting for him was that you don't have to travel to ends of the earth to find a cause to get behind: there's drama in every household from here to the Hindu Kush, and something worth fighting for in every family.

Another inspiration came while I was writing, when a journalist decided to tell the world that the Archbishop of Canterbury's father wasn't the man he'd always thought — as if it was anybody's business but his own. The Archbishop handled it with exemplary grace, but it struck me what a blow something like that could deal to your identity.

The original draft of the book stopped in 1984, but it didn't quite work. It was my wife Anuradha's idea to revisit Ben in adulthood, when he had problems of his own — it was also her idea, I should add, to give him a disastrous marriage that is happily nothing like ours. If the book works now, it's thanks to her.

This opened up new dimensions, and brought the book back full circle to that first inspiration. We always seem to be looking for something in our childhoods that will explain our failings, and Ben's obsessive quest embodies that. But in the end, the answers don't lie in the past. We invent ourselves as we go, and are the sum of the choices we make.

2) **The Return Home** *features two central male characters, Jack and Ben. Which of the two do you see more of yourself in?*

That's a hard question to answer, because there's some of me in each of them. The childhood Ben is probably the closest to me. Like him, I grew up on a small island where nothing much ever happened and you had to rely on your imagination to fill the days. I heard ghosts in the chimney at night, and played in the old German watchtower out at Les Landes. It frightens me now to think how we used to run around those old fortifications on the cliffs.

There's some of me in Jack, too. I was a reporter in Afghanistan, in the 2001 war rather than the eighties. Thankfully I never lost a limb and wasn't injured in the field, but I had problems with my legs as a child, and spent several months on crutches. The sores on Jack's hands are mine.

But a lot of Jack is invented. I have never mounted any rescue operations down the cliffs in Jersey or anywhere else, I am no womaniser and I could not keep up with his drinking.

The only thing I share with the adult Ben is his post-traumatic stress disorder, which I suffered for a time after Afghanistan and Iraq. I too wandered the streets of London trying to shake off the memory of bomb victims, bracing for an explosion that never came. The rest of the adult Ben, I'm happy to say, is pure fiction.

3) Jack suffers physically and mentally from his time reporting on an overseas conflict. Much attention is rightly given to soldiers returning from war zones,

but do you feel journalists and other civilians, such as aid workers, also need more help?

Yes, it's a real problem. There is still a macho culture among journalists that seems more rooted in the 1940s, if not even further back, rather than the 21st century. Instead of confronting their experiences, there's an attitude of "Another gin and tonic will do the trick." But of course it won't, and the world of war reporting is littered with casualties who never got a scratch physically.

I remember being sent on a chemical weapons course by a newspaper before the Iraq war. The ex-military types running the course brought in a therapist to offer counselling to journalists. This was a man who'd counselled soldiers, people who'd been in battle and watched their comrades die in front of them. And one of the journalists there started attacking him and saying anyone who needed counselling shouldn't be in that sort of job. Of course the soldiers soon put him in his place, but it shows you how backward the approach can be.

More recently there's been an issue with newspapers using young freelancers to go to places like Syria rather than send their staff, to save money. They're sending young and inexperienced people into the most dangerous place in the world without proper backup, and the result has been an epidemic of kidnapping. And on top of that, there is no proper duty of care to those who do make it back, to provide them with counselling and support.

I know the mental cost of working in war zones. I barely slept for a month when I got home from Afghanistan in 2001. I have gaps in my memories of some of the worst things I saw: moments that are simply missing.

4) *You now live and work in Berlin, do you miss your childhood Jersey? Is Jersey still your "home"?*

Yes — more so as I grow older. As a child I couldn't wait to grow up and leave. I spent so many years trying to get off the island and go out and see the world, but now I go back whenever I get the chance. Part of that is age: the quiet life starts to have its attractions when you get past forty. But I think it is also to do with getting married and taking my wife to Jersey. She'd never been before, and you see a place with new eyes when you share it with someone you love.

As everyone does with their home, I miss the way it was in my childhood. Jersey was a big holiday destination in those days, and I remember packed beaches and people enjoying themselves all summer. But also the change in the seasons, and how the place seemed to empty in the winters. These days it's still the same island underneath, only now you can have a deserted beach to yourself.

Like Ben, I'm not from an old Jersey family. My father moved to the island as a child, but even now some of the older islanders would consider us outsiders.

But like Ben, again, I never knew any other home. And anyway, I don't see what's so bad about being an outsider. We're all outsiders if you think about it: we're just temporary residents in this life, passing through.

5) *There are lots of charming details about life in Jersey, such as the presence of Centenier Falle. Do you feel that life on Jersey is still quite different from life in the UK?*

Yes, very much so. When I first visited the UK as a child, it felt like a foreign country to me, even though my father was born in London. I'd never seen things like trains and rivers before, except on television. And there was a different mentality, a different way of seeing the world.

One of the joys of researching and writing The Return Home for me has been rediscovering Jersey. It seems ironic now that I travelled so far and wide when there was so much that was exotic and mysterious in the place I came from.

There's a lot of things in the book people might think are made up, but which are true. There was a huge storm in the island when I was growing up, and the memory of sitting up listening to the trees falling all around that night is still as frightening as anything I encountered in Iraq and Afghanistan.

The tide really does go out a mile and leave strange desert landscapes behind. There is an Egypt Wood with a Wolf's Lair at the bottom. Jersey is full of fortifications left over from the German occupation, like the tower at Les Landes. It's also riddled with Nazi tunnel complexes. And there are houses like Tempest House, complete with towers.

And there's plenty I didn't manage to get in the book. To this day, you can still make any construction work stop immediately and force a judicial review simply by kneeling and invoking the aid of an ancient Norman prince — in French, naturally.

6) From which writers have you drawn inspiration as an author?

There are so many. I was conscious of Dickens as an influence while writing with a child's voice – Harper Lee too, although I would never claim to be able to write like either of them. The same goes for Thomas Hardy in the storm scene. Julian Barnes and Ian McEwan were influences when piecing together the past and understanding how it frames the present.

More generally Anthony Burgess, who gets a mention in the book, was always an inspiration to me for his use of language. Hilary Mantel, for her prose as well as her ability to bring the remote past to life. Graham Greene for his ability to see the wounded humanity in even his darkest creations.

7) *One key aspect of the book is the surprising and troubling relationship between Ben and his wife. Do you think he was right to try so hard to make things work?*

That's a difficult question. I certainly wouldn't want to generalise about what anyone in that sort of position should do. On one level, Ben believes he is trying to make things work with Naomi for the sake of his children, and of course that's a very noble thing to do. Children have to come first in any situation like that.

But that's not his only motivation. He's also trying to make the marriage work because that's who he wants to be. It's about his identity: he doesn't want to be the kind of man who walks out on a marriage or gets a divorce. And that's more troubling.

8) The Return Home *is something of a departure from your last work,* The Burden of the Desert. *What's next, and where's next?*

I'm working on a novel that tackles the refugee crisis, immigration and terrorism, but not in a conventional or obvious way. What I find deeply disturbing in Britain—and all over Europe—at the moment is the way refugees and immigrants have been stripped of their humanity. You have people who are fleeing Syria, where they could be crucified or burned alive, and we talk about them as if they're monsters. That's what fear does to you. But you can't do that in a novel. You can't write about some one without understanding their motivation. A novel forces you to look at everything from the other point of view and write about people as they are, in all their complexity.

As for "where", this next book is set in London. *The Return Home* touches on London a little, but I want to take on the great metropolis properly. I used to love riding the night buses in London and listening to people speaking in what seemed like every language on earth.

I'm also working on a non-fiction book, about my experiences as a reporter in places like Afghanistan, India and the Middle East.

After that, I don't know. I've been living in Berlin for a couple of years now, and I'd like to write a novel set here. It feels that so much has happened in Berlin that there's no room left for ghosts, only the living. They're still rebuilding the city, more than 70 years after the end of the Second World War, and I like walking the streets and trying to work out where the Wall used to run.

Justin Huggler on...

Afghanistan

I first travelled to Afghanistan in October 2001, a few weeks after the 9/11 attacks. The newspaper I was working for at the time, The Independent, called to ask if I'd be willing to go. The Taliban, the original Isis, fresh from blowing the Bamiyan Buddhas to bits, were refusing to hand over Osama bin Laden, so the US was turning the full might of a superpower on a country where half the population still lived in what seemed like the Middle Ages. Afghanistan, the country the world had forgotten, was suddenly the focus of everyone's attention. Who wouldn't want to be there?

I flew in on a rusting Russian-made helicopter. One of the pilots was crouched on the roof as we boarded, hitting the rotors with a spanner. I prayed the thing would stay up. It left us in a small village of mud-walled houses that was the capital of the Northern Alliance, the last remnant of resistance to the Taliban, and when it took off again, it was as if the whole of modern civilisation was leaving.

The only electricity in that village came from

generators, and there wasn't enough fuel to leave them on for long. At night we worked by the light of hurricane lamps, our faces lost in the shadows. The only connection to the outside world was long-wave radio, and people clustered around to hear the latest from the war through the hisses and pops of static.

Not that the war, or modernity, were ever that far away. Both flew over our heads every day in the form of American bombers, and at night I lay awake, listening to the sound of the bombs rolling up the valley.

I remember sitting in the remains of a fort built by Alexander the Great as the American planes passed overhead, and the Taliban tanks fired from across the Oxus river.

"But will you sit here with me when the real fighting starts?" the Afghan commander asked me.

I could hear the whine of a shell approaching. There was a puff of dust in the distance, followed by the dull thud of the impact.

Through it all, it was the Afghan people who impressed me. They had been through the Soviet occupation and the struggle to liberate their country, and the even more devastating civil war that followed. Then there had been the Taliban. But still they endured.

I remember once, driving across the country, we came to a bridge that had collapsed. Anywhere else, you'd call the authorities and wait for some one to come and fix it. But there was no phone, and there were no authorities to call. I thought we'd have to turn back, but the Afghans I was travelling with got out of the car and rebuilt the bridge themselves, with their bare hands.

A cold winter day, snow in the air, and one of the journalists was shivering despite her warm Western coat. The Afghan translator wordlessly unwound the brown woollen shawl he was wearing—all he had over his thin cotton shirt to keep him warm—and placed it around her shoulders. The buttons were missing on his shirt, and his skin was red from the cold. But he smiled and refused to shiver.

Further down the banks of the Oxus, we watched the wooden ferry that carried people across to Tajikistan on the far side. Night was falling and the lights were coming on in Tajikistan. They would have been warm inside. On the Afghan side everything was dissolving into shadow. The wind was bitter and there was no heating. I nodded across and asked the Afghan ferryman if he ever envied the Tajiks.

He gave a low, dry laugh. "They have electricity, but they have no freedom."

We tend to forget that Afghanistan was a civilised place until the Russians invaded. People don't know much history in the modern world, and there's a tendency to assume everywhere was always the way it is now, as if there's something inherently backward about Afghanistan. The Afghans had their freedom, but they had paid a heavy price.

All the bombs the Americans were dropping started to have an effect. The Taliban were in retreat, the Northern Alliance was advancing, and we followed deep into the country, across mountain ranges and through one-street towns that seemed like something out of a Western movie, where the only shops doing business were the coffin-makers.

One night I slept in an ammunition store, surrounded by crates of Kalashnikovs. We ate in restaurants where the Afghans would sit with their rocket-launchers propped against the wall beside them, and little hunks of meat were hacked from the body of a goat hanging from the roof.

I grew used to watching out for the red-painted stones that marked off minefields, until it became second nature and I avoided them without thinking. Twenty years of war had left Afghanistan with more landmines than anywhere else on earth, and there were people with missing limbs everywhere, one-legged children on crutches. The Americans dropped more mines out of the sky, bright yellow plastic anti-personnel devices that the Afghan children thought were toys.

We got hold of a Japanese mini-van with a cassette player, and I listened to Ahmad Zahir, the Afghan Elvis; a memory of times before the war. "You broke your promise," he sang to a former lover, "you abandoned me. If you came back now, it would be too late, you would find me dead."

He could have been singing to the West. The Afghan Mujahideen were our heroes when they fought the Russians. They even turned up in a James Bond movie. But we forgot them when the Soviets were driven out.

In the siege of Kunduz I accepted the surrender of a Taliban mullah. Mullah Hadi and his men had just walked across no man's land through American bombing and Taliban rocket fire, and he couldn't find anyone to surrender to. So we bundled him into the back of our mini-van. As he and his retinue were getting in some one screamed that the Taliban had fired a rocket at us, and the driver sped off with one of Mullah Hadi's men still hanging halfway out the door.

A little down the road the farmers were working as usual. They had spread rice on the road to dry, and asked us to drive over it to squeeze the moisture out.

The first time I nearly died was in Qala-i Jangi, a prisoner-of-war camp. Hundreds of captured Taliban had staged an uprising there. In response, the Americans had bombed their own POW camp, and there were bodies everywhere. I was looking around when I found the entrance to a cellar. I peered down into the dark. I almost went down but the smell of dead bodies was overpowering and I moved on. A few minutes later an Afghan started down the same stairs and was shot dead. There were Taliban survivors hiding in the dark below. One of them, it later turned out, was the American Taliban, John Walker Lindh.

The second time was just over the border in Pakistan, on the road to Kandahar. This was at the end of the war: the Taliban had made their last stand in the city, and it had just fallen to American-backed forces. I was with Robert Fisk, a colleague on The Independent, when our car broke down in a village en route. The mood in the street quickly turned hostile, and it wasn't long before the first stone was thrown. A bus driver across the road signalled to us to get on. We rushed over and I managed to climb on board, but the crowd grabbed Robert. I tried to pull him onto the bus but they dragged him away. The stones became rocks. I remember a big man laughing as he brought one down on Robert's head. I turned to the passengers for support, but none of them would look at me. I knew I had to find help, but stepping off the bus was the hardest thing I have ever done—I felt I was walking to my death.

The crowd, it turned out, was too wrapped up in Robert to notice me, and so I found our translator and sent him for help. Our driver made me wait in the car, hoping I wouldn't be seen, but we were soon surrounded again. I feared was only a matter of time before they dragged me out.

The translator returned with law enforcement in the form of a lone tribesman who charged the crowd with his gun and pulled me to safety. When we got to Robert he had been rescued by a local mullah but was badly hurt.

The newspaper, in the inimitable style of Fleet Street,

said his injuries meant it was depending on me to get to Kandahar. That meant going back down the same road. I went, this time with a different translator, a man called Habibullah who taught me about Afghan courage. We crossed the border on the back of a smuggler's motor-bike and were immediately surrounded again. I feared the worst, but Habibullah smiled and introduced me to the crowd. He told them why I'd come, and by the time he'd finished they were clapping me on the back and shaking my hand.

That night in Kandahar, we ate pomegranates and the Afghan men told dirty jokes from the villages. They asked for a joke from my country and, casting around for something that would appeal, I told them the Miller's Tale. They loved it. I wondered what Chaucer would have thought. Kandahar probably wasn't that different from his England, apart from the guns.

A couple of nights later, word came from the authorities that some Taliban were back in the city and were planning to kidnap a journalist. I moved to a government guest house, where we were advised to stay indoors for our own safety. In the evening Habibullah turned up and said he had come to invite me to dinner in the city.

"Isn't it too dangerous?" I said.

"You still don't understand Afghanistan," he told me. "Do you think these armed guards can protect you? If you stay in hiding here like a coward, they will come in and drag you out. But if you walk down the street at my side and look every man we meet in the eye, no one will touch you."

We ate at a restaurant in the heart of the city that night. We walked there and back unarmed through the streets, and as Habibullah had promised, I came to no harm.

Jersey

Jersey and the other Channel Islands were the only part of the British Isles to be occupied by the Nazis during the Second World War. In June 1940, as France fell to a German army that seemed to have swept all Europe before it, and British troops were evacuated from Dunkirk, Winston Churchill's government came to the reluctant conclusion that it could not mount an effective defence of the islands. Just weeks after Churchill vowed to fight on the beaches, the British gave up the Crown's oldest possessions without firing a shot.

It was a sound military decision. The coast of France is visible from Jersey on a clear day, and there was no way the islands, whose fortifications had barely been modernised since the Napoleonic wars, could be protected from a modern army.

But for the people of the islands, it was a devastating blow. It sentenced them to almost five years of military occupation that would continue even after France had been liberated, and bring them to the point of starvation, with the islands under siege and the Germans stubbornly holding out. For others, there would be no rescue, only deportation to the concentration camps and death in the gas chambers.

It caused a degree of mutual distrust and misunderstanding in the islands' 1,000-year-old relationship with England that lingers to this day.

Jersey and the other Channel Islands are the last remnants of the lands William the Conqueror controlled as Duke of Normandy before he captured the English throne in 1066. They have always enjoyed a high degree of autonomy, and have never been part of the United Kingdom.

But as the Second World War loomed, the islands threw themselves behind the British cause with patriotic enthusiasm. They voted to send money to help the war effort, and waived their ancient exemption from military service. Young men flocked to join the British armed forces.

In June 1940, Jersey found itself facing imminent German occupation with little idea of what to expect. Many of the men of fighting age were gone. A few thousand people were hurriedly evacuated, but most vowed to remain on their island home. As the last British evacuation ship left, they were on their own.

Things started badly when the British neglected to inform the Germans they had demilitarised the islands. Expecting resistance, Luftwaffe reconnaissance flights mistook farm lorries for troop carriers and carried out air raids that left 44 dead.

After that, the British government passed a message to Germany that the islands were undefended. Nazi troops landed in Jersey and Guernsey, and the occupation began.

At first, it was much less harsh than the occupation of continental Europe. The reason lay in the Nazis' grotesque race theory, which placed the British just below the Germans. Hitler apparently wanted to demonstrate how civilised a Nazi occupation could be, as a model for the occupation of Britain that he believed would follow.

But if the islands escaped the massacres and collective punishments of continental Europe, they did not escape all the horrors of Nazi rule. Most of the islands' Jews had evacuated to Britain, but those who remained, mostly foreign citizens who had fled to the islands to escape the Nazi advance across Europe, were subject to repression. Three Jewish women who had fled Poland and Austria were sent to Auschwitz, where they died.

Islanders with Jewish grandparents were stripped of their property, forced to close their businesses and ordered to remain indoors. The island authorities cooperated with the Germans in this, but refused to go along with a demand for Jews to be made to wear armbands with a yellow star. Official documents were also falsified to hide the Jewish heritages of islanders.

More than 2,000 islanders were deported and interned in camps in Germany. While they did not endure the suffering of concentration camp victims, conditions were harsh and many died.

Meanwhile the Germans began to fortify the islands—to an extraordinary extent. The fortifications were part of Hitler's Atlantic Wall, which ran from Norway to the Spanish border to prevent a possible British invasion. But remarkably, the islands Britain had not even tried to defend were to be among the most heavily fortified places on earth.

Nearly 8 per cent of all the concrete for the Atlantic Wall went to the Channel Islands, along with more German guns than 600 miles of the Normandy coast. Hitler appears to have been obsessed with holding on to the only patch of British territory he controlled, and his officers spoke of his "island madness".

The watchtower at Les Landes that features in The Return Home, more properly a range-finding tower, is just one of the remarkable fortifications still standing in the island to this day. There are vast complexes of tunnels dug under the surface of Jersey, where the Nazis planned to shelter entire infantry divisions from Allied air raids as they prepared to invade Britain. Construction went on long after invasion plans were shelved, and the islands became a place where the Nazis appeared to be pursuing a fantasy, cut off from reality, as the course of the war turned and the rest of their empire began to fall away.

All this construction required labour, and the Germans brought in more than 16,000 slave labourers including Jews, Soviet POWs and French Algerians and Moroccans handed over by the Vichy government. Many were literally worked to death on the islands.

An accusation that has been increasingly levelled against islanders by other Britons in recent years is that they did not do enough to resist the occupation. It is a claim that has led to a lot of ill feeling on both sides.

In fact, the islanders were not in a position to mount anything resembling the French Resistance. Most of the men of fighting age had left before the occupation and were serving with British armed forces elsewhere. The islands were extremely heavily garrisoned. There was one Nazi soldier for every three civilians in Jersey, compared to one for every 250 in France. There were more Germans per square mile in Jersey than in Germany. Jersey measures nine miles by five, meaning there was nowhere for a resistance to hide.

Yet despite all this there was a degree of resistance in Jersey and the other islands. Many islanders sheltered escaped slave labourers, and there was a clandestine network to move them around the island. One Jersey woman who took in an escaped Russian, Louisa Gould, paid for her courage with her life. Denounced to the German authorities, she was sent to Ravensbrück concentration camp in Germany, where she died in the gas chambers in 1945, just three months before Jersey was liberated.

Hundreds of islanders escaped by boat to Britain to hand over information about the occupation and join the armed forces. Many drowned trying to make the crossing undetected in the perilous waters off the coast. Dennis Vibert, a 21-year-old islander, made it successfully to Weymouth in an 8-foot wooden boat. When his outboard motor had fallen off he rowed the rest of the way. He carried the first full report on conditions on the island, only to be charged 10 shillings import duty on his boat by customs. He went on to serve as an RAF bomber pilot.

The mistrust and resentment went in the other direction too, from islanders who felt abandoned by the British authorities. In fact, the islands were not as thoroughly forgotten as they thought.

There really was a secret mission to Egypt Wood on Christmas night in 1943, as mentioned in *The Return Home*. A group of British and Free French commandos led by Captain Philip Ayton landed at the bottom of the wood, hoping to kidnap a Nazi soldier and find out about conditions on the island. They were unable to find a German and Captain Ayton was fatally wounded by a landmine on the way back to the boat. Memorial services are still held in his honour in Egypt Wood.

The mission was part of Operation Hardtack, a series of commando raids on the Channel Islands and the northern French coast in 1943, but they were discontinued for fear they were causing the Germans to bring reinforcements to the area.

In June 1944, four long years after the occupation

began, came D-Day and the Normandy landings. But there was to be no liberation for the Channel Islands, not for another eleven long months. Deterred by the now formidable German fortifications on the islands, the British decided to bypass them altogether.

As Allied troops liberated France to scenes of jubilation and began to press on towards Germany, the islands became the last Nazi possession for miles around. The British decided to starve the Germans out. The Germans responded by requisitioning food from the civilian population. Supplies of medicine began to run out. In January 1945, the electricity was cut off.

"Let 'em starve," Churchill wrote in a memorandum. "No fighting. They can rot at their leisure."

Vice-Admiral Friedrich Hüffmeier, a fanatical Nazi, took over as commandant. "We shall never surrender," he told Jersey's Bailiff, Alexander Coutanche. "In the end you and I will be eating grass."

It was a prediction that came close to being true. Only a Red Cross ship carrying food kept the islanders alive.

On 30 April 1945, with his empire in ruins, Hitler committed suicide. But still the Germans clung on in the Channel Islands, refusing to surrender. Two days later, Berlin fell to the Allies, but the islands did not. It wasn't until 9 May, the day after VE Day, that the Nazi occupations forces surrendered and the islands were finally liberated.

Justin Huggler was born in the Channel Island of Jersey.
A former foreign correspondent for the *Independent*
newspaper, he covered the occupation of Iraq from 2003 to
2004. He has also covered the 2001 war in Afghanistan, the
second Palestinian intifada, the 2004 Indian Ocean tsunami,
the overthrow of Slobodan Milosevic, and the Nepalese
revolution. He is the author of *The Burden of the Desert*. He
lives and works in Berlin.